2—

Shock Talk

Shock Talk

A Novel

Bob Larson

A JANET THOMA BOOK

THOMAS NELSON PUBLISHERS
Nashville

Published in Nashville, Tennessee, by Thomas Nelson, Inc.

This is a work of fiction. All characters are products of the author's imagination, and resemblance to actual persons, living or dead, is purely coincidental.

Library of Congress Cataloging-in-Publication Data
Larson, Bob.
   Shock talk: a novel / Bob Larson
     p. cm.
   ISBN 0-7852-7009-4 (pb)
    1. Television personalities—Fiction. 2. Mothers and daughters—Fiction. 3. Spiritual Warfare—Fiction. 4. Talk shows—Fiction. I. Title.
PS3562.A747 S56 2001
813'.54—dc21

                                00-069530
                                    CIP

Printed in the United States of America
1 2 3 4 5 6 7 8 9 10 PHX 06 05 04 03 02 01

To my family (especially my wife),
who sacrificed my time with them
to make this book possible

Prologue

A noise arose from the countryside. Slowly, deliberately, it built from a *tap, tap* to a pounding cadence. It descended upon a small English village where darkness had calmed the clamor of seventeenth-century daily toil. It was well past midnight and the hamlet was slumbering when the churning hoofbeats met the cold cobblestone. The sharp torque of each tread upon the stones ricocheted off the mud-plastered walls. A lone dog howled at the clatter but didn't gave chase. The mist from a night fog drifted in and out of each corridor, momentarily obscuring the view. Still, the rider proceeded without hesitation.

A few residents stirred, lit their candles, and peered out of windows trying to catch a glimpse of who was atop the racing mount. All they could see was the form of a man urging his large horse onward. Above the echo of the hoofbeats, those spying out the nameless rider heard the snorts from the horse's flared nostrils. The pair dashed through town in a few minutes, and the sleepy citizens blew out their candles and went back to bed.

At the outer edge of the settlement, the road changed from rock to a soft vermilion clay typical of this area in the king's realm. The horse's hooves welcomed the soft dirt. Loose footing wasn't a problem for this steed. He was a draft horse, with hooves broader than a man's outstretched hand. Horses like this weren't usually enlisted for such a speedy trip, but the rider was desperate, and this plow horse was all he had for the journey.

A scant quarter-mile beyond the edge of the village, the rider suddenly stopped and pulled the reins with all the force he had. The horse's huge body lunged and then halted. The sleek sheen of its body reflected in the light of the full moon that peeked in and out of drifting clouds. The rider patted the neck of the horse and strained to see what direction to take. Suddenly he jerked backward in fear. The horse sensed his alarm, shivered, and pawed the ground with its left front hoof.

Hanging from the lush limb of a fir tree was a batch of gnarled twigs, bound together with bark strips. The strange shape would have gone unnoticed by most people. But to this rider, the wooden emblem was a foreboding sign: a crude cross, suspended upside down and pierced at the crossbar junction with an angled stick, as if it were a spear piercing the heart of the symbol. The rider knew what it meant and the direction he should take next.

He nudged his horse slowly forward and then leaned hard left on the reins at the location of the strange emblem. There was no trail, and the beast hesitated at the base of the dark woods. Little moonlight penetrated the thicket of leafless, moss-laden branches. Deliberately planting each hoof, the horse veered first to one side and then the other in a serpentine pattern, bobbing its way through the woods. The rider leaned forward, his body pressed against the withers to duck under the tree branches.

The hoofbeats were quiet now. The occasional snapping of a fallen twig and the crunch of dried leaves on the forest floor interrupted the haunting silence. The far-off hoot of an owl and the swoosh of an intermittent breeze were the only companions to the silence. Every few seconds, the rider nervously peered over his shoulder as if he sensed something was following him. But no other traveler ventured into this uncharted thicket.

For a mile or more, horse and rider dodged the dense forest. An observer might have wondered how they knew what direction to take.

Their only compass was a hunch, and their guide an invisible force spurring them onward. The steed never once broke stride until the flora gave way to a small clearing where a puff of smoke slowly rose from an open bonfire. A cloaked figure sat next to the flames, his back toward the approaching rider.

In this alcove, the darkened canopy of the trees gave way to glowering clouds that dimmed the moonlight. The rider paused at the perimeter of the bower, halting the horse, which nervously twitched its neck against the reins. Near the bonfire was a small wooden shack, barely large enough to accommodate a single room. It was windowless and constructed of weathered, gray boards. It seemed out of place, as if it served no purpose in this setting. Its single door was closed.

The horse whinnied, but the rider remained motionless. A large black raven cawed sharply as it circled overhead. With his hood still covering his head, the figure by the fire stood slowly without turning. The rider nudged the horse in the ribs to get it to move forward. Fifty yards from the bonfire. Then, thirty. Twenty. The horse stepped cautiously in the darkness. Ten yards. The figure turned, his face still hidden by the hood, which hung low over his forehead. His head was turned sideways, the shadow from the hood obscuring his face.

"You're late!" his deep voice barked.

"I did everything I could to meet your demands," the rider responded, halting his horse and slowly dismounting.

He stood by the horse's neck, holding the reins in his right hand.

"Well, where is it?" the figure demanded.

The rider dropped the reins and approached slowly. He reached in his tattered cloak and handed a small leather bag to the mysterious figure.

For a moment the unidentified form did nothing. Then he shook the bag slightly and raised it in front of his face, inspecting its contents without opening it. In disgust he threw the bag to the ground. "It's not enough," he intoned solemnly. "If each coin were gold, the value wouldn't come close to what's owed. You know what's expected of you."

He gestured dismissively toward the bag. "There can't be more than half of what's due. Where's the rest?"

The rider stood speechless.

"Midnight tonight was the deadline! You're late, and you're short!"

"I've given all I can. There's nothing left."

"Oh, really?" the figure sneered.

"Take my horse. My last possession. You can have him."

The hooded specter slowly circled rider and horse, nodding his head up and down as if carefully surveying the offered beast.

"I can buy a dozen nags like this in the market for a fraction of what you owe. Don't trifle with me. Who do you think you're dealing with? Our people don't eat the dust of workhorses. Insult me no further!"

"If you'll just give me a little more time, maybe . . ."

"Time? Oh, I think we've been very generous with time. You sound just like your father. Your family is all the same. You should have thought of 'time' before you developed such a fondness for ale and wagers. Sorry, the debt is due and there is no more time. Your time has run out."

The rider grasped for any stalling tactic. When he did respond, his words took on a desperate tone. "Is there anything I can give you that will suffice until the charge can be paid? *Anything?*"

The hooded figure walked slowly forward. His right hand, covered with a black leather glove, rose toward his forehead. He tipped back the front corner of the hood and eased it off his head. His sleek black hair, pasted straight back on the top and sides, glimmered in the faint light.

"Anything? Well, now that you mention it, there is something." His voice deepened as the sentence trailed off. Than he said abruptly, "Your soul."

The rider froze. "You can't be serious? It's just a gambling debt. It's not like I owe you my life."

"Well, then, just exactly how are you going to pay?"

"Time. Just a little more time."

The dark-haired stranger threw back his head and flung out his arms with his hands thrust heavenward. The glint of a knife blade in his right fist shone in the moonlight. "Time? There is no more time. Not for you, not for anyone who belongs to you. Your father ran out of time, just like you have. And so has your son."

The rider's body stiffened. "My son? What's he got to do with it?"

"Your father belonged to me. Now you belong to me. And soon, so shall your newborn son."

"Never! A thousand times no!"

"No?" the stranger responded mockingly. "Let's not forget something. *You* owe me, I don't owe you. Your soul or your son, which is it?"

"All right. But leave my family out of it. My soul, if you will, but not my only child." He fell to his knees and sobbed. "Take me if you must, but let that be enough."

The stranger turned his back and walked toward the bonfire. He drew near the flames.

"It is enough. The debt is paid."

Without another word, he stepped directly into the fire. Flames leapt upward all around him. He was immersed in the blaze but not consumed. Slowly he turned and faced the rider, his face an expression of immeasurable evil. He stretched out his left arm, and with his index finger curled, he beckoned toward his adversary.

In fear the rider retreated from the scene, taking measured steps backward while he wiped his face with his hands. He glanced over his shoulder to pick up the horse's reins. He gripped the leather in his hands and turned to face the horse. As his eyes met the beast's, the horse shrieked in terror and suddenly reared up. Its front feet stabbed high into the air and then came sharply down with a sickening thud. The front edge of the hooves caught the top of the rider's head and sent him staggering to the ground. Blood coursed from the break in his skull as his body fell to the soft, muddy earth. He lay there lifeless as the spooked horse ran back into the forest.

A shadowy image holding a long gun emerged from the small shed.

He aimed toward the bonfire. The crack of gunpowder split the night. The flames of the bonfire exploded with a burst of heat and sparks. The hoofbeats of the horse faded into the forest as a baby's frightened cry pierced the cold air.

1

Jenny Owens peeked through the doorway. She noticed at once that the color of the room wasn't green. There wasn't a speck of emerald anywhere. Not the furnishings or accessories. Not even a hint of olive in the carpet. Why was this place called the Green Room? It made no sense to Jenny, but then not much about *The Billy McBride Show* made any sense. It was tabloid TV, capitalizing on the lowest common denominator of audience appeal. It was lowbrow, but it was a financial success. It was number one in the ratings, and Billy was at the top of his game.

Jenny stepped cautiously into the Green Room knowing that she was soon destined for a large dose of embarrassment. The thought of the *McBride* crowd chanting in her face almost made her bolt from the room. But she stopped and pondered. When you're desperate, you do desperate things. You'll allow yourself to be exploited, even humiliated, if it brings you one step closer to the answer. Jenny knew she needed an answer as fast as possible. At this point in her life she didn't care where the answer came from. Even if it came from Billy McBride.

What kind of answer could a shock-talk TV host possibly have for the disintegrating relationship with her daughter, Allison? Jenny admitted to herself that she had no idea. She was curious why *McBride* picked their story. Hadn't the viewing audience seen it all by now? She remembered the *McBride* show she saw entitled "Mouthing Off to Mother." The topic was children who defied their moms and dads. Billy took the side of the parents and championed the no-nonsense notion that they are the bosses of the household.

Jenny was impressed by Billy. Sure, he was sensational, but he really seemed to care about his guests. She knew that much of what went on was contrived, like a carefully choreographed WWF wrestling match, but Billy did hug and weep with abuse victims. He held the hands of distraught family members facing death and heartache. When shows centered on compelling human needs, the phone numbers of counseling centers were offered at the end. Billy wasn't a pastor or a priest. He wasn't a professional therapist, but he had a caring heart. Jenny was convinced of that. He was genuinely interested in the continuing welfare of those on his show. That must be the reason he sometimes featured short segments that reported on the progress of past guests who had found help for their problems.

Only Jenny's utter desperation could have brought her here. Pleading with her daughter hadn't worked. The advice of friends had done no good. But in spite of past failures to turn Allison around, Jenny would not give up. She was willing to allow almost anyone the chance to do whatever was necessary to bring back Allison. That's why two weeks earlier she had written down the 1-800 number listed in the *McBride* show credits. The number was highlighted, along with a list of upcoming show topics that scrolled down the screen. When Jenny saw "Families Out of Control," something inside her said, "Call!"

That first inquiry led to a series of preshow phone calls from Billy's producer, Jeff Steinberg, who gave Jenny a long list of very personal and probing questions. She guessed he was gauging what kind of guest she would be and whether her dilemma suited the upcoming show's format.

It must have been a fit. Two days after Steinberg's last grilling, a woman from the show called to say their story had been chosen. The producer was especially pleased that Jenny and Allison lived in Phoenix, where *McBride* originated. That made it easier for them to be on the show because they were just a limo ride away.

Jenny broke the news to Allison shortly thereafter. Jenny was surprised by Allison's response. She was receptive to the idea of going on national television and talking about their family problems. Jenny wasn't sure why. Maybe underneath her unconcerned exterior, Allison was just as desperate in her own way. Or maybe it was a chance to grasp fifteen minutes of fame in front of her friends. Allison's two-year-old daughter, Ashley, was too young to have an opinion about the baring of her mother's dirty laundry in front of millions of video voyeurs. So the matter was settled over a Domino's pizza. After that, neither Jenny nor Allison said a thing about what they were really thinking.

Jenny walked slowly through the Green Room and eased herself into a comfortable chair at the far end. Allison entered the room a few moments later. She approached the hors d'oeuvre tray on a shelf near the doorway. She picked up a piece of cheese pierced with a toothpick and sampled it.

"Not bad, Mom. A little stiff, but tasty. Want a piece?"

"No, thanks."

Jenny eyed the dozens of framed photographs adorning the walls. Billy was in every one of them, surrounded by an assortment of celebrities and distinguished guests from the past. A soundless television set in one corner played an endless loop of scenes from *McBride*, featuring the most outrageous moments, seamlessly edited together in a nonstop assault of offensiveness. Fists flew, chairs flew, sometimes bodies flew. Barely-clad hookers sauntered, extravagantly dressed drag queens paraded, and all sorts of individuals sobbed and screamed. Jenny was glad someone had punched the mute button on the remote.

She had watched *McBride* the day before, knowing that she would be on today. She wondered if there might be a promo about her appearance, and if what it said would indicate how McBride might handle her situation. The show was a panel discussing the theme "Wives with Younger Lovers." Jenny found the show disgusting, especially the vulgar comments made by one of the guests, comedian Mack McCormick. She wondered whether the plight of her relationship with Allison would be the subject of similar sarcasm.

She caught the smell of a pungent odor and sniffed the air to try to figure out where it was coming from.

"Mack McCormick sat in the chair you're in last night," Steinberg said, noticing her reaction, as he entered the room. He walked toward Jenny and extended his hand. "Hi, I'm Jeff Steinberg. You must be Jenny. That's probably McCormick's stale cigar smoke that you smell. He never touched any of the goodies we had to eat. He just sat here and smoked one cigar after another."

Jenny shook Steinberg's hand and nodded her head in acknowledgment. Steinberg wasn't at all what she had expected. She envisioned a short, dark-haired, wiry man who was on the serious side. Instead, Steinberg was middle-aged and balding. His undersized suit was off-the-rack quality and barely covered his portly frame. He smiled with a warmth that seemed at the same time genuine and beguiling.

"I understand that Kim Usher, my assistant, escorted you from the limo to the Green Room."

"Yes, she was most gracious," Jenny acknowledged.

"I presume this is your daughter," Steinberg said, motioning toward Allison.

"Pleased to meet you," Allison responded without diverting her attention from the food tray. She poked a cherry tomato with another toothpick and swallowed it whole.

"Relax. It's about twenty minutes until show time," Steinberg said. "Help yourselves to the food. There are drinks in the small fridge under

4

the table. Make yourself at home. I'll be back shortly to take you onstage."

As Steinberg exited, Jenny glanced in Allison's direction. She didn't look nervous at all. She was such a beautiful young woman, though life had taken a toll on her twenty-two hard-lived years. Jenny wished that she could get Allison's blue-green eyes to meet hers. Ignoring her mother was typical behavior. The two seldom made eye contact even when eating at home. Jenny assumed it was because Allison never got over the embarrassment of having to move back in after being on her own. That, plus the stigma of having a child out of wedlock, gave Allison a sense of failure and shame. Her uneasiness with life had made her an angry person, and the two of them frequently had words, embittered words, the kind that two people who love each other use unwisely and are sorry about much later.

After months of harsh exchanges, there wasn't much left to say now, on the verge of a televised confrontation. Jenny even felt strange being in the same room with Allison. At home, Allison secluded herself in her bedroom most of the time. When they were together, it was because of Ashley. They needed to discuss things such as what time Ashley needed to be put to bed or when Jenny's babysitting services would be required.

Jenny had tried to reach out to Allison and let her know she was welcome back home. She bought her presents, told her jokes, and even accompanied her on unannounced trips to the mall. All these attempts seemed to fail. Even trying to surprise her by announcing their being on *The Billy McBride Show* hadn't sparked the dialogue they both needed. Jenny's heart ached. She just wanted her little girl back, the innocent child who clung to her chest and cried out for "Mommy" over every scrape and bruise.

"Would you like something to drink? Pop? Juice of some kind?" Kim Usher's inquiry interrupted Jenny's thoughts.

Usher was an intense woman in her late twenties. She had brownish blonde hair, pulled back severely. Her dark business suit was accented by strap-on shoes. She moved quickly and deliberately, displaying her artificial friendliness in front of gritted teeth.

"I understand Jeff was just here," Usher said. "He asked me to look after you until closer to air time."

"An apple juice would be fine, if you have it," Jenny replied.

"One apple juice coming up." Usher knelt down in front of the small mini-bar-type refrigerator and took out a bottle of Snapple. "I've got to check things on the set," she said, as she handed the juice to Jenny, "but I'll be back to prep you for the show."

"Thanks." Jenny paused. "I have one question, if you've got a moment?"

"Sure. What's on your mind?" Usher put her hands stiffly on her hips.

"Why do they call this the Green Room?"

Kim laughed slightly. "I suspect most everybody we have on the show wonders, but they don't have the nerve to ask. They think everybody is supposed to know and are too embarrassed to say anything."

Jenny's question threw Usher off balance and slowed her down. She knelt again at the mini-bar, took out a Diet Coke, and popped the top. "I'm just an apprentice working while I'm getting my master's in communications at Arizona State, but from what I hear, it goes back to the days of the original *Tonight Show*. That was the first major network television show that featured guests. Before going on the set, the guests were kept in a holding room that was painted green. Johnny Carson kept referring to it as the Green Room, and the name stuck. It's a term that has no current relevance to its original meaning. Like using the word *Kleenex* when we want a tissue or saying we're making a Xerox when we photocopy a paper. You would think we'd at least have a green chair or something, but this is all we've got." Usher pointed to the rust wallpaper and tan-toned furnishings. Then she quickly snapped back into action and disappeared.

Jenny again turned her attention to Allison, who still hovered near the food as if it were a security blanket. Her eating was interrupted only by nervous tugs at the long sleeves of her black, designer-label sweat-shirt. It matched perfectly the floor-length, flowing black skirt she wore. Darkness dominated Allison's fashion sensitivities, with her tastes running from black to black to black.

Her clothing perfectly matched her mood. Her eyes were ringed with a thin line of black mascara, giving her a somber, defiant appearance. Many times Jenny had offered to buy Allison any article of clothing she wanted, something brighter and more vibrant, but Allison had flatly refused her offers.

Allison's menacing veneer was further enhanced by the half dozen rings that pierced the cartilage of both ears. The skin below her lower lip was punctured by a silver pin with a small round ball on each end. It looked painful, but Jenny presumed it had less to do with fashion conformity and more to do with intimidating anyone who crossed her path. From her straight, raven-colored hair to her black sixteen-hole Doc Martens, Allison's attire said, "If you're part of my crowd, you're okay. If not, stay out of my way." The wardrobe was not what Jenny envisioned as the proper clothing for a young mother striving to get her life together. It seemed as if Allison was living in her past, part single mom and part rebellious teenager.

It was painful for Jenny to see her daughter assume this dark demeanor. Jenny knew what was behind the facade. No matter how hostile Allison appeared on the outside, Jenny remembered the tender moments they shared when Allison was a child. She was always headstrong but had a sweet personality that broke through her aggressive exterior. Unfortunately, defiance was now her way of expressing herself.

Ten years ago Jenny and her ex-husband, Danny, had parted ways in divorce court. Since that day, Allison had been the sole object of Jenny's affection. Life as a single parent had been more difficult than Jenny ever imagined it could be. But no matter what the cost, every sacrifice was worth it for Allison's sake. The extra dish of macaroni instead of a night out at a restaurant, the sparse wardrobe replenished only occasionally with a visit to TJ Maxx, and the austere life of solitude in a cramped apartment were small prices to pay so that Allison could have the things she wanted.

Danny was delinquent with the child support he promised, and that made life a lot tougher. But Jenny didn't mind the shortfall. She gladly exchanged it for the benefit of keeping Allison away from Danny's heavy drinking and hard living. As far as Jenny was concerned, Danny could keep his money if she had Allison to herself to raise as a mother knew best.

A slight pang of hunger, or nervousness, shot through Jenny's stomach. The hors d'oeuvres looked delicious, so she decided to join Allison at the tray.

"You know," Jenny said, trying to strike up a conversation, "things could get quite personal out there." Jenny paused. "Are you prepared for that?"

Allison shrugged her shoulders.

"What if they get into our family history?"

"So?" Allison responded. "Everybody I know is a little messed up. Dysfunctional families aren't exactly rare these days."

Jenny pulled a dozen white grapes, one by one, from a bunch and put them, a few at a time, in her mouth. "I'm not talking about us in general . . . I mean you specifically."

"What are you talking about? Are you referring to Ashley? Raising a child without marrying her father is all the rage in Hollywood. Why should that shock anyone?"

Jenny put a couple of brownie squares on a napkin and headed back to her chair. Halfway across the room she paused. What she started to say wasn't something she planned to mention. In fact, she had never discussed it with Allison. But Jenny wondered if this was the time to finally tell her.

"When he was briefing me about the show over the phone, Steinberg hinted that they sometimes investigate the pasts of people they have on the show. He warned me that McBride likes to shock people on the set by telling something that they might have never revealed before, especially to friends and family. I wasn't sure whether Steinberg told me that as part of standard procedure or whether he was telegraphing me a warning."

Allison cocked out her left leg at the knee and put her right hand on her hip as a sign of irritation. "What are you getting at? If you have something to say, say it. You know there are plenty of skeletons in my closet that I wouldn't want anyone to know about, especially you. Hey, *I'm* the one taking the risk by coming on this show. What could you possibly be concerned about that would be more awful than anything I already know I've done?"

Jenny said nothing as she stepped away from Allison and slowly relaxed into a chair. She popped a couple more grapes. "Guess I felt like you always suspected it down inside. I mean, you and Danny were so much alike, and yet different in so many ways. I figured that some-day you'd ask about it and then I'd tell you. I just don't want it to come out on a show like this with the whole world watching."

"Mother! I'm getting really irritated! What in the world are you . . ."

"Allison?"

The voice came from the doorway. It was Kim Usher. She motioned toward Allison to come quickly.

"I need to see you for a few minutes. Can you follow me, please?"

Her voice was irritatingly matter-of-fact, almost disinterested. Allison moved away from her comfort food of cheese bits, olives, and small kosher pickles and followed Usher as she walked briskly down a long tiled hallway. With one arm, Usher clutched to her chest a clipboard with a dozen dog-eared papers attached. Her other hand twirled a lead pencil between her fingers. She vigorously chomped a wad of gum in time with her steps.

"I hear you and your mom don't get along," Usher said as she pointed toward a door on her left.

Allison nodded.

"That's okay. In fact, that's great. It'll add lots of tension to the show." They entered a small ten-by-ten room, with a dilapidated couch and a folding chair. Usher closed the door. "Over there," she said abruptly, as she pointed to the Goodwill-destined sofa. Allison sat down.

Usher wasted no time getting to the point. "Do you yell much at your mother?"

Allison held inside a loadful of anger and resentment toward her mother, but Usher's blunt manner annoyed her almost as much. She kept silent.

"I need to explain to you what Billy's show is all about," Kim said, staring sternly at Allison. "We didn't go through all the trouble to get you here to have a polite tête-à-tête. The success of this show depends on whether there's action on the set. Don't hold back. If you want to yell at your mother, go ahead. Forget about those cameras and the studio audience. Pretend you're in your own living room. If your mom says something you don't like, tell her off. Be yourself. Let your anger out. Be real. Understand?"

This wasn't what Allison expected. Sure, she understood that *McBride* thrived on controversy and conflict, but in her naïveté she assumed the outbursts were, well, a little more spontaneous. She didn't like being prompted to commit emotional self-destruction on national television. Allison admitted to herself that Usher was asking her to do nothing more in public than she'd done a hundred or more times in private—violently vent her frustrations.

What was the point of doing it here under the guise of reconciliation? She had long ago given up any hope of harmony with her mother. Too many bad feelings had been expressed and too many harsh words had been exchanged to think things would get better. Allison detested her mother, but she needed her and didn't like Usher's idea that she should go in front of the cameras and express open belligerence.

"But I thought the show was about . . . I agreed to be on because . . . what I meant to say was . . ."

"I know, I know. You thought this was some kind of counseling session or glorified family therapy. Sorry, honey. If you want to see a shrink, that's a different time and place. This is entertainment. Shock talk." Kim winked. "Hey, look at it this way. You're a cute gal, and you'll be on national TV. Just think of all the guys that'll be coming on to you after this show."

Allison lifted both legs off the floor and tucked them under her. She nervously pulled her skirt over her knees and rubbed her right wrist. Kim's callousness made her uneasy. She was scared and wanted comfort, not aggression.

The assistant producer ticked off a couple of items on the papers she held, as if she were going through a checklist evaluating Allison's qualifications for the *McBride* battlefield. She looked across the top of her clipboard. "Look, kid, I can relate. My mom and old man split when I was young, and I've had to make it on my own. It's a cruel world out there and you've gotta be tough. If I didn't need to look respectable to keep this job and pay the rent for me and my boyfriend, I'd probably streak my hair pink so I could thumb my nose at the world. I envy the chance you have tonight to make a statement in front of the whole country. Tell your mom off. Tell the world off. Tell everybody where to get off. Scream if you have to. Cuss if you want to. We have a slight time delay, so we can bleep that out. Hold nothing back!"

Kim handed Allison a sheet of paper. "Read this over. It's a legal release saying we have the right to do what we want with your appearance here and that no matter what happens, you can't sue us. You can't go on the show without it. Everybody signs it. It's just a formality, but the legal eagles say we have to do it, especially since that gay guy got shot after being on the *Jenny Jones* show."

Allison signed the release. She had just been introduced to the world of shock talk, where everything is coached and manipulated.

Kim stood abruptly and opened the door. "C'mon. Let's head back to the Green Room. Show time is less than twenty minutes away."

As Allison walked down the long hallway back to the Green Room, Jeff Steinberg approached Jenny.

"Time for us to talk, Ms. Owens . . . Ms. Owens?"

Jenny stared at him as he stood in the doorway where minutes earlier Allison had exited. Jenny wasn't sure how much time had passed. She was dazed, frozen on the spot. She had come so close to telling Allison the truth about her past, a truth she feared might come out during the show.

"Yes, of course. I'm sorry. I was deep in thought."

"This way, Jenny, if I can call you that. We'll step into a side room where we can talk in private."

Steinberg motioned toward a room entered by a door near the chair where Jenny had sat. The room was only big enough for two folding chairs and a small coffee table. Jenny sat down, while Steinberg stood, hovering over her. He seemed serious. His dark brown eyes bore down on her.

"We care, really care about you and your daughter. We're here to help. Billy wants you to leave the show with a sense that something has been accomplished, that you and your daughter—Allison, right?—are on the road to something better."

Jenny found it hard to concentrate. Steinberg sounded sincere and his eyes softened occasionally, but Jenny wasn't sure he meant what he said.

"What can I expect when I get in front of the cameras?" Jenny asked. "What if Allison won't talk?"

Steinberg grinned, almost a smirk. "Oh, she'll talk, we'll see to that." He paused. "What I mean to say is that Billy will encourage an atmosphere of open exchange. Your job is to pour out your feelings as a mother. Every parent in America will empathize with you."

"But I don't want sympathy," Jenny responded. "I want answers. I don't think you understand, Mr. Steinberg. My daughter's situation is desperate. My granddaughter's future is on the line. To you this is just another TV show," Jenny continued, "but to me it's a last chance to save my child's life!"

Steinberg knelt beside Jenny. "Please, try to calm yourself. Save this for when you're on the set. That's when Billy can do you the most good."

"Is that what you really want? A weeping, hysterical mother?"

"No, no. That's not it. I'm just saying that here and now I can't help you. I'm not . . . qualified. Billy understands these things much better than I do. This is going to be an emotional night for you, and you mustn't let all of your energy out now."

Steinberg took Jenny's hand and gently lifted her from the chair. "It's less than five minutes to show time, and we have to get you miked." He turned toward the door. "Oh, by the way, you'll need to sign these papers," he said, handing Jenny the same documents Usher had shown Allison. "They're standard legal releases every guest signs. Just leave them by the hors d'oeuvres."

Jenny slowly exited the room. She felt slightly used and wondered if her efforts to turn Allison's heart toward home might instead drive her farther away. She was determined to make one last effort to say to Allison what had eluded her earlier. She felt very alone.

"Microphone time, Ms. Owens." A burly guy in jeans and a T-shirt walked toward Jenny carrying a tiny microphone with a two-foot cord leading to a battery pack. "I'm Jim, the sound guy. I need to wire you and your daughter. Okay if I hang this pack on the back of your belt?"

"Sure. Whatever you need to do."

Jim gently lifted the back of Jenny's mauve suit jacket and attached the battery pack. He strung the cord underneath her jacket and carefully pinned the microphone to the jacket's lapel.

"Just don't take your jacket off anytime," he said. "And be careful not to gesture with your arms and rub the mike. Always keep your arms out from the front of your body. Now, count slowly to ten for me."

"One, two, three, four . . ."

Jim put one earphone of a headset to his left ear and listened carefully. "Great. Just keep that volume level when you speak. If you get louder, no problem, we can turn you down. Don't talk lower than that."

Jim turned to Allison. "You're next, little lady."

Allison rolled her eyes at the condescending comment as Jim clipped her microphone to the neck of her loose-fitting sweatshirt.

"Would you mind running the cord from this microphone underneath your sweatshirt and bringing it out the bottom. We'll put the pack in the pocket of your skirt."

"Oh, no!" Usher said stepping into the room. "The sweatshirt. Forgot about that." She turned to the production crew of a half dozen people gathered just outside the door to the green room. "Anybody have a jacket she can borrow? You know Billy's rules. No slogans on the show. He gets all the endorsements."

"What's the problem?" Allison asked.

"What you're wearing. I should have noticed it earlier." Usher pointed to the bold words TOMMY HILFIGER across the front of Allison's shirt. "We've got to at least partially obscure that. Billy has all sorts of licensing deals, and no one promotes anything on the show without him getting a piece of the action."

Usher turned again to the crew. "No jackets, anywhere?"

"This is Arizona," one of Jim's assistants said.

"Then give up your T-shirt," Usher said, pointing to a young man holding a roll of microphone cords. "She'll wear that."

"What!" Allison responded. "That dorky thing? It's plain gray. You expect the whole country to see my television debut wearing a gray T-shirt?"

"It's gray or you go away, sweetheart," Usher said in her brusque New Jersey transplant accent. "What'll it be?"

The young man quickly took off his T-shirt and tossed it to Allison.

"The bathroom's over there," Usher said, pointing to a door a dozen steps down the hall outside the Green Room. "Hurry, it's almost show time."

"I've got a light sweater," a female assistant called from a room nearby. "I keep it handy because you guys always have the air conditioning turned up so high." She handed the sweater to Allison. "At least this will partially cover that awful T-shirt."

Allison angrily stomped toward the bathroom and exited moments later, holding the offending sweatshirt in her hand. She stepped into the Green Room and tossed it on a couch. As she did, Jenny followed her and grabbed her by the hand.

"You've got to hear it from me."

Allison stopped in her tracks, frozen by the dread in her mother's voice. Outside the Green Room everyone frantically made last-minute preparations, but a brief moment of silence prevailed inside the room. Jenny took both Allison's hands in hers and looked directly into her eyes.

"I can't bear the thought of having McBride tell you what I should tell you as your mother." Jenny took a deep breath and swallowed hard. Her hands were shaking. "Danny isn't your real father."

2

Families Out of Control" was just another day in front of the cameras, as far as Billy McBride was concerned. He'd done the same basic routine hundreds of times. Tease the topic. Badger the guests. Shock the viewing audience. Push the language to the profane. Incite outlandish reactions. Yank opinions from one extreme to the next. Solicit physical responses. Annoy. Arouse. Agitate. Enrage. Incense. Infuriate. Humiliate. Exaggerate. Orchestrate—every imaginable aspect on the spectrum of human emotions. In the end, with everyone psychologically exhausted, bring on the sentimentality for a wrap that pulls heartstrings toward a melodramatic conclusion. Just another shock-talk episode. How could anyone know that this show would forever alter the life of America's most-watched talk show host?

Billy waited backstage, ready to face the millions who each weekday anticipated his show with perverse interest akin to gawking at a car crash. He huddled near the set in a private corner that the entire *McBride* staff knew was off-limits to any interruptions. He talked to himself, rehearsing over and over the one-liners he planned to use on the show. Occasionally he glanced at a stack of papers Jeff Steinberg had just handed him, show prep documents that outlined each of the guests. Billy read for a few seconds, then closed his eyes, committing as much as possible to memory. He always had the teleprompter to rescue him, but he wanted an additional backlog of information in his mind for more spontaneous interchanges.

The only person who dared break in on him was Angela Sudbury, his makeup artist. She intermittently stepped in front of Billy to fluff powder on his forehead or flick dandruff specks from his shoulders. She tugged at his tie to straighten it. She pulled at his lapels to take the wrinkles out of his jacket. Billy ignored her intervention, lost in thought about what he'd do in front of the camera. At one point, Steinberg approached and whispered something in his ear. Billy chuckled briefly and went back to his state of concentration.

On the set, joke after joke from the warm-up comedian, Andy Mallory, echoed off the concrete floor and tall, blank walls of the expansive network television facility. The crowd, known affectionately to the show crew as "animals," consisted of a hundred people, mostly young males. They were a high-energy bunch who reacted instantly to Mallory's off-color humor. They came in every size and shape. Many wore T-shirts that read, TAKE A RIDE WITH MCBRIDE. They hooted and hollered as if it were a college fraternity party.

Mallory was Billy's best friend, and Billy knew his show would fail unless the studio audience was properly prepped. He grinned as he overheard Andy's four-letter expletives. This was the kind of language Billy believed he needed to loosen up the audience so they'd display a no-holds-barred response during the show. Billy made no pretense that his program was family entertainment. If a little dirty talk got the audience revved up with anticipation, so what?

In the back of his mind, Billy counted down the final seconds before show time. He shifted his weight from one foot to another and tottered slightly on the high heels of his alligator-skin cowboy boots. For a brief moment he peeked around the stage props and looked at his fans. After all these years in front of a television camera, his stomach still churned before each show. He knew the people in his audience either loved or hated him, and both groups watched with equal enthusiasm. They told him about their devotion with e-mail that ran the gamut from marriage proposals to death threats.

Most network television executives sneered and dismissed him as the lowlife of talk TV, but Billy knew that enough people adored him to keep up his market share. His outrageousness was justified with exploding ad rates. Sponsors waited in line to pitch their products on his show. If the mainstream media considered him a cultural cartoon, so be it. The parade of guests who cheated on their spouses and lovers, plus the scandalous assortment of social misfits and transgendered oddballs, translated into ever-increasing ratings.

It wasn't easy being the icon of trash TV. Billy made sure his postproduction crew scrupulously edited out the constant stream of four-letter words and occasional displays of nudity. When the violence got too out of hand and someone was injured, the cameras pointed in another direction. He laughed off the critics by defending his show as entertainment. He wasn't out to change society or promote world peace. He wasn't attempting to teach people anything valuable. When he did emote, it was designed to bring a touch of pathos to the show, in the midst of hurled insults and flying fists.

He tried not to think about the lives that were ruined by his show. Billy admitted to himself that there were good people who took his format seriously and thought their appearance would have a positive effect on their problems, only to learn that they were just another bizarre guest for the gallery of goons. To Billy it was all in the game, and if some on his show didn't understand the rules, tough.

"Two minutes," called out the floor director from behind camera number one.

Billy rubbed his eyes and looked at himself in a small mirror he had taken from his pocket. He straightened the brim of his white cowboy hat. Most TV talk show hosts dressed in Armanis, but Billy preferred western-cut suits with wide lapels and bolo ties inlaid with silver and turquoise. At age forty-two, he wasn't as handsome as the rodeo circuit rider he once was when he broke broncos and hearts from Cody to Casper. Still, his face had that same jaw-jutting, rugged look. No Rogaine prescriptions were needed for his head of thick, dark brown hair. Billy's strong frame made him look years younger than most of his contemporaries, who had succumbed to love handles and sagging eyelids. His engaging grin, accented by two latent dimples, was so infectious that Billy hit it off quickly with almost everyone, male or female.

Billy took out a pencil and marked a couple of provocative points he intended to make with each guest, folded the cheat sheets, and put them in the left inside breast pocket of his coat. From this point on, he was on his own. He had to depend on ingenuity and experience to keep up the energy level of the show.

The sound of the applause and hoots generated by Mallory crescendoed into a deafening roar as the *McBride* theme music was pumped through large overhead speakers. This was it. An hour from now he would either be closer to another ratings sweep or chewing out Steinberg for not finding more nutcases willing to bare their souls and totally humiliate themselves.

The floor director tugged at Billy's sleeve and pointed his index finger in the air. One minute until the live network feed from L.A. to New York. Billy edged toward the rear of the show's set and took a couple of deep breaths to calm his nerves. The rush of facing a live studio audience and the challenge of titillating the curiosity of twenty million Americans were what he lived for.

A year ago, Billy had moved the production of his show from Los Angeles, California. He got sick of having to schmooz Hollywood executives, so he thumbed his nose at "elitists" and set up shop in Phoenix, Arizona. The move shocked television marketing geniuses. It couldn't be done. Everyone knew that L.A. and New York were the two poles of power in broadcasting. Phoenix was too far from anywhere, and way too conservative. Besides, hiring a staff of professionals with experience required access to a talent pool that only the two coasts could provide. At worst, Chicago might do. That's where Donahue went from Dayton. Phoenix? No way would it work.

But it did. Doing it his way fit the thumb-your-nose attitude Billy exuded during the show. Doing it in Phoenix said, "I don't need your buttoned-down Eastern intellectuals or your Tommy-Bahamas-shirted suck-ups."

The design of his set reflected local color. It looked like a cross between a Nevada bordello and a tack store. The guest chairs were covered in a garish, bright red crushed velvet. A Mexican style saddle, inlaid with genuine hand-hammered silver, sat atop a section of split-rail fencing. Several horse bridles and a set of spurs were strung over the fence posts. The backdrop was a hand-painted outdoor desert scene of saguaros and yucca plants that looked like a page from *Arizona Highways* magazine. One almost expected the Sons of the Pioneers to walk on stage and sing "Tumbling Tumbleweed." It was kind of corny, but that was the point. Billy was no urban Oprah. He was down-home, as real as the sting of a prickly pear cactus and as unpretentious as a ranch hand cutting cattle.

"Ride 'em, cowboy," Steinberg said, as he passed by on his way to the production booth. Billy's eyes were closed to memorize some last-minute lines from his script, but he knew Steinberg's comment was an alert that the show was seconds away. The next thing he'd hear would be the announcer's voice signaling the start of the show.

"And now, the host of America's most unscripted hour on television. The man whose boots were made for walking into your living room with the unusual, the outlandish, and the outright insane. Take a wild ride with the host who hog-ties topics others won't touch—Billllleeee McBride!"

The announcer's introduction brought the studio audience to its feet. Affectionate catcalls greeted Billy as he sprang into action. The technical director chatted incessantly through his headset, in constant communication with the control room where the monitors of ten video cameras were displayed.

"Tight on one," the floor director said. Quickly the camera directly in front of Billy zoomed slowly to catch his expression. It framed his face so closely that his intense eyes nearly filled the screen.

"Wide on three, fan shot!" The number three cameraman did a 180 with his lens and turned to capture an enthusiastic group of scantily-clad young women in the studio audience holding up a banner that read, L.A. LOVES YOU! COME HOME, BILLY BOY!

Unseen to the viewers, but in full view of the studio audience, Mallory kept punching his fists into the air to pump up anyone who appeared less than delirious with Billy. A man with a shoulder-cam crouched at the edge of the stage, near Billy's feet, and angled his lens upward. The director in the control room went to the floor camera, capturing its surreal angle. It caught a view that one might have if he knelt at Billy's feet and looked upward adoringly, exactly the feeling the director wanted on-screen.

Being the center of this hubbub of activity and experiencing the thrill of launching another show was Billy's adrenaline rush. So what if his personal life was a disaster of titanic proportions? Television critics panned him for breakfast, and the tabloids speculated about his trysts with young cowgirls. This hour, in this studio, was his moment of glory. If the network execs considered him a blight on their phony "quality" programming, Billy was immune to it. He wasn't looking for "survivors" or "millionaires." He was the angry white male's idea of manhood, a hero to those who drove trucks and drove nails.

He was at the top of his game, and no bucking bronco with a moralistic bent would sway him from the sleaze that was his stock-in-trade. All that mattered were the people who watched in droves and the companies who pitched their products shamelessly during his commercials: psychic hot lines, exercise aids, get-out-of-debt loan companies, bail bond barterers, and lawyers looking for clients charged with D.U.I.

Billy didn't see himself as a moral policeman worried that some mother's daughter might be tempted to try what she saw exploited on his show. He was an entertainer, and shock talk was entertaining, if not aesthetically uplifting.

"Billl-eeee, Billl-eeee," the crowd shouted over and over, as they punched their fists heavenward. McBride tilted his head down with a tinge of apparent self-effacement at such adulation. He wasn't actually embarrassed, but it looked good to appear that way. In fact, it made the audience shout all the louder. When Billy figured he had milked the audience's reception for all he could get, he put up the palms of his outstretched arms in a gesture of "That's enough."

Gradually the studio audience calmed down and Billy started his preshow monologue. It was a carefully contrived homily on how he did this show because he cared about people and wanted to give average Americans a chance to speak their minds in a free and open forum.

"My fellow Americans," Billy said with a Nixonesque tone, "saddle up your ponies. We're going to ride from the land of political correctness into the badlands of emotional honesty where politicians and preachers aren't welcome. What you'll see is uncensored and uncut, real people with real lives. This isn't about *Friends*, and it sure hasn't been *Touched by an Angel*."

The audience loved it. They were back on their feet stomping and cheering. "Billl-eeee, Billll-eeee!"

"People on our show want to be here," the teleprompter reminded Billy.

Billy raised his right arm to cool the crowd and looked earnestly into the camera, responding dutifully to the directive given him. "Everyone on today's show has asked to appear and understands that the discussions may be deeply personal," he said. "They have freely consented to have the most personal aspects of their lives explored because they believe that their honesty will help others. That, friends, is why we do this show, to help make the world a better place."

Billy lowered his voice in mock seriousness, and the studio audience hushed. It was as if Billy and his crazed crowd were in collusion with an inside joke. Rant one minute, and emote the next. Highs and lows. That's what made his show work. Take on the bizarre with an air of solemnity, like Chevy Chase singing "Moon River."

"And now," Billy raised his voice like an evangelist preparing to give an altar call, "the moment of truth has arrived. Tighten your cinch straps, check your bridle bit, and grab your saddle horn. Coming out of chute number one, families who are out of control. Moms and dads who are desperate. Their children are so far gone, all that stands between them and a juvenile detention facility is this show." Billy paused, waiting for what he said to sink in. "In other words, what you, the studio audience, say to these hapless parents may be their last hope to control their kids. So, listen carefully and choose your words wisely."

Billy touched the tip of his hat. Steinberg recognized the cue. In the control room he punched up the show's theme jingle. Billy stepped back from the front of the set to the part of the stage where four empty chairs were arranged.

"Ladies and gentlemen," Billy said, "our first guest is a father fed up with his son's Internet addictions. Would you please welcome Floyd Simpson and his son, Roger."

To the sound of studio applause, augmented by a prerecorded clap track, a father in his late thirties stepped from behind the curtain, stage left. The elder Simpson wore a blue and red plaid shirt accented by tan Dockers slacks and white Nikes. He glanced nervously around the room as if he were lost, even though McBride's staff had already run him through the preshow checks of which chair to sit in. Billy caught Floyd's eye and motioned to the proper place on the set.

The father was followed by Roger, a thin, slightly gawky teenager, who seemed overwhelmed to be on television. He wore baggy jeans and an oversized T-shirt with the NO FEAR slogan silk-screened in bright red over a black background. Billy took one look at the T-shirt and shot an angry glance at Kim Usher, standing just off the set. Usher winced. The younger Simpson wasn't wearing that when she briefed him. He must have changed his shirt backstage, but there was no way to tell Billy that now. Roger's wide-eyed countenance bore a silly grin. Repeatedly, he nervously tossed his head backward to get his long, straggly hair out of his eyes.

Once Floyd and Roger were seated, Billy put his hand on one knee and leaned in their direction. He tilted back his cowboy hat. "Let me get this straight, Mr. Simpson. You're upset that your fourteen-year-old son spends every evening at his computer and avoids any contact with the rest of the family, right?"

The elder Simpson squirmed in his chair. "It's not just that, Mr. McBride," he said deliberately. "Roger takes this whole computer thing too far. Like the time I caught him surfing one of those porn sites named . . ."

Billy raised his hand to interrupt. "Hold it right there, Mr. Simpson. I know how raunchy those cybersex come-ons can be," he said with a church-lady sense of seriousness. "Let's just say that Roger was being enticed, as a minor, by some very unscrupulous porn vendors."

Billy glanced over his shoulder and gave a knowing wink to his audience. Hardly repressed giggles of titillation rippled through the crowd.

"And he was using my credit card to do it!" Floyd continued. "He actually placed an order and downloaded some nude photographs. Why, that sex site had sounds and moving pictures and everything. It was like stepping into a triple-X-rated video store!"

"Oooh," the audience cooed in mock shock.

"If you knew Roger was doing this sort of thing, why didn't you put a blocking device on his Internet access?"

"Don't know much about that sort of thing," Floyd explained. "Hey, I don't even know how to get on the Internet. This is a different generation, and Roger always seems to be a step ahead of his mom and me.

But what really ticked us off was when he started ordering booze on the Internet."

"Alcohol?" Billy said with fake amazement. Steinberg had briefed him carefully to go for this issue aggressively when it came up. And now Floyd was handing it to him on a silver platter.

"That's right. No I.D. check, no liquor laws, no nothing. Roger just ordered the booze sent straight to the house while my wife and me were away one weekend. When beer and liquor companies advertise on the Internet for direct delivery, what can a parent do?"

Billy glanced at the studio audience out of the corner of his eye. The younger members had grins on their faces and exchanged knowing glances. The few older people among them appeared shocked and indignant.

"Roger, why did you do it?" Billy asked.

"Why not?" Roger replied cavalierly. "The old man downs a six-pack any time he feels like it, so why shouldn't I? Some weekends when he's watching football, he's so dead-drunk Mom can't get him to bed at night. He sleeps off his hangover on the couch. Once he threw up on the living room rug. Don't tell me what I'm doing is all that bad, and don't tell me he has any right to run my life when he can't control himself!"

Floyd's face turned red. The audience burst into applause at his being put on the defensive. Roger smiled at the audience's response to his revelation.

Billy motioned for the audience to quiet down, as if he wanted to invoke some seriousness to the discussion. In truth, he was delighted at the spontaneous reaction. Things were heating up. Relational conflict always made the interest level in the show increase. Having Roger and his father exchanging barbs was perfect. If he was really lucky, they might threaten to strike out physically or throw something at each other.

Billy moved backward from the stage, seeking someone in the studio audience toward whom he could thrust a microphone. He spotted her, a middle-aged woman in the third row who seemed equally disgusted with both Floyd and Roger.

McBride inched toward her and asked, "If Roger were your kid, what would you do?"

At first the woman flinched as the cordless microphone neared her lips. Then she quickly offered her unabashed opinion with a Southern drawl that pegged her as an immigrant to the desert Southwest from somewhere in Alabama. "I'd pull the plug on that newfangled computer and send that kid back to the basics with enough books piled up for homework each night that he wouldn't have time to look at naked women and drink booze."

The woman paused, rolled up her right blouse sleeve, and pointed her arm and index finger in Floyd's direction. "As for this father, he's a pathetic parent! He needs to dry out, straighten up, and start setting an example. It's not the kid who's out of control in this family, it's that dad!"

The audience cheered, not so much for the logic of her analysis as for the dogmatic exuberance of her opinion. From behind camera number two, Billy saw Steinberg trying to get his attention. When their eyes met briefly, Steinberg waved his left arm in a circular motion, signaling to Billy it was time for a station break.

"Hold on, everyone," Billy said, "If you think Roger and Floyd's situation is bad, in a moment you'll meet Jenny and Allison Owens. Jenny says her daughter Allison is so out of control that she fails to take full responsibility for raising her two-year-old daughter and dumps her on Grandma. To make matters worse, Allison has moved back in to sponge off Mom. Should Mom kick out Allison, or endure her immaturity for the sake of her granddaughter? Stay tuned for our next segment, 'Moving Back with Mom.' But first, a brief break to sell some stuff so we can afford to keep bringing you 'quality' programming designed for the well-informed to stay informed. Now, don't you jump the fence for greener pastures. Stay tuned while I rein in the next segment of our show on 'Families Out of Control.'"

Andy Mallory stepped from the shadows and, just off camera, cajoled the audience into another clapping frenzy. Then, as the cameras went to black for four minutes of commercial inserts, Mallory made a cutting sign with his left thumb across his throat to silence the audience.

Instantly, he broke into another monologue of obscene behavior peppered with profane humor to keep the studio audience fired up. Billy quickly reached inside his coat jacket and pulled out his producer's notes and glanced at them. Angela Sudbury bounded onstage and powder-puffed Billy's nose and forehead. Technicians scurried everywhere, readjusting where microphone cords lay, rearranging the placement of guest chairs, and checking lighting and camera angles. A production assistant offered water to Floyd and Roger and moved them from the center-stage chairs to two chairs on the far left end. As they did, father and son looked at each other disgustedly.

"Fifteen seconds!" the floor director yelled. All production activity promptly ceased, and everyone involved with the show went back to their respective stations. Mallory delivered his last punch line.

"Five, four, three, two . . ."

Off-camera, Mallory encouraged another round of return cheers. "Welcome back," Billy said to camera one. "Our next guests are a forty-two-year-old mother named Jenny and her twenty-two-year-old daughter, Allison, who Jenny says needs to act her age. Jenny is here today to get some help before Allison totally self-destructs. Would you welcome Jenny and Allison Owens."

As the audience applauded, Jenny stepped on stage first. In her creased, A-line, Liz Claiborne slacks, relaxed cardigan sweater, and summer-weight suit coat, Jenny appeared to be the quintessential suburban soccer mom. Her medium-length brunette hair gently touched her shoulders and framed her pale face and delicate blue eyes. She was pretty, but her troubled expression detracted from her good looks. She was tired, like any parent who has fought a long family war with a troublesome child. The audience applause subsided, and both Jenny and Allison were seated.

McBride immediately directed his first question to Allison. "Just who do you think you are to act so irresponsibly? I hear that you go to raves, do Ecstasy, stay out until all hours of the night, and leave the parenting of your two-year-old to your mother. When are you going to grow up?"

Allison stiffened. She hadn't expected Billy to attack her so quickly. *Who told him about the raves and Ecstasy? What else did he know?* Her mind raced.

Billy went on. "From what I understand, your mother has spent the last ten years as a single parent, sacrificing to give you a good life. Is this the way you pay back her years of hard work and self-denial?"

The audience loved it. They were hardly a more responsible lot themselves, but the show wasn't about logic. It thrived on emotion, any kind of emotion directed at anyone. Allison was getting it, and that meant there would soon be sparks.

Allison glared back with a frightened gaze. "I don't have to take this!"

"What about the grief your mother has taken for years?" Billy shot back.

Jenny hadn't expected this either. She was angry with Billy for so suddenly getting after Allison.

"Just a minute, Mr. McBride," she chimed in. "My daughter may be thoughtless and even stupid at times, but she doesn't deserve being treated like this."

Another "Oooh!" from the audience.

"Maybe *you're* the problem," Billy challenged her. "Perhaps you shouldn't have taken her back home. If she messed up her life, let her pay the consequences and come to her senses. Is this what you've done every time she failed, prop her up with a pillow?"

"And what about my granddaughter? There's an innocent child involved. Little Ashley didn't ask for this. I'd let Allison pay for her mistakes, but not Ashley."

"Oh, Mom, I'm not a charity case. I can take care of Ashley. You talk like I'm incapable of raising my own child."

"If you were 'capable,'" Jenny interjected, "you wouldn't have become pregnant in the first place."

The audience was on its feet cheering and booing first one side, then the next.

Billy loved every minute of what was happening. It was just the way he wanted it. Mother and daughter at each other, and both upset with him.

"And what about your father? Where is he with all of this happening?" Billy asked.

"Leave my so-called father out of this," Allison responded angrily. "He doesn't deserve to be called a father. He never was one."

"Which one?" Billy asked sarcastically.

"And what's that supposed to mean?" Allison shot back.

Jenny's fear had come to pass. Now she was glad for what she said to Allison back in the Green Room. Even if Allison didn't yet understand, she wasn't being completely blindsided.

Allison jumped to her feet. "That's it! I've had enough. I'm outta here."

Without warning, she started off the stage. As she did, Billy instinctively reached out to slow her down by grabbing her left wrist.

The studio audience jumped to their feet, yelling, "Stop her, Billy! Don't let her get away!"

Members of the production crew went into action untangling cables as every camera operator jockeyed to get the perfect shot of the outburst. In the control room, Steinberg yelled out a stream of directives as he switched from one camera to another. These moments of unrehearsed conflict could create indelible impressions in the minds of viewers and advertisers. He wanted to make sure the drama was hyped to the max.

As Billy held on to Allison, she winced in extreme pain. Her knees buckled slightly and her left shoulder twisted. For a moment she strained against his grasp. He checked to make sure he was not holding on too tightly. She glared at him, shook off his grasp, and sat back down in her chair.

Billy was glad the incident was over. He didn't want to take any chances that his restraint would result in a lawsuit later, so he examined Allison immediately. Without asking, he reached for the sleeve of the sweater she was wearing and pushed it up to her elbow. Blood oozed from a scab his grip had dislodged. Billy looked closer and saw that Allison's forearm was crisscrossed with more than a dozen reddened gashes and at least a dozen more wounds with whitened scar tissue.

To Billy's amazement, Allison wasn't just an undependable parent. She was also suicidal.

3

What Billy should do next wasn't in any preproduction briefing book. Nothing Usher or Steinberg had told him prepared him for this moment. Pushing people to their limit was Billy's forte, but he wasn't sure how to handle someone who was suicidal. His entertainment instincts told him that Allison's outburst was good theater. Her scarred arm would be great shock value, especially if one of the handheld cameras could get a close-up. If he said nothing, he'd pass up an opportunity to further dramatize an already sensational incident. But deep inside, something told Billy to keep silent about the blood and scars, at least for now. He quickly pulled the sleeve back.

Was he going soft? Hardly. There were practical reasons for saying nothing. There was plenty of show left. If he exposed Allison's suicidal inclinations too early, she might leave and scuttle the remainder of the show.

Billy needed time to decide what to do. Unlike most television shows where the timing of commercial breaks is the director's call, Billy liked to pace his own show and reserved the right to format on the fly. Out of camera range, he clenched the fist of his left hand, a sign for the floor director to alert Steinberg that a commercial was coming. Seconds later, the show's theme music intruded and Billy opted out with a quick, "We'll be right back after these messages from our sponsors."

Instantly, Mallory was at it again diverting the confused reaction of the audience back to ribald jokes. He delivered a series of sophomoric one-liners so worthy of the description "locker room humor" that they almost smelled of sweaty socks. Everyone in the crowd quickly forgot Allison's averted exit. As far as Billy could tell, his quick look at her forearm went unnoticed.

Steinberg bounded from the control room to point D, short for "damage control." That's the place behind the set that he and Billy were to meet anytime something went wrong during the show and they needed to talk confidentially.

"Billy, you're five minutes ahead of your scheduled break," Steinberg sternly said. "You've dug yourself a big hole that'll be tough to get out of. What's the point, dude?"

"Jeff, you couldn't see that girl's arm. She's all sliced up, man. She has scars all over. Dozens of them. It's like her arm was the choice meat of the day in a butcher shop. Worse yet, one of the cuts is recent. It's bleeding. I think that I tore loose a scab when I grabbed her."

"Yeah?" Steinberg grinned. "I'll tell the hand-cam to move in tight. We'll fill up the whole screen with it. People all across the country will be grabbing for barf bags."

Billy looked serious. "Are you sure we should do that?"

"Sure? I'm dead certain. What do you think this show is all about, anyway? We're not *E.R.* We don't close wounds, we open them. You know that's what the audience wants."

"That's what they want, but what about Allison's mother?"

"What about her? What's she got to do with it? It's probably her fault her daughter is so screwed up, anyway. Besides, she's on the verge of breaking into tears. Arguing with her daughter in front of the cameras really got to her. If you hadn't gone to a break, we'd still have millions of people riveted to their TV sets right now, watching close-ups of her anguished, tear-stained face. These are the moments we live for around here. You know our motto, 'lowlife and high drama.'"

Robert Demrod, the floor director, peeked around the corner of the set. He pushed his headset off one ear and held up his middle and index fingers. "Two minutes, boss. Anything you want?"

"Nothing."

Steinberg put an arm on Billy's shoulder. "Stay cool. Get back out there and milk what's going on for all it's worth. Shove Allison's arm in her mother's face and demand to know how she messed up to make a kid like this go bad. Taunt her or Allison. Get somebody to break. We'll be ready with tight shots of which face flashes the most emotion. Remember, ratings sweeps. What you do in the next few minutes might make the difference in whether you are renewed in a dozen shaky markets. Some stations have been tottering on the verge of cancellation over the crazier stuff we've done. But if you can push this episode over the edge and show them point shares, it'll shut up all the naysayers. If that kid detonates, it could mean a jump to eight figures on your next contract."

This wasn't the first time Steinberg and Billy had talked like this. Billy knew the rules of the television game. The audience of network TV had been declining for years. Niche cable programming was swallowing up the tech crowd, and syndicated shows like *McBride* were the last hope of local affiliates. All the network executives gave lip service to the idea of shows with good taste, but what they really wanted was shows that tasted good at the financial bottom line.

Steinberg was right, Billy reminded himself. This was no time to play armchair psychologist and wonder what might happen if Allison went over the edge. He wasn't responsible for whatever made her slice up her arms. His job was to capitalize on the episode.

"Thirty seconds." Demrod's voice broke into Billy's thoughts. Less than half a minute for his brain to come up with a segue back into the topic.

"Go get 'em, guy," Steinberg said as he punched a fist into the air, like a boxing coach shoving his combatant back into the ring.

Instantly it struck Billy. He knew what to do, tasteful or not. He was grateful for Steinberg's reality check, which had jolted him back from a brief moment of concern for a messed-up child and her mother.

As the show's theme song mingled with the audience-augmented clap track, Billy jumped back on the set and looked earnestly into camera one. At the same time he grabbed Allison's right hand and pulled her out of her chair. "Stand up, young woman," he demanded. "Look into that camera and tell America why you want to die."

Allison jerked free and folded her arms across her chest and stiffened. Intense hate filled her eyes, a look Billy guessed Jenny had seen many times.

"What's the matter? Can't talk? Does it take a sharp edge to pry you open, if you know what I mean. Let's get real. You're a self-mutilator, a cutter. Whatever it's called, something inside you is sick."

The studio fell silent. Everyone was too shocked to react. Jenny sat back in her chair with a stunned look.

"Has your mother seen that arm? If you're 'brave' enough to cut yourself, why not let the whole world in on your nasty little secret? Quit hiding behind long sleeves. You're not a character in an Anne Rice novel. You're the daughter of a loving mother, and it's time you leveled with her about your problems. Tell us, how much blood have you spilled to ease your emotional pain? Are you some kind of vampire or just an overaged brat using your own body as a butcher block for some sickness inside your head?"

Allison was boiling with anger, and Billy expected her to explode any moment. She did.

A string of profanities flew from Allison's mouth. Suddenly she reached into a pocket of her skirt and whipped out a razor blade. The harsh television klieg lights glinted off the blade. Billy's bodyguards-for-hire, on duty for every show to keep things from getting completely out of hand, lunged toward Allison.

It was too late. In one swift motion, she slashed her forearm. Blood spurted everywhere. A piercing scream shot from Allison's mouth, and she collapsed on the floor, unconscious.

From all over the studio, cameras converged on her bleeding body. Close-ups of her mutilated arm filled the television screen. After several dramatic seconds of such images, Steinberg decided that such a scene, played out too long, might even be too much for Billy's audience. He abruptly signaled a commercial break without the benefit of any lead-in.

"Someone get a doctor!" a member of the studio audience screamed.

"We've got one," Billy yelled back.

In seconds a doctor bounded from backstage and attended to Allison's wound. Some months ago Billy had made arrangements for the show to always have a physician on call. That decision was prompted by an incident involving a guest who went berserk and broke two of Billy's ribs by flinging a chair at him. After the episode he joked about how much more dangerous it was being a shock-talk host than riding Brahma bulls back in Wyoming. In fact, Billy's broken ribs were no laughing matter. For months he struggled with breathing and was only able to carry on his work with the aid of steroids and prescription painkillers.

"She'll be okay. It's just a flesh wound," the doctor said. "She hit a vessel at the most vulnerable point, and that's why there was so much blood. The good news is that she coagulated quickly." The doctor covered the wound with gauze and wrapped it with tape. "Right now she's in shock. We need to take her to a place she can rest." He motioned for the bodyguards to help him.

"Put her on the couch in the Green Room," Billy directed.

Four men knelt and gently lifted Allison's limp body. As the commercial break ended, the cameras rolled again, just in time to see the men slowly carry Allison offstage.

As soon as Allison was safely off the set, Billy went to Jenny and consoled her with an arm around her shoulder. Jenny burst into tears and buried her face in Billy's chest. Billy had been so absorbed with what went on, for a few brief moments he forgot that he was on television. When he realized that what happened had been witnessed by millions, he sensed that the television audience was due some kind of explanation. He knelt by Jenny's chair, took off his hat, and stared straight into the camera.

"Look, folks," Billy said above the sound of Jenny's sobs, "I had no idea this was going to happen. That was real blood. This wasn't an act." He paused for dramatic impact. "We tell you to expect the unexpected," Billy went on, "but not even I expected this." Billy looked at Jenny. "Did you have any warning she'd do something like this?"

Jenny sniffled for a moment. Her voice cracked, "No. Sure, I knew she had problems cutting herself in the past when she was a teenager, but I got her to a therapist who helped. I thought the worst of it was over." She looked earnestly into Billy's face. "What are you going to do?"

It was an uncomfortable moment. Billy's job was to create shock, not pick up the pieces afterward. Whatever emotional litter was left behind once the credits started rolling was a problem for his staff producers. When a show got out of hand, the director scrolled a special announcement during the credits: *"The Billy McBride Show* is interested in the well-being of our guests. For those in crisis we offer counseling referrals and transitional support." Billy knew the truth. This only meant handing out a list of phone numbers to contact local psychiatrists.

Jenny stood to her feet and clasped her hands in a prayerful gesture. The cameras caught her reddened eyes and her strained countenance. "Mr. McBride, will you help me save Allison's life?" Jenny asked.

Initially, Billy was caught off guard. Then, his shock-talk instincts kicked in. This was the perfect setup for a continuing saga. By agreeing to help Jenny, he could drag out the pathos of this family crisis over several shows, like a continuing soap opera: "Rescuing Allison from the brink of death!"

He would ask people all across the country for advice on how to help her. They'd respond by letters, e-mails, phone calls. Perhaps he'd set up a 900 number. Those were financially lucrative, and Billy surmised people would spend real bucks to offer their suggestions. A calculator ran in the back of his brain. *This wasn't a tragedy. This was a moneymaker.*

Steinberg knew Billy's knack for the dramatic was in full swing, so he directed the cameras to switch from a tight shot of Jenny's tear-stained eyes, to a slow zoom of Billy. Gradually, camera one went from a frame of Billy from the waist up to a full screen of his earnest face.

"Will you heed this mother's tearful plea? If Allison were your daughter or granddaughter, would you sit there and do nothing? Of course not. You'd spare nothing to rescue this precious child."

Billy was surprised at how warm and sincere he sounded. It reminded him of the missionaries who used to come to his church when he was a child and take up offerings to feed starving children in some faraway country overwhelmed by poverty. They showed slides of babies with bloated bellies and lifeless youngsters, their gaunt faces covered with flies. "For less than a dollar a day, you can provide a child like Juan with food and clothing." Billy remembered the plea and locked the image in his mind as an emotional anchor.

He pulled off his jacket and dramatically flung it on the floor. He unbuttoned his right sleeve and pulled it to his elbow. With his left index finger he made a series of slashing gestures across his forearm. "From her wrist upward, there were dozens of scars from Allison's repeated attempts to kill herself. This desperate woman's life is at stake. Will you join me in an effort to rescue her before it's . . . too late?"

The audience was on its feet responding with an emotional fever pitch. "Yes!" they shouted in response to Billy's eloquence.

It was surreal. The same crowd that minutes earlier hooted in response to Mallory's jokes about private parts and bodily functions now pledged themselves to an unselfish humanitarian mission. For a moment, Billy silently wondered if he'd missed his calling and should have been an evangelist.

"Will you help Allison find a reason to live before she turns up in a morgue somewhere?"

The crowd's enthusiasm reached a frenzied pitch. "Yes, yes, yes!" they yelled over and over and then broke into cheers.

In truth, Billy had no idea how to fulfill his crusade on Allison's behalf. The rhetoric and the reaction were great, but he feared that he was promising more than he could deliver.

Demrod gestured frantically, trying to catch Billy's eye. In the excitement, Billy hadn't noticed the clock ticking away. It was time to wrap the show, and only seconds remained.

"America, I love you," Billy said. "Tomorrow, same time, same station, be here. We'll take on the topic, 'Transsexual Dating—How to Know Who Is What!'"

As the theme music blared over studio loudspeakers, Billy made his way off the set and down the hallway to his office. Staffers of every level greeted him with high-fives. Everyone, from the lowliest gofer to every staff producer, knew that today's show was a home run out of the park.

Within seconds, Billy was ensconced in his small but well-furnished den. He retreated there after every show to decompress. His assistant, Mandy Manchester, knew what to have waiting: a cold can of diet cherry Pepsi to drink, a bowl of fresh Planter's mixed nuts to munch, and a hot towel to wipe the perspiration from his face.

Next was a shower. Billy's contract stipulated that wherever his show was taped, he had to have an office nearby with running water. Showering was his way of relaxing and letting go of the tension. That, and a change into blue jeans and a polo shirt, calmed him.

Billy handed Mandy his sport coat. "It's got a spot on the left sleeve," he said. "Better get it laundered. I might wear it again in a week or so, unless Carter's Clothing boosts the wardrobe budget." Billy took off his tie. "Tell Carter's I want my clothing allowance increased to ten shirts a month if they're going to keep getting a promotional announcement in the credits. If they don't come through, shop the endorsement avails to someone else. I'm sick of their shirts anyway. With our ratings we ought to move up to something *Italian*."

"I'll do my best," Mandy answered dutifully. She popped the top on Billy's Pepsi and handed it to him as someone knocked on the door.

"See who it is," Billy said as he hung his tie on a rack.

Mandy opened the door slightly and poked her head through the crack. Then she closed the door and turned toward Billy. "Better hold off on your shower. That Owens lady wants to talk to you."

Billy paused. He didn't like to be interrupted after the show by anyone, especially a guest. On the set, every guest was important, but once the cameras were off, they were on their own, yesterday's news. But Billy felt drawn to Jenny's plight. Not only that, if he was going to string out her saga, he needed to assure her of his concern.

"Tell her I'll be right with her. I'll meet her in the Green Room."

Minutes later Billy entered the Green Room. The faint smell of fruit and cheese from the half-eaten food tray pervaded the room. Allison lay on the couch with her eyes closed. Jenny sat in a chair, her face buried in her hands.

"How's Allison?" Billy asked.

"I spoke with the doctor. He says she'll be all right. It'll just be one more scar to add to the others." Jenny rose from her chair and walked toward Billy. "You meant what you said out there, didn't you?" she asked.

Billy paused. "Of course."

"You were serious when you said you'd enlist the help of the whole country to help my daughter, weren't you?"

Billy knew that he hadn't really meant what he said, at least not the way Jenny meant it. This show was in the can, and now he had to prepare for tomorrow's topic, and the day after that. So what if he overstated things a little?

"Ms. Owens, I understand why you're so distressed at what happened today. You have every right to be concerned. But you've got to understand that . . ."

"It's all an act, isn't it!" Jenny squared her shoulders and defiantly placed both hands on her hips. "You used us out there! Friends warned me that's what you were about, but I hoped against hope that there was a chance, just a small chance . . ."

Jenny burst into tears. She turned her head aside and hid her face against her right forearm.

Billy froze. It wasn't the first time a disillusioned, angry guest had exploded at him. Some had to be taken away by security. But Billy never worried. A phalanx of lawyers kept him just far enough from the edge of a lawsuit to avoid any recrimination.

But he was uneasy with Jenny. Something about her situation seemed different. In a strange way, he connected with Allison, even though he had never entertained self-destructive impulses. His mind raced for an answer—why couldn't he just walk away and turn things over to a subordinate, like every other time?

"Ms. Owens, you're right, the show is an act. This is show biz. We're in the business of entertaining. Without a certain amount of sensationalism, we couldn't survive. So, in a sense we were using you. But we weren't exploiting you. Even you've got to admit that this show brought things between you and your daughter to a head. Now you both sense how serious the situation is and can get some help."

"Help? You mean this?" Jenny waved a sheet of paper in Billy's face. "Your 'faithful' staff gave me this list of shrinks. Well, I've taken Allison to see shrinks before. For ten years she's been in and out of therapy, until our health insurance ran out. There aren't any answers on this piece of paper that will save my daughter's life."

Jenny wadded up the paper and threw it at Billy. The crumpled paper bounced off the side of his face and fell to the floor.

"You were my last hope. You were right when you said that there's something sick inside Allison. You can see it in her eyes. But whatever it is can't be cured by any more $200 sessions with some psychiatrist!"

Jenny paced back and forth across the small room. "So what about your pledge to help her? Was that just as hollow as everything else you said?"

Billy realized that he was in too deep to run for cover. His integrity had been challenged, and he couldn't back down. Like the luck of the draw in getting a bad bull to ride back in Cheyenne, he had to see this thing through to some kind of conclusion.

"No, I meant what I said. We will help your daughter."

"When?"

Billy searched for an answer. Then he blurted out. "Day after tomorrow. We'll have you back on the show, and we'll bring in a panel of experts to hear both sides of the story and offer advice."

The answer didn't satisfy Jenny, but it was better than anything she'd heard so far.

"Listen. Can you hear it?"

It was Allison speaking. Her eyes were open. She raised herself up on one arm. Jenny quickly went to her and took her hand, pulling her up to a sitting position.

"Hear what?" Jenny said.

"That sound. It's like a train, clickety-clack . . . no, it's not a train. It's the sound of . . ."

"Of what?" Billy joined in.

"I don't know. There's breathing. Heavy breathing. And that sound. It's like a drumbeat. It's incessant. It's getting louder and louder. My God! I can't stand it. It's pounding in my head like it always does. Stop it, Mother. Tell them to stop it. That's the sound I hear when I cut myself."

Allison turned to Billy. "You can make it go away."

"Make what go away?"

"The sound. You must hear it too."

"I have no idea what you're talking about."

Allison fixed her eyes on Billy. He was taken aback by the force of her gaze. His spine shivered, and he felt something cold move up and down his arms. Somewhere deep inside he knew she was right. In his soul he could hear it.

4

Billy didn't like early mornings. Especially mornings like this, the day after his encounter with Jenny and Allison. No matter what he did to calm his nerves—a cup of hot herbal tea, two capsules of Tylenol PM—sleep eluded him. The sight of Allison's blood-stained body stole his repose. But the look in Allison's eyes haunted him the most. Something in her resonated with something in him.

Billy lived alone, and solitude never bothered him. But today his two-bedroom townhouse seemed more secluded than ever before. He'd been a loner most of his life. Madalyn, his mother, was the only person he'd ever felt close to. No aunts, no uncles, no grandparents ever visited their small, white clapboard, ranch-style house. When Madalyn died of cancer at the early age of fifty-seven, Billy was unmarried and unattached. Her passing ended any connection he might have had with an extended family.

Memories of his dad were hard to recall. Brogue McBride disappeared when Billy was just four. In the back of his mind he remembered harsh words, a slammed automobile door, and the sight of a car driving away. He saw himself standing on the front porch of the house in Cody, Wyoming, with Madalyn's arm around his shoulder. Billy couldn't remember what the man in the car looked like, and he had no memories of life before that incident. In fact, he had little recollection of anything until his early teenage years.

Someone must have taken snapshots of his father and him. Every proud daddy has at least one picture holding his new baby. But Billy never saw a single photo. Why hadn't his mother ever shown him any photographs? If there were wedding portraits of the man who fathered him, they were hidden away. In fact, Madalyn never once spoke about the man she married. He was a living dead man, if indeed he was still alive.

Billy never asked about his father. He knew better. The subject was taboo. A code of silence willingly agreed to, without coercion or logic. A few times Billy thought about broaching the subject but backed off when he saw the approaching sadness in his mother's eyes. He desperately wanted to know the facts about his father, but not at the risk of hurting his mother.

That avoidance made him angry. Those who knew Billy described him as outgoing and friendly to a fault. But Billy knew that his cavalier attitude toward life masked a deep inner resentment that bordered on bitterness. While she was alive, he never dared challenge his mother's embargo on information about his father. Because he never spoke to her about it before her death and couldn't confront her now, the rancor had to have a way out. Billy suspected that his sarcastic attitude in front of the camera was a public expression of his internal frustration. The pain of no paternal connection had to go somewhere. So, his suffering was the root of his success. As he stumbled toward the bathroom, Billy understood why Allison had such an effect on him. Both were running from a father they didn't have and plunging toward a future without any anchor in the past.

No bathroom should be this well-lit so early in the morning, Billy thought.

A bank of bare lightbulbs, like those in dressing rooms, framed either side of the mirror in front of him. The bags under his eyes seemed baggier than usual. His hairline looked as if it had receded several centimeters overnight. He brushed the hair out of his eyes and pulled at a couple of graying ones that he thought were out of place for a man his age. He ran a comb through an obstinate strand, and held it to the side of his head while he applied a pump spray of Sassoon Super Hold.

Billy turned his face first to one side, then the other, studying his reflection from every possible angle. Whose nose was this? Why did it veer slightly to the left? Why were his eyes brown? Madalyn's were blue. He never liked the way his upper lip veered slightly upward on the right side. That's why he grew a mustache. By clipping the hair straight across, it evened out the line of his lips. Billy's careful study of his characteristics wasn't an exercise in vanity. It was a quest for genetics. Who was he biologically? He had half an answer, Madalyn's half.

Billy opened the shower door and turned on the spigots. Someday he'd have a place with instant hot water. Living here convinced him of that. Whoever built these townhouses didn't know much about plumbing. Some mornings it took as much as five minutes for the water to get hot. He didn't have a lot of time today to get ready. It was already 10:00 A.M., and he was due at the studio for today's show briefing in less than an hour. While he waited for the right mix of water temperature, his mind went back to Allison.

They were a lot alike. Both were rebels who didn't fit in well with life's mainstream. To them, life was a fishbowl, and they saw it from the outside. Others were content to swim in concentric circles, seldom questioning their course. The Billies and Allisons of the world wanted a larger perspective. That's why they looked at things differently. But it was lonely outside the bowl. Not many wanted to take the risk and jump out of the safe, warm waters of confinement. Allison had done that by adopting her own brand of rebellious individualism, and Billy had accomplished it by bucking the definition of TV stardom.

Ouch!

Billy quickly withdrew his hand from inside the shower. He was so lost in thought that he had put his hand under the spout without thinking. The hot water was hot enough, but the cold was still tepid and the mix was scalding. The burn on his hand jolted him from the introspection he had been undergoing since awakening.

The box!

The thought came to him out of nowhere. Maybe the answers about who he was could be found there? He never looked inside it while his mother was alive. He remembered her lovingly holding it as if it contained treasure. It was a jewelry box that played "Sentimental Journey" when you lifted the lid. Madalyn had kept it locked in a chest at the foot of her bed. Billy saw it on just a few occasions. Once, when he was a teenager, he had asked to look inside. Her firm "No" permanently settled the matter. Now it was somewhere among her personal effects. Everything that belonged to her was contained in a dozen cardboard boxes sitting in Billy's garage.

Billy turned off the shower. This was more important. He stumbled from the bathroom, barely awake, and quickly dressed. He grabbed a soiled sweat suit and donned his oldest knock-around New Balance sneakers, the ones he had retired from running. His task was going to be a dirty one, and there was no sense in dressing up for the occasion.

On the way to the garage, Billy stopped in the kitchen long enough to slap some low-fat, strawberry cream cheese on a cinnamon raisin Einstein bagel. He reached in the refrigerator for a carton of orange juice, the "contains no pulp" kind. Five bites and three big gulps later, he was out of the kitchen and in the garage. He hit the door opener, backed his black Infiniti out the door, and parked it in the driveway. He left the door open to let in more light and turned his attention to the boxes.

They were piled at all angles, one on top of another, all the way to the ceiling. They came in various sizes, with the corporate logos of Bekins and Allied plastered on the outside. Some were full and rigid.

Others, half empty, were slightly crushed and lopsided from the weight of the boxes stacked on top. Several tilted sideways like a moving company's tower of Pisa.

Billy hadn't touched these boxes since the day they were packed in Cody. They contained clothes, personal effects, knickknacks, and the other memorabilia of Madalyn's life before she moved. If Madalyn had had her way, she'd have spent the rest of her life in Wyoming, but Billy wouldn't hear of it. He flew home one weekend and insisted that she move to the sunny Southwest. Two weeks later, she was living in Sun City, Del Webb's paradise for the senior set. The boxes went into Billy's garage.

The one-bedroom patio house that Billy had bought for his mother wasn't home for long. A stroke left her paralyzed on one side and unable to eat or attend to bodily functions. Even with the help of a nurse visiting once a day, it was too hard for Madalyn to carry on life as she had before. The stroke eventually confined her to a wheelchair, and there was no choice but to put her in a nursing home with constant caregiving.

Billy didn't think there was much "care" to the giving, during those brief six months his mother languished in bed. The minimum-wage staff probably did their best, but it wasn't like living in Cody. Billy went to see her almost every day. One night he got a call saying he needed to come quickly because his mother was fading. She died before he got there, before he had one last chance to ask about his father.

He stayed with the body for an hour, and talked to the lifeless form as if Madalyn were still there. Billy said the things he always wanted to say in the living years. Mostly he talked about his dad. He asked the questions he was never bold enough to ask in life. Why had Brogue and Madalyn parted? Why was he forbidden ever to see this father? What kind of a man was he? Was he tall or short? Handsome or average? Bright or a regular guy? What color was his hair? Was he bald? Fat? Athletic?

There were no answers to the questions that echoed off the barren walls of his mother's death chamber. When the doctor finally came to close her eyes and pull the white sheet over her head, Billy collected a few items from her room. A copy of a Monet that hung on one wall. A pot of silk, red roses. A cup inscribed with the words WORLD'S GREATEST MOM.

The Monet, the roses, and the cup were dispersed in his townhouse. But Billy wanted more, something that would give him a sense of his past. Perhaps he would find it in these cardboard coffins. He would roll away the stone and resurrect whatever had been sealed inside.

Where should he start? Which box held the treasure? Billy hadn't a clue, so he began at the top.

He placed an eight-foot ladder next to the boxes and started dismantling the stack, setting each box on the floor, spread out over the space of the empty garage bay. Billy took a pocketknife and slit through the wrapping tape. He flipped back the lids and scrounged inside every box looking for *the* box.

Most boxes contained personal items his mother had planned to use decorating her new Sun City quarters: a small painted porcelain rabbit, several pillows with stitched maxims ("Prayer changes things," "Home is where the heart is," and similar sentiments), souvenir dishware from the few trips she took in life ("SEATTLE WORLD'S FAIR 1962," read one decorative bowl), and a foot-high china poodle with an electrical cord sticking out of the tail. Billy couldn't resist plugging it in. He smiled as the eyes blinked from a bulb inside.

More porcelain figurines, commemorative teacups, and doilies, crocheted with intricate designs, the stuff of social finery in far-off Cody. Billy carefully removed the newspaper surrounding each item, looked at it, and then wrapped the boxed memory again. When each box had been carefully examined, he used a black marker to make a check on top, indicating its contents had been inspected.

An hour later, only two shipping boxes were left, both Bekins. Billy stood over them. Somewhere inside was what he was seeking, or so he hoped. If nothing turned up, the search was still worth it. He had journeyed through his mother's world in a way he never felt close enough to do while she was still alive. The last hour had been a journey marked with smiles and an occasional tear. The resentment he felt toward her partially dissipated when he saw her existence so warmly pass before him. Madalyn was a special woman, even if she had hidden the secret of her soul that he was seeking.

The first of the two remaining boxes yielded more of what he'd already seen. One box left. He hesitated to open it. If the treasure chest was there, this ordeal must be some kind of cosmic joke.

With one deft slash of his knife, Billy cut the tape. He snapped back the flaps from both sides. Newspaper. Like all the other boxes, this one was packed with yellowed newsprint hastily stuffed inside as a final cushion against breakage. More and more newspaper. Then, he saw it. A cheap, metal storage box, the kind that unsophisticated folks with few private documents to hide purchased at Wal-Mart. It was locked. Billy hastily grabbed a screwdriver and began prying at the thin metal latch.

Snap! The yellow plastic handle to the screwdriver was still in his hands, but the metal stem had broken and bounced across the garage floor. This time Billy took a hammer and, using the claw tip, easily snapped the rivets holding the lock. He laid the hammer down slowly, almost reverently, as if he had unsealed fabled booty. He lifted the lid, only to find another box.

There it was, just as he had remembered it. He slowly lifted the lid.

"Gonna take a sentimental journey, gonna set my heart at ease." The words coursed through his mind as the tinkle of the melody drifted through the musty air of the garage.

Another box was inside this one. It was a hand-tooled leather case with a scene of Mount Rushmore chiseled into the top and the words *Rapid City, S.D.* underneath the presidents' faces.

Billy closed his eyes. He imagined himself being held by strong arms. He gazed, with his neck bent back, at the granite images of Jefferson, Roosevelt, Lincoln, and Washington. He clung to a hairy neck. It was a warm, safe memory.

Solemnly Billy placed the leather case on a paper towel, lest it become soiled by one of the many oily stains that dotted his garage floor. He opened the hinged lid and saw three smaller packages inside. Each was wrapped in thin paper, the kind that upscale stores use inside folded shirts to keep them from creasing. Each was bound by a single red ribbon, immaculately tied in the exact center. The ribbons showed no sign they had ever been wrinkled by being untied, and then tied again. Whatever was inside the paper and ribbon had been permanently sequestered, never to be seen.

Billy picked up the first packet and held it momentarily before untying the ribbon. South Dakota. Deadwood. The museum. The memory was distinct.

Mommy, Daddy, see what I found. It's a black widow spider on a pin. Billy closed his eyes again. There in the midst of flat, glass-enclosed display cases were specimens of local insect life.

It was all so clear, as if it were occurring this instant. A part of Billy was in the now. He wasn't traveling down memory lane. He was there on his tiptoes, his small hands gripping the edge of the case and pulling his body up just far enough to see inside. The same strong arms that lifted his gaze to Rushmore had reached under his armpits and held him higher so that he could see the entire exhibit of creepy, crawling things.

Look over there, in that other case, Billy heard a deep male voice say. *That's a Colt 45 like the kind Wild Bill Hickok used.*

Billy blinked himself back to the present. How could such distant remembrances be so vivid?

He unraveled the ribbon and pulled back the paper containing a stack of photographs. The top one was of a handsome soldier, standing ramrod-straight, his hat folded flat and tucked under his belt. His grin was broad and toothy, a genial sort of person whose eyes flashed with personality. HELLO FROM SEOUL, MAY 1950 had been scratched into the emulsion of the fading black-and-white photo.

It was Brogue. Billy was sure of it. He fought back the lump in his throat and gently ran his fingers around the edges of the picture. Under that photo were others. The same man, the same uniform, but different settings: standing in front of an Oriental temple, bending over a plate of food while wielding chopsticks.

Different circumstances, but the same smile. A smile that burned itself into Billy's soul. This was the treasure he'd spent a lifetime searching for, preserved for this moment by some unknown photographer. Billy felt suspended between life and death, born again to a man he never knew, and separated by death from a mother he couldn't question.

For a moment he considered not opening the other packets. Maybe it was best to stop now and let the truth die with his mother. The thought lodged in his mind briefly, but he couldn't stop. He had to know more about this man, every picayune thing he could find out. Maybe there was a dog tag in the next package. A draft number. Some official piece of paper that could be traced.

The next ribbon yielded a single document. Billy tenderly unfolded it, afraid that a twist of the paper might tear it. "Department of Defense," read the masthead across the top.

August 11, 1952

Dear Corporal McBride,

I regret the circumstances under which this letter must be written. However, a grievous situation has come to the attention of your commanding officer concerning certain events while you were in Korea.

A Korean woman has filed charges with the U.S. consulate in Taipei claiming that you are the father of her child and that on or

*about June the 13, 1948, you were married to her in a civil cere-
mony, duly recorded in documents forwarded to my office.*

*Our records indicate that you were previously married to
Madalyn Prior of North Platte, Nebraska, in 1947, the year before
you were drafted. We have no record of your having been divorced
from her. As you know, the Army takes seriously the morals of its
fighting men, and these accusations call into question your pending
honorable discharge.*

*Perhaps there is a reasonable explanation for this matter. It is not
the intent of the Army to pry into the personal lives of its soldiers;
however, if the accusations against you are true, your conduct would
violate the Military Code of Justice.*

*The Formosa High Command is pressing my office for an imme-
diate explanation. Please respond quickly. Thank you.*

> *Yours truly,*
> *General Alfred Kenyon*
> *Undersecretary of the Army*
> *The Pentagon*
> *Washington, D.C.*

This wasn't what Billy wanted. Before this moment, he knew nothing about his father. Now he knew too much. Worse yet, he was forced,
absent any living witnesses, to make sense of a messy situation.

In his fantasies about his father while growing up, Billy had filled in
the blanks with heroic proportions. His dad was tall, muscular, athletic,
handsome, personable, charming, intelligent, kind, compassionate,
loving. This letter from General Kenyon contradicted the immaculate
image his mind had constructed. What should he believe about a man
he couldn't cross-examine?

If true, this letter explained a lot. No wonder his mother sent his dad
packing. Two wives and two families! But what other facts influenced
this situation? How much of a chance did his father have to explain?

Did his dad ever see this letter, or did he come home one day to find his belongings packed and sitting on the front porch?

Billy was angry and confused. Events from the distant past now had power over him with no sense of resolution. Then, he heard it.

Thumpity, thumpity, thump.

At first he thought it was the pulse of his own heart, but the rhythm was more like that of a galloping horse. This was the sound Allison had talked about. It was coming closer.

Billy rose to his feet and looked around the garage. The rhythmic pounding stopped. His garage was a mess, with rumpled newsprint strewn everywhere. He bent over to stuff it back in the box when he realized he hadn't opened that last ribbon-tied packet. He didn't want to. He had enough surprises for one day, even for a lifetime. But curiosity prevailed, and he found himself kneeling next to that Bekins box and once again holding the leather-bound case in his hands.

Even more slowly this time he unraveled the third ribbon. The contents were much heavier than that of the other packages. As the ribbon came undone, a metal object fell out and struck the concrete with a clang. Its oval shape caused it to oscillate for a few seconds. When its vibrations ceased, it lay silently on the cold concrete. Billy knew instantly what it was. He'd seen many of them on the rodeo circuit.

He cradled the oversized championship belt buckle in the palm of his hands and read the ornate inscription: FIRST PLACE, BULL RIDING, CHEYENNE FRONTIER DAYS 1956.

Inside the paper that wrapped the buckle was a handwritten note. The penmanship was sloppy but legible. The words were eloquent in their simplicity:

My dearest Madalyn,

> *Since that day you told me to leave and never show my face*
> *again, I've prayed God would give me some way to show you how*

sorry I am and how much I still love you. My life hasn't amounted to much without you, and I don't have many skills to get a good job. So I travel the circuit from town to town hoping for a big win to keep up the payments on my pickup. It's hard to make a go of it with no college education and a dishonorable discharge from the service.

Last week was the best win yet in Cheyenne. Now I'll be able to buy a small trailer to pull so at least I'll have somewhere to sleep on those overnight drives between rodeos. I've searched for some way to say you still mean the world to me. This buckle, the most important thing in my life, outside of you and Billy, is my way of showing I still care.

My darling Madalyn, there will never be another woman in my life besides you. I was lonely, mixed up, and did a very dumb thing. Forgive me. If you can find a way past your pain to take me back, I'll be there in a New York minute. If you can't, I'll always understand.

Hug Billy for me and tell him that his dad misses him something fierce. I know he's a little man by now and doing his best to look after you. When you look in his eyes, please remember me, if we never see each other again.

I still love you, Brogue

Reality struck like lightning. The toughness Billy had acquired from years of bronco riding and taking on Hollywood crumpled like the newspapers scattered all around him. He dropped to the cool concrete and wept like a baby.

He determined he'd find his father, dead or alive!

5

Allison Owens flew down Forty-fourth Street in her black '92 Honda at thrill-ride speed. When the road dead-ended at University Street, she pulled a sharp right, accelerating past the south end of the Phoenix Sky Harbor Airport. This section of University was lined with nude bars, strip joints, and XXX-rated video stores on either side. Massage parlors assured "private rooms" with "sensual" techniques available. Voluptuous airbrushed sex sirens beckoned from dozens of billboards inviting customers to take advantage of "the most beautiful women in Phoenix" and "all nude" cabaret shows. Allison was oblivious to the blatant erotic appeals. She'd driven through this part of town so many times that her eyes blocked out the selling of sex.

All was quiet on the street. Allison looked at her watch and gasped, "Eight o'clock. My mom's gonna wring my neck!" She knew that her mother would be furious when she awakened to find that Ashley had been left alone with her again. Allison rubbed her bloodshot eyes and pressed the accelerator even harder. She had to get back to the house as quickly as possible with a good explanation for her absence.

She glanced at her wrists where she'd cut herself on *McBride* the day before. The tightly woven threads of her long-sleeved black sweater pulled at the fresh, tender scabs, irritating them. She was glad it wasn't one of those infamous Valley of the Sun summer days when the thermometer hit 115 degrees. On those days, the planes she saw now on final approach wouldn't be taking off again, grounded by the overpowering heat that reduced aerodynamic lift. At least in early January she could wear something to cover the darkness that pushed her to end it all.

What am I thinking? She mused. *All of America has seen my cutting job. How embarrassing.* She shook her head. *Why do I do this crazy stuff? I need help!*

Allison slammed on her brakes to stop at the intersection where Thirtieth Street crossed. As she waited for the light to change, she tapped impatiently on the steering wheel with her long fingernails. Every nerve in her body seemed on alert. She didn't like making this trip so early in the morning, but she was desperate. Her thoughts raced frantically, and the voices she always heard inside her head were especially loud today. It was like an internal family conflict, with relatives all vying for dominance. Some shouted. Others screamed. They told her she was worthless and deserved to be punished, that the mistakes she'd made in life were all her fault. The voices insisted she'd never amount to anything and was only good to be used and abused.

Allison knew why she cut herself. It was the only way to vent her inner chaos.

As the light turned green, she turned left and headed toward the southern outskirts of the city. Two miles later she approached a pre-stressed concrete warehouse surrounded by a chain-link fence. A sign on the front entrance read "OTOROLA," minus the giant *M* of the communications company that had abandoned the facility in favor of cheaper south-of-the-border labor.

She had never been here at this time of day and was surprised to find the front gate to the complex unsecured. She drove through the opening and parked near a white trailer, like the ones used to house offices at construction sites. The trailer rested on gray cinder blocks, its wheels suspended above the asphalt. There was no sign on the structure, which was dented in places and had paint peeling on every side. Gang graffiti, which had been sloppily spray-painted over, was barely legible on one end. A "No Admittance" sign was screwed to the door.

Allison got out of her car and walked slowly toward the trailer, located behind the building that was the home of the raves. She stepped on the small steel riser in front of the door and pushed the button of a buzzer near the handle. The sound was irritating, as if whoever installed it wanted to be sure that nothing would drown out its signal.

Allison waited a few seconds and pushed the buzzer again. No response. She muttered a curse under her breath and started back to the car. Just as she put the key in the door to unlock her Honda, she heard the door to the trailer crank open.

"Allie? Is that you?"

A tall, gaunt man in his early twenties leaned out the door, looking half asleep. He was bare-chested and wore string-tied, khaki cargo pants.

"It's me, E-Man."

He looked like a middle-aged man, even though he hadn't hit his thirties yet. Too much hard living had taken an early toll. The platinum, spiked hair looked harsh, not hip. His weathered skin appeared tight and yellowish, like someone three times his age suffering from malnutrition. His smile was friendly, but it had an empty pretense, as if he were a salesman ready to pitch a product with an overrehearsed spiel.

"Hey, Allie, whatcha doing here before sundown? The rollin' doesn't start for another twelve hours. You usually don't show up until we've been ravin' for a while. Me, I've been up all night, and I'm gonna try to make it until tomorrow without crashing. Hey, what do you say we have our own little party. Got some pacifiers?"

Allison looked up at the early morning sun, shielding her eyes from its angled rays that were unusually warm even for a sunny, wintertime Phoenix day. She rolled her eyes. "No thanks. I just need some 'E.' Are you selling?"

"We'd have a lot more fun sharing."

Allison was irritated. "Look, I didn't come here to be hustled. All I need is your pharmaceuticals. Are you selling, or not?"

E-Man didn't appear to be the kind of guy who spent his time worrying about how other people used his psychotropic wares. In fact, he looked like a loser who didn't care much about anything in life.

"Is this some kind of a trick?" he asked.

Allison wondered if her untimely presence created suspicion.

"Drop the defense. I'm alone. I'm not a narc on a mission. You know me. I've risked the wrath of Social Services' taking my child to use what you've got. It's just that I'm in a bad way today, and I need some Armanis."

E-man was as casual as a candy vendor assessing his assortment of sugar. "All out. Second choice?"

"Constellations?"

"Sure, baby, those I got. It'll cost ya."

"What's that supposed to mean?"

E-man tilted his head back and looked out the corner of his eyes seductively at Allison. He checked her out, with an up-and-down once-over, trying again.

Allison folded her arms across her chest in disgust. "Knock it off, E. I told you, you're not my type. Five bucks."

"Eight."

Allison was getting agitated. "If I want to barter, I'll go to an Oriental bazaar! Six. Or I'll take my business elsewhere."

"Hold on, Allie. No need to get pushy. How many?"

"I need two dozen. Seven bucks. My last offer."

E-man put out his hands, palms first, in a calming gesture. "All right, I'll deal. It's just that you took me by surprise. I'm not used to seeing you until around midnight. In fact, you're lucky to find me here. I usually don't show up until the crowd starts arriving around nine o'clock. But we had some trouble with outside dealers barging in last night, so the boss had me stay here until things completely cleared out. That's why I'm burning some E-fuel."

E-man glanced around the complex looking for anyone who might overhear their conversation. He motioned for Allison to step inside the trailer. As he did, he reached in his pocket and pulled out a plastic bag. "I got some K. Want some of that?"

"You know that I only do those when I'm cocktailing. Not today. Besides, I'm in a hurry."

"Okay, okay. That's cool."

Allison ducked her head as she entered the metal structure. She glanced around the interior of the trailer. At the nearest end was a tattered couch, with the sharp edges of springs randomly poking through the cracked leather cushions. A couple of soiled, smelly blankets had been thrown on the couch along with two throw pillows with the stuffings oozing out of various tears. A beat-up wooden desk piled with empty plastic zipper bags was against the wall across from the door. A half-collapsed director's chair was at the other end, next to a weathered beanbag chair. Behind that was a wall. A sign, taped to the door with masking tape, read: "ENTER AT YOUR OWN RISK. ROTTWEILER INSIDE."

"Is there really a vicious dog behind that door?" Allison asked.

"You get one chance to open it and find out. Be my guest," E-man answered, with a sinister gap-toothed grin. He flopped himself on one end of the couch and shut his haggard brown eyes.

"It stinks in here." Allison exhaled and wrinkled her nose.

"What can I say?" E-man replied. "Some kids threw up in here last night. A bunch of high school gangsta wanna-bes combined the Ecstacy with ketamine, that animal tranquilizer stuff, and wine, cheap wine. It's bad news, but when you're on Ecstacy, nothing much bothers you."

"Now that's really cocktailing," Allison observed, rolling her eyes in disbelief. "Don't the cops ever check out this place?"

"Yeah, like they check out the fourteen-year-olds who roll here every weekend," E-man answered sarcastically. "Get real, Allie. The pigs are for show. They frisk a couple of wide-eyed geeks who are here for the first time to make it look good, and that's it. What are they going to do? All at once, arrest two thousand kids who are high and dancing in that building over there? I don't think so. It's a rave, for crying out loud, and most of the general public doesn't even know where we are, let alone what we do. We're not exactly a high-profile law enforcement priority, and we like it that way. Our stuff used to be legal, until do-gooders had to ruin a good thing. C'mon, our drugs don't hurt anyone, do they?"

Allison shrugged and thought, *If you were the poster boy for E, I'd quit today.*

She began to get nervous. "What if someone walks in on us now? I'm used to buying when there are lots of people around. Safety in numbers, you know."

E-man laughed. "This is our 'office.' Every 'business' has to have an 'office.' The cops would need a warrant to come inside. Hey, they don't look in here at night, and they're certainly not going to look in here during the day. Now, let's get down to business. You know the rules, cash only."

Allison said nothing. She walked over to a rusted sink and fiddled with the faucet handle. "Got something to drink? I haven't had breakfast yet."

"Allie, this is an Ecstasy lab, not a concessions stand. If you want a Pepsi on location, you'll have to go to the Diamondback's Bank One Ballpark," E-man chided. He looked at Allison seriously. "Do I detect a certain hesitation to come up with the cash?" he said, rubbing together the index finger and thumb of his right hand.

"I've got it, that's not a problem. It's just that . . . I don't have it on me right now. I had to run out of the house early this morning, and Mom . . ."

E-man interrupted. "I get the picture. Mom wasn't up yet, and you couldn't lie to her to get the goods. I don't care how you get the money.

I just have to be paid in cash. You know the rules. Besides, you owe me for a couple of weeks. You understand the law of supply and demand. I supply, and I make the demands."

"I'll have it tonight."

"Then that's when you'll get the E."

Allison's body stiffened. "You don't understand! I *have* to have it now. Tonight's too late. My head needs help. The voices are getting louder. I promise I'll pay."

"What's so serious that you need to roll now, in broad daylight?"

"This!" Allison rolled up her sleeves.

"That's definitely not cool," E-man said, slightly sobered by what he saw. "I'm not so sure I should sell to you anytime."

Allison walked toward E-man, put her arms out, and clasped his hands. She pulled him up from the couch and put her arms around his waist. She leaned back and softly looked up into his eyes. "My head is churning. Like I told you before, your stuff is the only thing that will quiet the voices. Help me, please."

E-man gently forced her arms away from him and plopped back down on the couch. He crossed one leg over another and rubbed the short stubble on his chin. "I'm just a businessman, you know," he said. "Like any good entrepreneur, I can only stay in business if I show a profit. And something for nothing isn't good business."

"I'm begging you, E, please. If not a couple dozen, just a few pills. Enough to get me through the day."

E-man assumed a thoughtful gaze at the ceiling, then leaned forward toward Allison. He reached in the pocket of his jeans and pulled out a small plastic bag with four tiny pills. He dangled them in front of Allison's face, barely three inches from her nose.

"Who's deejaying tonight?" Allison asked, an obvious stalling tactic.

E-man continued to swing the bag like a tempting pendulum. "The best, man, Amondo XT. The nod, man, he gets the nod. But get to the point. Yes or no, do you have the money?"

Allison clasped her hands in a prayerlike gesture. "For the last time, no, but I will tonight. I just have to get some E now and get back to the house. You know I'm good for the money. I just don't have it on me. What do you expect me to do, sell my soul?"

E-man snapped his fingers around the plastic bag and doubled his fist, imprisoning the cache Allison begged for. He put the bag back in his pocket and stood to his feet. "Allie, baby, we already have that."

Allison's eyes winced with a questioning gaze. "Have what?"

"Your soul."

"Yeah, right," Allison said, not taking the comment seriously.

E-man stepped to the door and, with a mock gesture of chivalry, bent at the waist and motioned for Allison to leave. He held out the plastic bag with the four pills. "My compliments," he said.

Allison stood to her feet, snatched the bag from E-man's hand and stepped outside. As she passed through the doorway, a cold chill swept across her body. Her arms rose with goose bumps. At first she thought it was the cooler outside air, but the sunlight glancing off the tarmac was too intense for that.

As she neared her car, Allison paused momentarily and glanced over her shoulder. E-man stood in the trailer doorway with an evil grin on his face. He leaned against the door jamb. With the thumbs of both hands he thumped on the metal frame of the trailer. *Thumpity, thump. Thumpity, thump.* The rhythmic throb spooked Allison. She quickly unlocked her car, jumped inside, and drove away.

As Jenny got out of bed, she, like Billy, encountered an image that reflected facts as they were. Her antagonist was the full-length mirror that hung on the back of her bedroom door. It exposed every droop, sag, and pocket of cellulite. Jenny feared that any day the battle of the bulge would start in earnest. Being in her forties scared her. It was the first step into the previously inconceivable era of early middle age. She noticed that most men still checked her out when she walked by, but she wondered how long that would last, with Allison's behavior robbing the last bits of youth from her.

As she prepared to take her first look in the mirror, she pulled back her brunette hair, which hung over one side of her face. It did that the first thing when she woke up. And it was always the left side. Jenny figured it must have been from her tendency to sleep on her left side with her hair tucked under her left cheek. Her blue eyes looked especially tired. The whole night she had thought about nothing but what to do next with Allison.

Jenny took the day off from work. After the ordeal of *McBride* the day before, she called her boss the minute she had awakened and cashed in some vacation time rather than face job pressures. That wasn't her original plan. She had expected to return as a minicelebrity, but Allison's suicide attempt changed things. When Jenny called her boss, an ambulance-chasing, personal-injury attorney named Larry Ludlow, he agreed that everyone in the office would have felt uncomfortable and at a loss for words to comfort her if she came back to work so soon.

Jenny was surprised that Ludlow let her take the day off so readily. He wasn't known for his generosity or his compassion with his office staff, especially Jenny. Her job was crucial to the firm. She worked as a telephone receptionist, answering lines that rang constantly. One potential client after another complained about injuries they were certain must be worth a million dollars or more if the right lawyer had their case. She had a soothing voice that exuded compassion and trustworthiness. *At least my caretaking quality is worth something*, she thought.

Larry was the man wanted by every person intent on suing. All of them had seen television ads where Larry promised the aggrieved they'd "get the money they deserved." Behind the boss's back, in the lunch room, the office staff "affectionately" referred to their employer as Larry

Lowlife. Jenny never made any derisive comments. She was grateful for a steady paycheck, even if she knew her income was based on the tactics of lying to insurance companies and threatening them with public disgrace if they didn't settle quickly. Her conscience bothered her every once in a while, until the reality of taking care of her precious granddaughter and her irresponsible but loved daughter hit home.

It hadn't been easy. Ever since Allison moved back into the house, she had done nothing to help. Jenny did it all: housekeeping, making the car and mortgage payments, and balancing the checkbook on time. She also scheduled doctor and dentist appointments for all three and fixed at least two meals a day. She tried to keep some personal "quiet time" for her own sake but wasn't very successful.

Jenny wrapped a robe around herself and headed for the kitchen for a morning round of decaf vanilla mocha. There on the kitchen center island was a note in Allison's handwriting:

> *Mom, keep an eye on Ashley for me. I'll be out for a while. Not sure when I'll return. Back as soon as possible.*
>
> *Allison*

Jenny crumpled the paper in her hands and threw it in the garbage. She muttered a profanity. How typical of Allison, to be so selfishly unconcerned for Ashley's welfare! Allison didn't say where she was going or how to contact her. Jenny spotted Allison's cell phone next to the microwave. She didn't even have the courtesy to take her phone in case there was an emergency with Ashley.

Jenny knew that she made a mistake when she told Allison last night that she planned to take off work today. That was Allison's ticket to go AWOL from her responsibilities as a mother. She'd done it before, and the last time she had been gone for three days without any contact.

Jenny thought back to what Billy McBride said on the show. He was right when he told Allison to grow up. Having a child might have been an accident, but now a child's life was in Allison's hands, and Ashley's well-being should come first. Jenny couldn't understand why Allison was so self-centered, to the point of attempting suicide without a thought of what that would do to an innocent two-year-old.

"Mommy, Mommy. Come get me!"

Jenny heard Ashley's voice cry from her bedroom. The shrill plea cut to the core of Jenny's soul. She wanted to ignore it. That's what Allison did when she didn't want to deal with the pressures of being an unwed single mother. But Jenny couldn't.

"Coming, sweetheart. Jen-Jen will be right there."

Jenny rushed to Ashley's crib and lifted her over the rails. Ashley clung to Jenny and nestled her head in the nape of Jenny's neck.

"Where's Mommy?" Ashley asked, as she looked toward the door.

"Gone. She'll be back soon."

"She bye-bye. Bye-bye no more, please." Ashley straightened up in Jenny's arms and looked her directly in the eye. "You be my Mommy."

Jenny wept inside but kept her composure. "I'm your grand-mommy. You have me all to yourself today."

"Mommy no love me." She looked down and pointed her finger at her heart.

"That's not true. She loves you very much."

"Why she go bye-bye?"

Jenny looked away in anger. "Don't cry, sweetheart. Let's get some breakfast. Would that be all right?"

"Can I have some nana?"

"One banana on the way."

Jenny set Ashley down to walk to the kitchen. Her tiny fingers wrapped tightly around Jenny's index finger as she walked alongside her grandmother and looked up at her. Halfway across the living room, Jenny heard the sound of the garage door opening to the stall where Allison parked her car. Jenny's back stiffened with resentment, knowing that Allison would walk in the door any minute.

"Run to the kitchen, sweetie. Jen-Jen will be there in just a minute."

"Grandma."

"Hush, Ashley. Do what I say."

Ashley dropped her head in a pout and shuffled toward the kitchen. Jenny folded her arms and faced the front door. Seconds later it opened. Allison was startled to see her mother standing there.

"I know what you're going to say," Allison offered. "I didn't want to wake you up. We were both up so late last night. I had some errands to run, and you know Ashley is hardly ever up by eight or nine o'clock. Sorry. Hope you didn't mind."

Her words were apologetic but well rehearsed. Jenny had heard similar speeches a thousand times before. Her irritation reached an explosive level.

Jenny threw her arms in the air in disgust. "Is it ever going to end? You're a mother and an adult, for Pete's sake. Is it too much to ask that you extend just a few courtesies, like letting me know where you are, when you'll return, what's going on? What if Ludlow hadn't let me off work today? Where would I have left Ashley? What if something had happened to you?"

Allison stomped across the room toward the kitchen and stopped short of the door. She reached for an apple in a fruit bowl and took a bite. She stared at the apple and then looked up at Jenny. "Is that what being a grandmother is all about? I thought that grandparents loved their grandchildren like their own children. You know I can't afford babysitters when I have to be out. Excuse me for thinking you'd want to have some quality time with your granddaughter! I suppose you'd feel better if I were a permanent prisoner in this house and never left."

Jenny shook her head. "I can't believe what I'm hearing. You've got it all twisted. *I'm* the one who really cares about Ashley's welfare. I'm the one who spends more time with her than you do, when you're out doing God-knows-what. Grow up. You're a mother. Act like it or . . . or . . . get out!"

Allison's eyes flashed with an intense anger Jenny had seen before when they had harsh words like this. She walked menacingly toward Jenny. As Allison passed a small desk at one end of the room, her hand brushed across the top and gripped a sharply pointed letter opener that lay there. Wielding it like a knife, she waved the tip in Jenny's direction.

"Don't threaten me, young woman!" Jenny shot back.

"I don't threaten," Allison responded, as her voice deepened with a tone Jenny wasn't sure she had heard before. "I'm not going anywhere. Back off or else."

"Or else what?" Jenny said, her voice slightly quivering.

A hideous sneer crossed Allison's lips. Then, with one swift motion she stabbed the apple with the opener. She drew the impaled fruit to her lips, took another bite, turned, and walked back toward the kitchen. Just as she approached the door, she stopped.

"An apple? I hate apples," she said, as she tossed the half-eaten core in a wastebasket.

Before she could go further, the phone on the desk rang. Allison quickly grabbed it.

"Hello . . . yes, this is Allison."

Jenny stood silently waiting to see who was on the phone. She shook with fear. She'd never seen Allison act like this before. *What has gotten into her?* she thought. *What if she hurts Ashley when I'm not around?* She shivered at the idea.

For a while Allison said nothing to the caller. Then she grinned as if she were privy to some inside joke.

"Sure, I'll be there this afternoon. See you later."

Allison put down the phone. "See who later?" Jenny asked. "This day has been tough enough on Ashley already. You're not heading out again!"

Allison pushed her left hand inside her jeans pocket and felt the plastic bag she had been given earlier. "Relax, Mom. Chill out. Everything will be just fine."

6

You know I keep a tight control on what happens on my show. This is the first time you've ever scheduled something without my knowing it!" Billy McBride slammed his fist down on his desk and glared at his producer, Jeff Steinberg.

Steinberg didn't flinch. His eyes were cold and steely. "No one questions whether you're the boss, Billy, but we both know where the ultimate power lies. The ratings don't lie, and yesterday's show with Jenny and Allison was off the charts. You don't think I'd do something without asking you first, unless I knew it was for your own good, do you? When I saw the Nielsen ratings this morning, I had no choice. So I went ahead and scheduled today's show."

"Choice? I'm the one who doesn't have a choice. You've changed the topic, booked the new guests, and notified the newspaper television guides–all without my having any idea what was happening."

"I tried to reach you on your phone, but you weren't available," Steinberg argued. "Where were you, anyway? You always have your cell phone on when you're out."

"I was in the garage."

"The garage? All morning? What in the world were you doing in your garage all that time?"

Billy waved off the question with a "Never mind."

Steinberg walked toward Billy's desk. He placed both hands flat on the desktop and leaned forward. "You've got to trust me on this one. I talked to both of them separately, and they individually agreed to come on the show. In fact, at the time, neither of them realized I had talked to the other. Billy, you really don't have a choice about going for the throat. The *McBride* distributors called me Monday with an ultimatum. You've been getting closer to the X-rated edge with every show, and a dozen advertisers are threatening this week to pull the plug, unless . . ."

"Unless what?"

"You know the answer to that. Unless the ratings are up. Advertisers aren't moral policemen. They don't care what you say or do, so long as they don't get too many complaints, and, most important, so long as . . ."

"The ratings are up. I know, I know." Billy looked away for a moment at the leather box in its new location on his desk. He reached over to trace the words *Rapid City, S.D.* with his fingertip. "You're sure this will work?"

"I'll stake my professional career on it."

"You might have to," Billy responded soberly.

Steinberg turned to leave. "We've got some incredible footage to open the show with, close-ups from yesterday that will gross out even the hardiest of souls. No one will switch channels. It's one of those defining moments we wait for in live TV. Remember, eight figures in that next contract. Today's the day we make the jump to the big leagues."

Billy glanced again at the paperwork Steinberg had accumulated to prepare him for today's show. No question about it, Steinberg had done his homework. The lineup for the show was top-notch and provocative. It was a coup to get both Jenny and Allison back on the show, especially when they'd both face a psychiatrist, a psychic, and a preacher.

"And now, the host of America's most unscripted hour on television. The man whose boots are made for walking into your living room with the unusual, the outlandish, and the outright insane. Take a wild ride with the host who hog-ties topics others won't touch, Billllleeee McBride!"

Once again the audience was on its feet to hoots and shouts of "Billll-eeee, Billll-eeee!"

"My fellow Americans," Billy started out, as he always did. The opening was so rote that he could say it under the influence of melatonin with bombs bursting in air. It was mechanical and calculated. But this time, he didn't follow his monologue with an immediate introduction of the topic.

"Watch your screen closely," he warned, "and for heaven's sake, if you have small children, get them out of the room." He paused with a sincere look on his face. In truth, Billy knew Steinberg didn't care what children saw. The warning was contrived for shock effect, designed to get the viewers' attention. "What you're about to see," Billy went on, "is some of the most graphic video ever captured on live television. And it happened yesterday, right here on this stage."

The television screen immediately cut away to footage of the moment when Allison slashed her forearm. One camera after another converged on her, zooming in as close as possible to the wound and the blood that shot from her veins in pulsing spurts. The sounds were almost as disturbing: Jenny's scream, the frantic calls for a doctor, the show personnel scurrying about, and the low-level reverberation of a pounding throb. Billy listened closely. He didn't remember the sound when the incident originally occurred. Perhaps he was too preoccupied at the time to notice. The timbre of the tone sounded live, like it wasn't on the videotape. But it had to be.

The final scene froze on Allison, her bloody body lying on the floor just before being carried from the studio. The camera first framed her face, showing a haunting smile on her lips. Then the camera slowly zoomed toward her eyes, which evoked an evil intensity, the pupils dilated and the eyeballs distended as if they were widening for a deeper look into her soul. The camera came closer until both eyes filled the entire television screen with an unblinking, trancelike gaze.

Then the screen gradually dissolved to Billy. "A little later in the show, that young woman and her mother will be back onstage to face you, America. But first, you're going to meet three people who think they have an answer to keep that young woman from killing herself. Please welcome our guests, a psychiatrist who specializes in treating people who self-mutilate, a psychic who specializes in past-lives regression, and a minister who says the devil made her do it."

McBride theme music blared from the studio speakers as two men and a woman stepped from backstage. Each nodded politely to the audience and sat down in the chairs set up for them. As the applause of the audience subsided, Billy stepped closer to the trio. He deferred to the middle-aged woman who was seated between the somber psychiatrist and the distinguished-looking clergyman.

The psychic's bleached blonde hair hung straight, resting gently on her shoulders in a style worn by women half her age. From her ears dangled earrings with oddly-shaped symbols. A long black scarf was wrapped loosely around her neck, accenting her long, flowing maroon dress, unbelted at the waist. Every finger of each hand sported a silver ring fashioned with the same symbols as her earrings. Her expression was vacant, as if she were bored with life. She sat erect with her hands folded in her lap.

"Gloria Stern is a self-proclaimed psychic," Billy said, as he reached for a hardcover book handed to him by the floor director. He held the book toward one of the cameras and slightly tilted it downward so that the embossed words of the title wouldn't catch the glare of the lights. "*Who You've Been Is Who You Are* is Ms. Stern's latest book." The complimentary plug out of the way, Billy turned to the unsmiling guest. "Like the rest of us, you've seen the footage of Allison. What do you think?"

"I saw the whole show yesterday," Stern informed the audience.

"That's better yet," Billy said. "Why do you think she attempted suicide, and what can we do to help her?"

Stern shuffled in her chair for a moment to relax her body and raised a finger as if lecturing the audience. "That poor woman is acting out what was scripted for her many, many lives ago."

"You mean, years ago, don't you?"

"No. I meant what I said. Lives ago. You see, each of us, in our genes, has the imprint of who we've been in other incarnations." She took a dramatic pause and pressed her pink lips together. "For example, in another life I was a member of Genghis Khan's harem in the thirteenth century. I was his favorite concubine, but he beheaded me when I fell out of favor after I fell in love with one of his courtiers. That's why I've never been married. I have issues with men, especially controlling men."

Several members of the studio audience groaned in disbelief. "And you want us to believe that your difficulties with the opposite sex are because of what happened to you hundreds of years ago?" Billy chided his less-than-credible guest. "Maybe you're just too tough to live with."

Billy's audience loved it. "Billll-eeee, Billll-eeee!" they chanted.

Billy raised his hand to quiet them.

"You don't have to believe me," Stern said, "but even the Holy Scriptures teach reincarnation. John the Baptist was the reincarnation of Elijah. It says so right in the Bible."

"Wait a minute," the preacher on Stern's left interrupted. "That passage of the Bible clearly says that John came in the *spirit* of Elijah, in other words, in the manner and calling of the ancient prophet. It doesn't say he was actually Elijah come again in the flesh."

Billy turned to the guest who was speaking. "Ms. Stern, meet Dr. Joseph Kingman, professor of biblical studies at Arizona Baptist Seminary, and according to the paperwork handed to me by my producer, an actual, bona fide exorcist!"

That job description met with howls from the audience, which seemed even more skeptical of Kingman's occupation than of Stern's psychic assumptions.

Dr. Kingman reacted immediately to the mockery directed toward him. "I'd prefer to be referred to simply as a Christian who believes in the Bible cover to cover."

Kingman's response momentarily quieted the crowd. He certainly didn't look like someone who was spiritually eccentric. His full head of silver-gray hair gave him a dignified demeanor. In his dark blue suit, white shirt, and stylish tie, he looked like the kind of pastor you'd expect to see in the pulpit of a respectable congregation. The graceful lines on his face spoke of maturity, and his pleasant expression was disarming. He was the kind of minister someone could trust and talk to.

Billy was anxious to exploit the differences between the preacher and the psychic and get the conflict between them started early. "So what do you think about Ms. Stern's idea that Allison's suicide attempt is somehow related to a previous incarnation?" he asked Kingman.

"Ridiculous," Kingman replied. "She can't even prove that she herself lived another life. Her idea of who she was in another reincarnation is subjective conjecture. Furthermore, she's in violation of the biblical commands against spiritism. She may call herself a psychic, but according to God's Word, she's a witch."

"A what?" Stern said, glaring at Kingman.

"You heard me, a witch. The Bible says you're practicing witchcraft."

Stern turned her back toward Kingman and looked in Billy's direction, a syrupy smile on her lips. "This man is typical of the fundamentalist bigots who burned witches and think that everyone who doesn't agree with them is going to hell. Now, let me tell you about that young woman who tried to kill herself. That is what we're here to talk about, isn't it?"

Billy nodded in agreement.

Stern went on. "If I could hypnotize that precious child of God, I'd take her back in time, through her past lives, until we encountered which existence injured her soul. Chances are, in another life she was brutally murdered. That disaster scripted her to think she deserves to die in an untimely, tragic fashion."

Billy leaned toward Stern and listened intently. "And what would your advice be to save her life?"

Stern closed her heavily mascaraed eyes and said nothing at first. Then she seemed to emerge from a quick trance. "The voices on the other side are telling me that she needs to understand that Supreme Intelligence gave her the body she's in now. The Spirit's purpose for her life is to love, laugh, and shed the shackles of her past incarnations. She is already one with the Universal Mind, if she will only realize it. She must forgive herself for seeking to destroy the Light Body that Intelligence gave her."

"If this woman was incarnated in the thirteenth century," the balding psychiatrist chimed in, "she's still living there," he said sarcastically. "As for the reverend, he's just as bad. An exorcist, you said? He's lost somewhere in the Middle Ages."

Billy loved it. Only minutes into the show, and the guests were jumping on one another without being prompted, just like Steinberg coached them to do.

"Ladies and gentlemen, you just heard his opinion. Now let me introduce our third expert, Dr. Wilford Andrews, chairman of the psychiatry department at the University of Arizona Medical School," Billy said. "Dr. Andrews, you obviously disagree with our other guests. What's your take on Allison's behavior?"

Dr. Andrews leaned forward in his chair, behaving like the consummate university professor about to address his class. He looked every bit the part in a white shirt, dark bow tie, and beige cardigan sweater. His salt-and-pepper full beard was neatly trimmed, in contrast to the slightly bushy eyebrows above his dark brown eyes. His heavily rimmed glasses emphasized his air of authority.

"She's a cutter. That's the short term for those who practice self-injury. As a self-mutilator," Dr. Andrews went on, "she's releasing some inner pain of her psyche. This business about past lives is hogwash. This young woman doesn't need a psychic or a preacher—she needs antidepressants. A prescription of Naltrexone should be the answer."

"Jesus is the answer!" Kingman shot back.

"Jesus? Which Jesus? Your judgmental Jesus or the Jesus of light, love, and understanding?" Stern interjected.

"Whoa, wait, everybody. One at a time," Billy said. "I want Dr. Andrews to finish. I'm confused. I thought Allison was trying to kill herself, but you're telling me she's actually doing something she thinks is helping her."

"Precisely. Many of my patients who are cutters tell me they actually feel better when they injure themselves. For example, before she died, Princess Diana admitted that she intentionally harmed her arms and legs. She had so much pain on the inside, hurting herself was a way of crying out for help."

"Is Allison typical of what you call 'cutters'?" Billy asked.

"Yes and no. She's female, and most self-mutilators are women. Half of them were sexually abused as children. The key to understanding this is that Allison didn't cut herself to die. She cuts herself to stay alive by releasing the inner angst."

"So how do you treat someone like this?"

"Sometimes they have to be institutionalized or undergo special therapy. But I must tell you, the cure rate is low."

"Low if you leave God out of it," Kingman again interjected.

Billy turned to the preacher. "You keep trying to bring God into this. That's a very simple way of looking at what seems to be a very complex psychological issue."

Kingman leaned sideways to face Andrews. "I don't disagree with everything the psychiatrist says, but locking people up or pumping them full of pills isn't the way to heal them. People like Allison have sick souls. Stopping them from self-injury or keeping them from killing themselves can only be done if God heals the original point of their pain."

"What's that—the point of the pain?" Billy wanted to know.

The crowd grew quiet.

"The place where their soul was first scarred," Kingman answered. "I've worked with lots of people like Allison, and they all have the same thing in common: a sense of worthlessness. Some trauma or abuse caused them to detach from emotional pain. Physical pain is a release from that hidden emotional pain that must be uncovered."

Billy grinned. "Now you sound like a shrink. I thought you were a preacher, not a therapist."

Kingman relaxed slightly and smiled back. "Freud would have made a great faith healer if he had believed in God and the Bible. He understood a lot about what makes people hurt. He just didn't know what to do about it."

"And I suppose you do!" Stern jumped back in the conversation. "If Allison were my daughter, I certainly wouldn't want a kook like you doing some religious hocus-pocus on her, flinging holy water, waving a crucifix, and yelling at the devil." She looked defiantly at Kingman, then shot an equally disdainful glance at Andrews. "A pox on both your houses. You're both clueless. Like I said in my book, *Who You've Been Is Who You Are*, she needs to get in touch with a past life, not some sad circumstance in this life. If she needs healing, it should come from recognizing the truth of her past incarnation, not the charlatanism of an Oral Roberts-come-lately like you."

Billy was overjoyed. Steinberg was right; this was the show that could put *McBride* over the top. The guests were chewing each other up, and Allison wasn't even onstage yet. Billy was so absorbed with the interchanges between his guests that he had almost forgotten it was time for a commercial break. Robert Demrod was frantically trying to get his attention. The moment Billy spotted him, he jumped in front of his guests and pointed at camera one.

"Hang on, partners. This is better than a Brahma bull snorting before the chute is opened. We'll hear more from our guests in a moment. Stay tuned. After this break we'll be joined by the young woman you saw yesterday whose suicide attempt, right here on this stage, is the subject of our discussion. Maybe she can tell us if the devil or Genghis Khan made her do it. We'll be right back after these messages."

The cameras went to black, and the commercials started rolling. Mallory jumped onstage to pump the crowd. Meanwhile, Billy darted to a back corner of the studio where Steinberg was waiting. Angela Sudbury delicately powdered his forehead and squirted short bursts of spray on hairs that popped up errantly. Steinberg slapped him on the back.

"Great job, Billy! This is the show we've needed for a long time. You're hot today."

"The guests are hot. That's the secret. I've got you to thank for that." He put up his right palm to high-five Steinberg. "Where do you think I should go with this thing now?"

"Get Allison out there. Let her face all three experts and see which one she reacts to the most."

"But what are we really going to do to help her? The shrink can't counsel her in thirty minutes, and we don't want that weird psychic woman doing some kind of trance thing to bring out a past whatever."

"How about an exorcism?" Steinberg suggested with a grin.

"You've got to be kidding. I'm on the edge, but not that far out. What do you think that preacher would do anyway? Do I look like I want to be puked on while Allison's head spins 360 degrees?"

Steinberg groaned.

"Just kidding," Billy responded. "Okay, let's get serious. What would that preacher do if he tried to exorcise Allison?"

Steinberg shrugged his shoulders. "Why don't you get out there and find out?"

Demrod gave the thirty seconds sign, and Mallory wrapped up his monologue. Billy was back onstage to whoops and hollers. The stage crew had moved the three guests slightly off center and added two more chairs for Allison and Jenny. Billy was in front of the camera again.

"Welcome back. Well, we've heard from experts in psychology, para-psychology, and . . . pseudopsychology." Billy looked straight at Kingman. "Now I want you to put your hands together as we welcome back our guests from yesterday, Jenny and Allison Owens."

Offstage, Kim Usher gently nudged Jenny and Allison up the steps toward their chairs. Jenny stepped forward hesitantly to greet Billy, but Allison passed her mother by. She looked strange and driven as she grabbed Billy by the hand, but didn't look him in the eye.

As they were seated, the camera went straight to a tight shot of Allison, who leaned forward as if to tie her shoe. In a split second, she lifted the pant leg of her jeans and whipped out a switchblade that had been taped to her ankle. Instantly she flipped open the blade. Everyone in the studio and on the stage froze in horror. Deliberately, she stood and headed toward the psychic, waving the blade ominously.

"Yesterday it was me. Today it's you," she mumbled.

Stern gripped the arms of her chair with both hands and leaned back as far as possible. Billy signaled his security team to hold steady. He didn't want some overzealous tough guy to lunge at Allison and worsen the situation. Just as Allison got to Stern's chair, she stopped and leaned forward slightly, extending the knife's blade in Stern's direction. Abject fear filled the psychic's face.

Allison held the knife a foot short of Stern's throat. The look of anger on Allison's face softened slightly, and the corners of her mouth turned upward with a sneer.

"Which life do you think I'm living now?" she asked. "The one this body is in, or another one from another time? What if I'm a reincarnated satanist and you're about to be my sacrifice?"

"Allison! Don't do anything crazy!" Jenny called out with tears streaming down her face.

Allison glanced momentarily at her mother and then directed her penetrating gaze back at Stern. Allison leaned forward until her face was inches from Stern's. "Hypnotize me now, you phony," she taunted the psychic. "Take me back in time to when I first walked in here and pulled out this knife."

Stern gulped and leaned back so far that the front legs of her chair lifted off the floor.

"Let's suppose I'm a reincarnated killer and that I've come back for another go-round of murder and mayhem. Do you really think your voices from the other side can stop me?"

Before Stern could answer, Allison turned her head toward Andrews. "Got a pill for this, Doc?"

Beads of sweat ran down the psychiatrist's face. He said nothing.

"Want to write me a prescription right now and medicate our psychic 'expert' out of this predicament?"

Allison looked back in the other direction toward Kingman, who sat calmly in his seat, seemingly unfazed by what was happening. "Got a Bible verse, Reverend?" she taunted.

"As a matter of fact, yes," Kingman answered. " 'I can do all things through Christ who strengthens me.' "

With that, Kingman stood and held out his hand toward Allison. "Hand that knife to me."

Allison laughed. "Why should I?"

"Because I command you to, in the name of Jesus!"

Allison stood up straight and withdrew the knife from the direction of Stern's throat. This time she aimed it at Kingman.

7

Let me get this straight. You are commanding me to drop this knife?" A macabre chortle rumbled deep inside Allison's throat. "Just who do you think you're talking to?" She approached Kingman with the knife clenched in her hand. Her eyes bore down on him, menacing and wild. Her body seemed strangely poised and threatening. As the crowd watched, she got closer and closer to Kingman.

"You tell me," the preacher replied.

"If anyone is going to do any commanding, it's me. I've got the power of death in my hands."

"You have no power," Kingman said, without flinching. He returned her intense stare.

"No power?" Allison swished the air with her knife, like Zorro making his mark. "Do you have anything more powerful than this?"

"God's power."

With her right hand Allison once again flourished the sharp steel blade in an intimidating manner and stepped closer to Kingman.

"If your God is so powerful, where is He now? For that matter, where was He my entire life? He could have . . ."

Allison stopped herself midsentence.

"He could have what?"

"It's none of your business, Reverend."

"You don't have to tell me. I can see it in your eyes."

Allison glared. "And exactly what do you see in my eyes?"

"The pain, the hurt, the rejection."

"If I want psychoanalysis, I'll pay a professional. Don't mess with my head. What makes you think you're any better than this worthless shrink, or this phony fortune-teller?" Allison gestured in the direction of the other guests. "I've got my own way of dealing with my problems, and it doesn't include your God. He never did anything for me anyway."

Billy stood back and watched in shock. He was caught between his impulse to protect everyone on the set from danger and his show business instinct to milk the suspense to the max. At some point Allison's threatening behavior could get out of hand, but now wasn't the time to try anything. He considered enlisting the *McBride* security guards, but Allison might cut someone before they intervened. Undoubtedly they were getting into position as inconspicuously as possible.

Billy was sure of only one thing: no one in the television audience was switching channels. In his mind's ear he could hear millions of telephones ringing as viewers called friends and relatives telling them to watch. This was better than the O. J. Simpson chase, minus the helicopters and the backseat driver.

Crash! Everyone turned in the direction of the noise.

The psychiatrist had tipped his chair over sideways. Andrews dived to the side of the stage, rolled across the floor, and bolted for safety behind the set. His escape triggered the exit of the psychic, who took advantage of the confusion and scrambled in the same direction. She ran toward the Green Room, losing her brown leather pumps as she fled.

For a brief instant, Allison looked away to see the cause of the commotion. She quickly returned her attention back to Kingman. "So why are you still here, Preacher? Too scared to run?"

"Quite the contrary," Kingman answered. "I have nothing to fear.

What's in me is a lot stronger than what's in you." Kingman sat steady, his eyes unwavering. He stared deep into her soul.

"And just exactly what do you think is in me?" she asked with a challenging smile.

"The devil. And more."

"More what?"

"More like you."

"Like me?"

"Yes, parts of Allison's soul."

Allison lowered the knife slightly. "If I'm not the devil, I'm sure acting like it. Who am I?"

Fear flashed through Allison's eyes, and her cheeks started to flush. Her glance darted around the room, and she uncomfortably fingered the knife blade.

"A frightened part of Allison. I don't know how you got there, but you have no intention of harming me with that knife. You're angry and dark inside, but you don't really want to kill me. You were created for Allison's survival, not for harming me or anyone else." Kingman gave a faint smile, as if he were talking to someone whose friendship he wanted to win.

Allison's body relaxed a little. Kingman reached toward the blade. When he did, Allison jerked it back into a threatening position.

"Don't underestimate what I'll do with this!" a guttural voice inside Allison warned.

Kingman didn't flinch. "I don't miscalculate what you'll do. You're capable of extreme evil."

Billy was confused. What did Kingman know that Billy didn't? Was he playing head games with Allison? Whatever was behind his strategy irritated Billy. This was *his* show, and he had watched from the sidelines long enough. He stepped toward Allison and the preacher.

"What's going on, Kingman? First you say she has the devil, and then you say she doesn't. You get inside her head, analyze her emotional makeup, and you don't even know her. You're a minister, not a mental health professional. Somebody is going to get hurt if you don't know what you're doing, and I don't want any more blood on my set."

"Shut up!" Allison looked directly at Billy and brandished the knife in his direction. "Let the preacher have his say."

Had he heard right? He realized that Allison was defending the same man she menaced.

"This isn't the first time I've faced someone like this young lady," Kingman said, looking at Billy. "The evil inside Allison typically threatens some kind of harm. I'm used to it."

"Quit talking in circles. Get to the point, Kingman," Billy insisted. "What's inside her?"

"Demons . . . and other identities."

"Demons? Oh, I forgot. You are an exorcist," Billy said sarcastically. He paused. "Other identities? More demons?"

"No, not demons. Personalities. Little children. Fractured parts of her soul."

"There you go with the psychobabble again."

"Enough! All of you keep quiet!" Allison screamed. "I'm sick of all of you treating me like I'm some freak. This isn't a horror movie. This isn't Stephen King. This is for real! I've lived my whole life in fear, and now all of you know what it's like. Welcome to my nightmare."

Suddenly, with tears streaming down her face, Jenny rose from her chair, stretched out her arms, and walked toward Allison. For a moment, Allison pointed the knife toward her. "Back off! I'm here to finish what I started yesterday and no one, not even you, Mom, is going to stop me." Allison drew the knife to her own throat.

Jenny didn't flinch. Slowly she came closer. "Give me the knife, Allison. I won't let you hurt yourself or anyone here. This insanity has to stop." Jenny paused and gave Allison a tender look.

"I'm warning you! Don't try to stop me!"

"Hi-yahhhh!"

It wasn't much of a karate call, but Billy knew from the action movies he'd seen that a loud yell gets an attacker off guard. Any other time it would have been humorous, but this was a serious situation. He lunged at Allison from behind, grabbed her right forearm, and twisted it violently. With his other arm, Billy grabbed Allison's left wrist and held her in a hammerlock. Allison screamed in pain and spewed a stream of profanities as she and Billy vaulted back and forth across the stage, struggling for control of the knife. Billy tightened his grip on Allison's arm, and the knife sliced the air in wide arcs.

Kingman grabbed Jenny and pulled her aside to safety. Billy didn't have the finely tuned physique of his rodeo days, but he was stronger than most men. Nevertheless, Allison jostled Billy about as if he were half her size. The audience was stunned by the strength Allison exhibited. How could this small woman fight so ferociously?

After a brief struggle that resembled the dance of two drunken sailors, Billy and Allison tumbled to the floor of the stage. They rolled to one side, then the other, like a sinking ship tossed by tumultuous waves. First, Billy was on his left side, his right hand restraining the knife. Then Allison jerked sharply and they both listed starboard. Lying on his right side made it harder to control the knife, and he was worried Allison might accidentally roll over and stab herself. Then Billy spotted Andrews's toppled chair and wiggled their bodies snakelike toward it. The maneuver worked.

Whack!

Billy yanked Allison's arm down hard against the chair's upturned leg. The knife fell from her hands. A beefy security guard swiftly grabbed the weapon while another guard helped Billy restrain Allison. Billy grabbed one arm and shoulder, and the guard held down the other. Just when it seemed things were in check, Allison thrust both legs into the air and heaved her shoulders forward. The maneuver broke the hold of the two men, who tumbled backward. In an instant she was on her hands and feet, crouching with knees bent catlike, and moving slowly backward. Billy and the guards collected themselves and prepared for another assault. The crowd was silent. The usual jeers had been replaced by gasps.

"Stop!" Kingman yelled. He jumped between Allison and the two men. Without saying another word, Kingman looked directly into the young woman's eyes and moved slowly toward her. Allison froze. She sat back on her heels and clutched her arms across her chest. A pained look filled her face.

Her body gradually relaxed, and she leaned to one side. Then she fell onto the floor and curled up in a fetal position. Deep sobs poured from inside her soul. She covered her head with her arms and buried her face in her chest. Jenny rushed to Allison and sat down by her. With motherly tenderness, Jenny cradled Allison's head in her lap. Kingman approached slowly, gently took Allison's hand in his, and sat on the floor.

Billy sat down on the edge of the set to regain his composure and catch his breath. He was exhausted and more confused than before. Why had Allison turned from a deranged assailant into a whimpering child? For now his curiosity would have to wait. This wasn't the time to answer questions. He had to get his mind back on the show. After all, his heroic efforts had been seen by millions, and the cameras were still rolling.

Steinberg did his job with professional precision. While the confrontation was unfolding, he canceled all commercial breaks. He might face the wrath of advertisers today, but he was convinced they would be pleased with an even larger viewing audience tomorrow. The cameras covered every face with close-ups and wrung out every emotion. The shots were tight and crisp, a succession of snapshots that captured an unprecedented moment in broadcast entertainment. It had been a dangerous on-the-edge drama, perhaps too close to the extremity of shock talk for even someone as controversial as Billy McBride.

Gradually, Allison's sobs subsided. One of Billy's assistants had brought a box of tissues over to her. She raised herself on one arm and looked around the studio. Her other hand held a wad of used tissues. She looked at her mother in confusion. "Mom, why are you crying?"

Jenny gently touched the sides of Allison's face with her hands. "It's okay, honey, don't worry. We're going to get you some help today."

"McBride. That's where we are. I remember the telephone call. But . . ."

Allison didn't seem to know where she was or the events of the previous day.

"I understand," Kingman said in a reassuring tone. "What happened wasn't your fault." He squeezed Allison's hand.

She looked at Kingman curiously. "Who are you?"

Kingman smiled. "I'm a minister they booked to be on the show with you."

Billy shook his head in bewilderment. The show already resembled the *Twilight Zone*, but this was too much. He wanted to jump to his feet and call Allison's bluff. What an actress! No wonder she manipulated her mother so easily. This clever woman could jerk people first one way, then the next, and afterwards claim no responsibility for her actions with some amnesic excuse. Worse yet, she had conned this gullible minister into going along with her ruse.

Allison tried to stand up but wobbled precariously when she tried to straighten her legs. That gave Billy the opportunity for one more heroic intervention. Now he could bring down the curtain in style. A signal from the floor director told him there were just two minutes left in the show. Billy rushed to Allison and picked her up in his arms. He held her toward camera one like a limp trophy and looked straight into the lens.

"This is a very troubled woman. You heard my pledge yesterday to help her any way possible. I'm keeping that promise." Billy glanced disdainfully in the direction where Andrews and Stern had retreated. "What our 'experts' couldn't do, I think I can."

"Billll-eeee! Billll-eeee!" The audience chanted.

Billy swallowed hard on his pride. "I realize I can't do this by myself. Reverend Kingman, you seem to have some special insight into what's going on with Allison. Will you help me?"

The request was a spur-of-the-moment thing. Billy wanted the glory for himself, and his show. But he knew deep inside that he really didn't have a clue about what to do.

"Certainly," Kingman responded. "I'll be happy to help, on one condition."

"You name it, Reverend."

"We must include God in whatever you have in mind."

Billy was caught off guard. "Sure, uh, no problem. We believe in a higher power, don't we?" He looked at his audience for a reaction.

The studio audience jumped to its feet and cheered. Shouts of "Higher power, higher power!" mingled with the standard "Billll-eeee!" chant.

Billy's mind worked overtime. He looked down at Allison, whose eyes were closed. "Tomorrow we're going to roll a tape from last week. I'm taking the day off so I can help this woman get in touch with her soul. When she does, I'll bring her right back here on this stage. She'll be a different woman. In the meantime, we're going to a rodeo!"

Billy had no idea where that outlandish thought came from. It just popped into his mind. He remembered earlier that day seeing an advertisement in *Western Horseman* magazine promoting the upcoming National Western Stock Show and Rodeo in Denver, Colorado. Where the inspiration came from didn't matter. It was a hit. The audience jumped up and down with shouts of "Rodeo, rodeo!"

Billy nodded farewell to the camera and walked offstage to shouts of acclaim. Steinberg caught him as he headed toward the Green Room.

"You're huffing and puffing with that woman in your arms. A little out of shape, cowboy?"

"This isn't the time for smart remarks. Just tell me if you can do it."

"Do what?"

"Pull a show from the can that aired last week and give me a day off."

"We'll have to tweak the commercial content a little to match this week's spot contracts, but the answer is 'yes.' That's not the problem."

Billy breathed so hard he could barely speak. "What is the problem?"

"You, and what you told millions of people. What came over you? If you don't watch out, you'll get too carried away with this Allison Owens thing. First it was a suicide attempt. Then a violent outburst. That's good for share points. But now you're on some kind of mission with an exorcist to solve her problems overnight. I'm afraid you're in over your head. What do you expect, a miracle?"

Billy entered the Green Room and headed toward the couch. He was so tired, he dropped Allison like a sack of potatoes on the couch. Allison covered her face with her hands.

Steinberg and Billy walked out of earshot. "You're right. A miracle is exactly what we need," Billy said.

"Don't act so serious. I was just joking. Get real. Kingman's an exorcist, not God Himself. I'm not even sure what he does is legit. I just thought he'd add something sensational to the show. I've seen video footage of what he does, and it's pretty far out."

"How far out?"

Jenny walked in and sat down on the edge of the couch beside Allison. She sat there silently, stroking Allison's brow.

"He's either a con man or some kind of magician. You should see what he does. People scream, foam at the mouth, and writhe in all kinds of contortions. Weird voices come out of their bodies. Then he tells the devil to leave them, and they go bananas. You know me. I've seen it all, especially when I was a reporter for the *National Exposé*. But even I have never seen anything quite like this."

"What kind of voices?"

"Bizarre sounds. Often they speak in other languages. I planned to give some of the videos to a university language department to see if they can figure out what's being said. Sometimes people speak what sounds like German, Gaelic, even Chinese. It's spooky, man. I just want you to know who you're going to hang out with. This guy is one strange dude."

"Maybe he pays these people to put on an act."

"I thought of that, but on some of the videos the people possessed by the devil are openly identified. They live in places where others know them. Plus, he has hundreds of hours of video from scores of cities. If it is all contrived, it would cost a fortune to pay these people and require incredible complexity to set it all up. Personally, I don't think it's staged."

Billy reached in the Green Room's refrigerator. "Not a single cherry Pepsi in here," he lamented. He settled for a Diet Coke and popped the tab. "Sounds like he's got you convinced."

"Not really. My theory is they're somehow hypnotized. These are religious people with an expectation level. They want to blame Satan for their problems, so Kingman gives them an easy way out. They don't have to be responsible for their actions. You know, 'the devil made them do it.' He convinces them that their difficulties in life are the result of some horrible situation in their past when the devil got them. Then, presto. He waves a Bible at them, throws on a little holy water, and tells the devil to go to hell, quite literally."

Billy rolled his eyes. "I wish I had known all this before I decided to involve this guy. I don't want to spend my time with some nutcase who sees spooks and goblins. Besides, I'm not serious about actually getting him to do an exorcism on Allison. I've already got a psycho woman on my hands who has tried to commit suicide and threatened to kill in front of a live television audience." He looked over at Allison and Jenny, who couldn't hear the conversation. "That's enough excitement for me to handle. I draw the line at levitating bodies."

"There's nothing like that on the videos. Why don't you see for yourself?"

"When?"

"How about now? Want me to get the videos?"

Billy paused and took a drink. "Sure. I'll shower and then check it out."

"Should I be making travel reservations?" Mandy Manchester asked as she popped her head in the room. "I overheard. You'd better lower your voices or your guests will hear you."

Billy rubbed the back of his neck to let go of the day's tension. "Yeah, I guess so."

"I heard what you said about the rodeo. Were you serious? Should I get tickets too?"

"Yes, of course."

"Where?"

"The National Western Stock Show in Denver. This is the last week, and the finals are tomorrow night. I know some people who run that rodeo and can get us great seats."

"What airline?"

"None. Get a private jet. You know I don't like airport hassles, especially at Sky Harbor. I want privacy." Billy started toward his dressing room. He yelled at Steinberg, who had made it halfway down the hall. "Hold off for now on those videos. I'll take them on the plane and look at them en route. That way Allison can see them too."

Billy ran back to the Green Room to say good-bye to his guests. They were gone. *I guess I am a little rattled*, he said to himself. *Maybe a little refreshment will get my brain back in gear.*

Billy went back to his office and headed for the shower in the back. He reached inside and turned on the water. *Wish they'd get the boiler fixed. It still takes forever for the water to get hot.*

He stepped from his bathroom back into the main part of the office and called out, "Didn't you call the repair people like I asked, Mandy?"

"Boss, being in hot water is your specialty. Why would anyone think you needed more?"

"Cute. Yes or no, did you tell them?"

"Yes, they said they'd send a plumber around some time this week. By the way, I said good-bye to your guests for you."

"Thanks. In all the confusion I lost it back there."

"Will it be just the two of you on the plane?"

"No, three."

"Oh, I forgot about her mother. Good idea to have a chaperone along." Mandy said.

Billy rolled his eyes in mock irritation. "Jenny isn't coming. It's me, Allison, and . . ." Billy paused to add a Transylvania-like roll to his tongue, ". . . the exorcist."

8

Billy McBride looked out the window of the plush departure lounge of Executive Travel International, a private air charter company that operated out of the Scottsdale, Arizona, Air Park. Fifty yards away on the tarmac sat the sleek, six-passenger Lear jet that would whisk him, Allison Owens, and the Reverend Joseph Kingman to Denver, Colorado. Billy was glad he'd made the decision to travel by private plane. No lines at the ticket counter, no stiff plastic seats in the waiting area at the gate, and, most of all, no crowds. He liked being a star, but the fervor of his fans sometimes got out of hand. Once, on a connecting flight in Dallas, a near riot had ensued when competition for his autograph heated up into a fistfight between several young males. Airport security had to be called, and Billy himself was nearly ejected from the concourse.

Not today. Billy was all alone in the lounge. Freshly brewed, steaming Starbucks was waiting, along with an assortment of breakfast rolls and juices. Classical music was piped in over the sound system, and comfortable chairs offered relaxation. Billy didn't take full advantage of the luxury. He paced the room nervously, glancing periodically at his watch. It was 6:50 A.M., they were due to depart in ten minutes, and he was the only one there. At $1,500 an hour, every minute was big bucks. He didn't want to keep the flight crew waiting.

For a moment, he was struck by the sheer absurdity of what he was doing. He still wasn't sure how he had gotten himself into this situation. When he rode his last bull in Cheyenne ten years ago, he'd sworn he would never see another rodeo. The cowboy motif was okay for his image, and he loved to dazzle people at parties with stories about the adrenalin rush of easing down on two thousand pounds of Brahma in the chute. But the truth was he didn't want to be reminded of his past. One reason was his need to keep the mystique alive. The other was Chauncy Wilhite.

Chauncy was his best friend, and his stiffest competition on the circuit. Week after week they had traded places at the top of the winnings list for all-around cowboy. Outside the arena, they were drinking buddies who traded tales of wild women and wild rides. But once it was time to mount up, they were the two toughest antagonists on the circuit. They were very close in ability and results. Sometimes no more than hundredths of a second separated them in an event like calf roping. But bull riding was the specialty they both claimed, and, from a professional standpoint, it turned them into bitter adversaries. Until that day in Cheyenne.

It was the last competition of the day, and they were neck-and-neck in the standings. Billy and Chauncy had both drawn tough bulls, the most feared of the stock. They agreed with each other that the winner would depend on the luck of the draw. So, at the last minute, to tempt fate, they secretly agreed to switch bulls without telling anyone. Billy got Haywire, while Chauncy ended up with a bull named Dangerous.

Billy rode first and made the whistle after eight seconds of bone-busting agony. Chauncy rode last and had to do it in style to impress the judges. Billy still recalled every twist of the tail and thrust of the horns as Dangerous pulled out every trick to dislodge his rider. Chauncy lasted the full ride, but Dangerous wasn't finished. One last kick of the bull's hind legs sent Chauncy sailing toward the animal's front feet. The cowboy landed head first, twisting his neck and driving his skull into the soft dirt. The rodeo clowns did all they could to divert the raging beast from Chauncy's body, which lay motionless in the arena, but Dangerous lived up to his name. His right front hoof came down squarely in the middle of Chauncy's back, crushing his spine with a crack so loud it could be heard in the stands. The pickup riders loaded Chauncy's lifeless body into an ambulance, but it was too late for medical intervention. To this day, Billy was still haunted by the sound of "Amazing Grace" being played at Chauncy's funeral.

"Thanks for asking me along." It was Kingman. Billy's thoughts were yanked back to the present reality, and he turned to shake the minister's hand.

"To be honest, I'm not sure why I did. But now that you're making the trip, I'd like a personal explanation about what's on these videos." Billy patted a soft black leather briefcase that was slung over his left shoulder. "They've got a VCR on the plane, and I figured it would be an interesting way to pass the time on our way to the rodeo."

Kingman looked puzzled. "Oh," he said, "your producer must have given you some of my exorcism footage. I'll admit it can look pretty far out to someone who doesn't know much about deliverance."

"Deliverance? What's that?"

"Just another term some Christians use to describe the casting out of demons. *Exorcism* is the classic term. But some associate that with ancient Roman Catholic rituals. I don't mind calling it exorcism. Many people who aren't familiar with the process, like you, don't relate to the word *deliverance*."

"Deliverance, exorcism, whatever. Steinberg warned me I'd see some things that would be hard to believe."

"He's right. And not just you. Even some in the clergy don't know how to handle it. In fact, most of the other professors at my seminary think I've gone off the deep end."

"Have you?"

"I'm just doing what's biblical." Kingman reached for the maroon, leather-bound Bible tucked under his arm. "Every time Jesus gave the Great Commission . . ."

"The great what?"

"Excuse me. Being a seminary professor, I take for granted that people know what I'm talking about. The Great Commission. The command of Jesus to take His message to others. Every time He said 'preach the gospel,' He also said 'cast out demons.' In fact, Jesus declared that exorcism—deliverance—would be the first sign that His message was valid."

Billy stepped over to a wall-mounted drinking fountain. He leaned down to take a drink and wiped his lips with the back of his hand. "I hate to sound so clueless, but I never heard that in church. Of course, I haven't spent a lot of time there the last few years. My mother took me to a Methodist church and a Presbyterian church when I was a kid, but they never talked about deliverance or demons."

"For that matter, you could have gone to a Baptist church, or a Pentecostal church, or any other kind of church and never heard a single word about the devil. It just isn't taught today."

Billy glanced again at his watch, ticking off the cost of keeping that Lear jet on the ground. He saw the two pilots scurrying around the exterior of the plane, doing their last-minute check of the engines and tires. "So where did Hollywood get its idea about this exorcism stuff? That's the only time I've come across it."

Kingman reverently ran his finger across the spine of his well-worn Bible. "The Hollywood version is the only account of exorcism that most people ever hear. But what you see in movies isn't very accurate. It's hard to put into words what goes on. Hopefully the videos will make it more understandable."

"Frankly, I can't wait to see you in action. Steinberg isn't easily impressed, and he was moved by what he saw."

"Mommy, Mommy, don't go." Ashley's cry interrupted the conversation. The door to the lounge opened, and Allison, Jenny, and Ashley entered. Allison carried Ashley in her arms, hugging her tightly while Jenny gently stroked her granddaughter's brow. "Mommy will be gone for just one night. That's all. Jen-Jen will look after you."

"Don't forget, your big Pooh Bear is waiting for you at home," Jenny reminded Ashley. "He'll be so glad to have you all to himself. Jen-Jen has taken the rest of the week off from work, and we can play together all day today. Maybe we'll even go to the zoo. You know how much you like the lions and tigers they have there."

Ashley's big, round, brown eyes peered out from under her long, brown bangs. One arm clung tightly to Allison's neck while the other nervously twisted a lock of hair behind her right ear. "No. I scared!"

Kingman flashed a grandfatherly smile and approached the child. "Hello, Ashley. I've heard so much about you from your grandmother. Can you shake my hand?"

At first, Ashley drew back, clutching Allison even more firmly. Then she looked at Kingman and tentatively stretched out her right hand. Kingman gently took it and gave a miniature handshake. "You have very pretty eyes, just like your mother."

Allison pulled a tissue from her pocket and wiped Ashley's nose. The little girl smiled slightly.

"I'm going to be with your mother, and I'll look after her, just like Grandma will look after you. And do you know who else will be looking after you?"

"Who?" Ashley asked quietly.

"A very special friend of mine–God."

Ashley looked puzzled. "You mean that man up in the sky?"

"He's much more than that. Let me show you something." He reached his arms toward Ashley. To Allison's amazement, her daughter responded. Kingman cradled Ashley with his left arm and walked over to the window. With his right hand he pointed to the McDowell Mountains that loomed a few miles in the distance. "You see those hills over there? God made those big, big mountains. And that's not all. He made the birds and the butterflies and the kitties and puppies."

"She has a puppy. His name is Puddles. We call him that because he makes puddles," Allison said.

Everyone laughed. Ashley broke into a big smile.

"You see," Kingman said. "The God who made those mountains, and Puddles, loves you and your mommy and your Jen-Jen very much. While Mommy is away, He'll be with you."

"Okay. Mommy, you go." Ashley patted her tiny chest. "God with me. Bye-bye."

Allison's face softened. Billy thought he saw tears in her eyes.

The roar of the Lear jet's engine burst into the room as the pilot opened the door. "Ready to take off, Mr. McBride? We're doing a final engine check. Just want to make sure you're ready before we power down so you can board."

"We're all here. Ready, everyone?"

Jenny took Ashley from Kingman's arms. "Mommy will miss you," Allison said, leaning to kiss her daughter.

"I'll have my cell phone on if you need me," Allison said to Jenny. She gave her mother an awkward hug.

"All the bags are loaded," the pilot said. "In less than two hours we'll be landing at Arapahoe County Airport, just outside Denver. I assume you've got transportation from there?"

"My assistant arranged for a limo."

"Great. Name's Winston. Brent is my first name," the pilot said.

"Let's wave good-bye to Mommy," Jenny said as the three passengers picked up their carry-on bags and started out the door to the aircraft.

"Mr. McBride, Mr. McBride!" A young, handsome Latin-looking man came running toward the lounge entrance. He threw open the door and rushed inside. Perspiration dropped from his brow. A large video camera was slung over his left shoulder. In his right hand he carried a small navy bag, the kind with wheels and a retractable handle.

"I was told to be here at 7:00 A.M. to join you on this flight and do video coverage of your trip. Sorry I'm late. The traffic on the 101 freeway was terrible. An automobile accident had cars backed up for miles. My name is Gabriel, Aaron Gabriel. I just got the message last night that I'd be needed. I was down in Mexico yesterday doing a shoot. I was the only bilingual cameraman they could find for the job."

"There's room for him, if you want to take him along. It's your call," Winston said to Billy.

"Steinberg!" Billy muttered a curse under his breath. "He's always doing something like this at the last minute and never telling me." He shook Gabriel's hand. "I can't blame him for wanting you along. I should have thought of it myself. Some action footage from the rodeo would be great to show as highlights of our trip. It's a great idea. If Steinberg said he wants you along, he's the boss when it comes to the show. Let's all get on board."

Allison and Kingman were already making their way to the plane, waving last minute good-byes to Jenny and Ashley.

"Let me help you with that suitcase." Billy reached to pick up Gabriel's luggage. It was heavier than he expected, and he paused momentarily. "Wow, what's in this? Are you sure it will pass weight restrictions?" he joked.

"It's full of videotape. I wasn't sure we could find some on the run. Since I was told to shoot everything that had a human-interest angle, I brought as many rolls as I could stuff in there."

"Great camera." Billy said admiringly, as they both approached the steps leading to the jet. "I've been wanting to get one of those digital models myself. You can really shoot under low light conditions. I've heard you don't need any light poles if you're shooting impromptu, like at a sports contest or concert."

"Exactly. And since the rodeo in Denver is indoors, we're going to have low-light conditions that are perfect for this camera."

"After you, Mr. Gabriel," Billy said gesturing for his new passenger to board.

Billy followed him up the steps. *Even if this guy's coming along was a good idea, I'm going to give Steinberg a piece of my mind when I get back. First he changed the show yesterday; then he invited someone to tag along without my permission. This is the last time he's going to spring something like this on me.*

The ramp to the jet retracted, and the entry door sealed shut. Then the copilot leaned out of the cockpit. "Fasten seat belts, everyone."

Billy glanced out the window and saw the reflection of the jet in the huge lounge windows. The sun peeked over the McDowells, and its rays struck the shiny skin of the plane. The angle of the sunbeams gave a yellow sheen to the aircraft as it taxied down the runway. The image of the Lear jet was reflected so brightly, it seemed surrounded by a golden halo.

9

The jet slid effortlessly through the atmosphere, past the cloud cover, and glided to its cruising altitude of nearly forty thousand feet. Billy leaned back in his chair and closed his eyes to block out the stress of the past two days. Across the aisle from him, Kingman thumbed through his Bible, stopping from time to time to focus on something that caught his attention. Allison, seated in front of Billy, gazed out the window at the retreating landscape of rocky boulders and cactus-covered flat lands. The sunlight illuminated the clouds in a mystical way. The passengers were temporarily miles away from phones and interruptions.

Gabriel had taken the seat ahead of Kingman. He sat motionless with his eyes closed, as if asleep. He was dressed in baggy, dark green camouflage pants and a tan safari shirt. His curly, black hair clung tightly to his scalp. Dark sunglasses hid his eyes. He was strangely peaceful and quiet.

"Mr. Gabriel," Billy called out over the roar of the plane's engines, "we were in such a rush to get aboard the plane, I didn't have a chance to introduce you to the others."

Gabriel opened his eyes and turned toward Billy. "That's all right. I know who everyone is. I was briefed before accepting this job."

Gabriel reached across the aisle. Allison hesitantly put out her hand in response. She kept her eyes diverted downward and mumbled a barely audible "Pleased to meet you."

"That's Dr. Joseph Kingman behind you," Billy said.

Gabriel reached over the top of his seat to greet the minister.

"I hope you didn't think I was rude back in the departure lounge," Billy went on, "but we were late to leave. I'm pleased you're with us. I just wish Steinberg had warned me that he invited you. I'm sure he felt he was doing the right thing by hiring you to shoot video."

"No problem. I'm accustomed to last-minute assignments and being placed in awkward situations. I'll fit right in. You won't even know I'm around. In fact, I'll get better video shots if everyone tries to ignore me. It will look more natural and less posed."

The copilot emerged from the cockpit and pointed to a door near Allison's feet. "If anyone wants a drink, just help yourself. They're in this refrigerator." He reached inside a small cabinet above the refrigerator and pulled out a tray of snacks, covered in plastic wrap. He peeled back the thin cover and passed the food to Allison, who helped herself to a finger sandwich. "Is there anything else I can do?" the copilot asked.

"Yes, I was told there was a VCR and TV screen on board," Billy said.

The copilot pulled out a recessed drawer just in front of Gabriel and pointed to a VCR. Then he reached toward the ceiling and popped down a flat-matrix video display screen. "I'll turn up the volume of the overhead speakers so you can hear better." He handed the VCR remote control to Billy. "Anything in particular you'd like to watch? We have a small selection of movies available."

"No, thanks," Billy responded. "We brought our own entertainment with us." He reached in the briefcase he had stowed under the seat in front of him and pulled out one of the Kingman exorcism videos. "Would you mind putting this in the VCR?" he asked as he handed the copilot a video marked "HOUSTON, 1999, PHILLIP/ANGER DEMON."

The copilot obliged and returned to the cockpit. All eyes were focused on the video screen. Even Allison looked away from the window to the color bars that first appeared on the video. The screen went to black and came up on the scene of a huge auditorium packed with people. A handheld camera followed a man from behind as he walked briskly toward the back of the building.

"Soul and spirit, I divide soul and spirit," said the man, whose voice Billy recognized as Kingman's.

Kingman waved his Bible up and down like a swordsman, slashing the air at some imaginary opponent. Periodically, he stopped and looked at someone carefully, and then moved on. Each time he approached an individual, his right arm, which was holding the Bible, shot out as if it were being symbolically thrust through them. Some of the people he approached winced as if they were in pain.

Billy hit the PAUSE button. "What's that all about?" he asked.

"The Bible says in Hebrews 4:12 that the Word of God is powerful and sharper than any 'two-edged sword.' It divides soul and spirit. That's what I was doing—dividing soul and spirit."

"I assume you meant that figuratively."

"No, Mr. McBride, you assumed wrong. I meant it literally."

"Call me Billy. How could you have meant it literally? You were holding a book in your hand. I don't mean to be offensive, but that Bible you were swinging around is just ink on paper."

"To you it's just paper and ink, but to the devil it's actually a sword. Of course, if you use it like a sword, you must have faith to believe it really is one."

"Why were you dividing soul and spirit?"

"The devil can't touch the spirit of someone who belongs to God, but he can torment their soul, their mind, and emotions. By separating the soul, I isolate that part that is affected by evil spirits. When the humanity of the person, as expressed by their spirit, is set apart from their soul, the evil can be more easily detected. If you'll go back to the video, you'll see how that happened."

Billy hit PLAY and the video resumed.

Kingman approached a handsome young man seated on the aisle. His blond hair and deep blue eyes gave him an all-American look. In his blue jeans and ASU Sun Devils T-shirt, he was indistinguishable from hundreds of others in the huge auditorium. Kingman drew near the man and waved the Bible like a sword, shouting, "I divide soul and spirit."

Immediately, the man's demeanor changed. His body stiffened so much that his back lifted off the chair. The nape of his neck rested on the top of the chair back, and his legs extended straight and stiff toward the floor. His arms twitched spasmodically, and his distended eyes glazed over, staring upward without blinking. Nothing but guttural and indecipherable growls could be heard from deep within his body.

A woman seated near the disturbed man got Kingman's attention. "He's my cousin. His name is Phillip. I invited him to the meeting. Last week he tried to commit suicide with an overdose of pills. I brought him here as a last hope." She wrung her hands and looked up with a hopeful gaze. King was undistracted by anything but Phillip. The minister focused on every movement and expression that Phillip made.

Kingman stared straight into the man's eyes and once again used his Bible like a sword. With the spine of the Bible pointed toward the man's face, Kingman started at the forehead and slowly brought the sacred book downward to the chest, as if slicing Phillip's head in two. "You must obey," he demanded in an authoritative voice. "Christ commands that you tell me your identity."

Once again Billy hit PAUSE.

"Now what's happening?"

"I'm directly confronting the demons in him."

"How did you know he had demons? Maybe he was just a mental case who freaked because of your intensity. What you do is pretty sensational. Some would probably accuse you of hyping the audience into a state of suggestibility. "

"If someone didn't understand what I'm doing, I can see how they might think that, but you saw the change that came over him. More than that, it was his eyes that tipped me off."

"Why are the eyes so significant?"

"An old proverb says the eyes are the mirror of the soul. When you want to converse with someone, you look into their eyes because facial expression may fool you. The eyes give you soul-to-soul communication. When someone has a demon, the evil spirit in their soul looks outward through their eyes. I teach that people with demons have a certain look."

"C'mon, Preacher," Allison interjected. "I've seen a lot of people with weird looks in their eyes, like when they're spaced out on meth or coke. Are you saying they all have demons?"

"That's not the kind of look I'm talking about. It's hard to describe, but once you see it, you never forget it. Start the video again and watch Phillip's eyes."

Billy hit PLAY and the camera zoomed in on Phillip as his head turned toward Kingman and his blank look changed to an intense glare.

"I told you to obey God's will and tell me your name."

"Anger!"

"Who's there with you?"

"Hate and Rage. We've been here a long time, and we're not leaving."

Kingman bent over and stared down the foreboding voice. He was nearly nose-to-nose with the man. "That's not all. There are others in there with you." Kingman straightened himself and pulled back several steps. "Murder, come to attention!"

Phillip sprang from his seat and lunged toward Kingman. Just as quickly, three brawny men standing nearby grabbed the man and wrestled him to the floor. A violent struggle ensued, but the men couldn't prevail. Phillip broke free and leaped again to his feet. This time, three more men joined the fight, and the six of them finally pinned Phillip to the ground.

Billy hit the PAUSE button. "Those men must be your bouncers. Are they with you everywhere?"

Kingman laughed. "I wish I could afford to have them with me every time the devil attacks. No, they're not hired hands. These were men I met before the meeting who agreed to protect me if violence occurred. They are loyal friends of our ministry and are ready to assist whenever I call upon them. I briefed them about what might happen, and fortunately they were ready. That's not always the case."

"Do you ever get hurt?"

Billy was surprised to hear Allison ask the question, especially since she was the one who threatened harm to Kingman less than twenty-four hours earlier.

"I've been kicked, scratched, bruised, spit on, and a lot more. Once I was tackled from behind by a woman who knocked me off my feet and grabbed my necktie. She twisted it until my breath was momentarily cut off. Another time a man pulled a gun and pointed it directly at me, threatening to pull the trigger. But God has not allowed me to be seriously injured."

"Thanks to your bodyguards," Billy interjected.

"No, thanks to my angels."

Allison tilted her head to one side with an incredulous look. "You don't mean real angels, do you? I believed in a fairy godmother when I was a child, but I never *really* thought she could grant a wish. I suppose your angels have feathery wings and all that. Oh, and don't forget the harps."

Kingman chuckled. "No harps. Wings? Maybe. Some said they saw wings."

"Who saw wings?" Allison asked.

"The demons. They see the angels. Sometimes they look over their shoulders at the angels who surround them. While they control the bodies of people they possess, I've watched demons dart about a room, trying to escape the attack of angels."

"You can't be serious."

"Oh yes, I am, Billy. I believe in angels more than I believe in talk show hosts."

Everyone laughed.

"Well, no one ever accused me of being an angel," Billy said.

"Hit that PLAY button again, and you'll see one of the times when angels intervened to protect me. In fact, why don't you give me the remote control so I can do a narration and stop and start it at the more interesting parts."

Billy handed the remote to Kingman.

Gabriel spoke. "Show them what happens when the angels take over and restrain the demons."

"I thought you were asleep," Billy said.

"I was preoccupied, but this is too interesting to miss."

"How do you know what's next? Have you seen this video before?"

"I told you I was well-prepared for the job. I needed to see what kind of shot angles would work best. The angel part is incredible. Let the reverend show you."

Kingman started up the video. On the screen they could see Phillip as he continued to fight against the men who tried to hold him. One man held his left leg, another his right. In like manner, different men held each arm. A fifth man pushed down on his chest, while another gripped his head. Suddenly, with a supernatural surge of strength, he pushed away the men and broke free. Once again he lurched toward the preacher.

"I loose angels from the throne of God to restrain you!" Kingman shouted. "I call for angels to seize you on your right side, your left side, in front, and in back."

Phillip's body was instantly immobilized. For a moment, Billy thought Kingman had hit the PAUSE button to stop the picture. All around Phillip the audience was in motion, scrambling for safety, but he was frozen in place, unable to move. A hideous look of evil contorted his face.

"You can't have him! He's mine," the voice inside Phillip taunted. "We are many, and we've been here for generations. We'll kill anyone who gets in our way!"

"You don't scare me, Murder! And you can't harm this man."

"I hate you, I hate you!" Phillip screamed until the veins popped out on his neck.

Billy thought he saw the look Kingman described. He couldn't be sure, but he was certain that whatever controlled Phillip now wasn't normal and maybe wasn't even human.

"We have rights! You can't tell us what to do," the demons said.

"If you have legal rights, we'll discover them," Kingman replied.

"You can't. It's too complex. You'll never find out!"

"Go to torment, awaiting the hour of your judgment. I call Phillip back to full consciousness now."

The entity that had overtaken Phillip's face, the one Kingman had identified as Murder, reacted with terror. Phillip's body convulsed as if the demon were fighting an invisible power against which it couldn't prevail, no matter how much force was exerted. Gradually, the look of evil on his face dissolved into a relaxed expression. He rubbed his face with his hands, shook his head as if waking from a sleep, and breathed deeply. Perspiration poured from his forehead.

Kingman reached out and put an arm around his shoulder. "You'll be all right. God has everything under control."

The man tilted his head to one side in bewilderment.

"Let me introduce myself. I'm Dr. Joseph Kingman. I'm a seminary professor, and I teach about the supernatural."

"Stop. I want to ask a question," Allison interjected.

Kingman paused the video.

"I don't get it. This guy came to see you. He was in the audience listening. Why are you introducing yourself to him? Didn't he already hear you say who you were?"

"Some part of him heard the beginning of my lecture, but not the man you see."

"I don't understand what you're getting at," said Billy.

"The person on the screen now isn't the person—or I should say 'personality'—who came to the seminar. That was a completely different part of his consciousness."

"What do you mean by personalities? Aren't you dealing with demons? These 'personalities' must be demons. That's the way I see it, for what it's worth," Allison said.

Kingman looked directly at Allison. "I understand why you think that. Even most people who do deliverance can make the mistake of thinking that personalities, or 'dissociative identities' as they are more properly called, are demons."

"Hold it. This is way over my head. Give it to me in simple terms," Billy insisted. "I'm a TV host, and I don't have a Ph.D. in clinical psychology."

"If you did, you still wouldn't know what I'm talking about," Kingman explained. "Most psychiatrists have little knowledge about multiple personalities."

"Ah, that's a term I understand. We did a show on that subject a few months ago. We featured the story of a murderer who tried to get off by claiming he had multiple personality disorder. He argued in court that, without his knowing what happened, one of his personalities pulled the trigger when he shot his wife."

"I know the case you're referring to," said Kingman. "John Byers, who was convicted and sentenced to death. I visited him in prison."

"Well, then," Billy responded. "I'm curious to know what you think. Did John do it, or did some other personality do it?"

Kingman leaned forward slightly into the aisle as his three fellow passengers strained to hear his explanation. "During a crisis in John's life, he got involved in the occult. The night of the murder, he consulted a Ouija board regarding a decision about taking a different job. The last thing he remembered was asking a question and placing his hands on the board. He came back to consciousness thirty minutes later, holding a gun and standing over the body of his dead wife."

"I'll tell you what I think," Billy said firmly. "Byers was fooling around and wanted to get rid of her. So he shot her and concocted an ingenious explanation to get off the hook. I had people on my show who knew him, and every one of them said he lied to save his neck."

"Perhaps, but I think he told the truth," Kingman countered. "The real John Byers didn't pull the trigger. Byers in his core consciousness did not technically kill, but the evil personality did, and John's core identity gave permission. You see, when I talked with John in prison, he told me that he was molested as a child. In my opinion, that abuse created a personality who wanted to violently strike back at the world. Demons added their influence, and the result was a verdict of first-degree murder. The 'bad' John inside his soul turned him toward evil and was given free rein to take human life. Both evil alter personalities and demons can be violent, but a demon can't act against the will of the person. On the other hand, an evil alter can, because that alter is the person, even if it is only a part of the consciousness."

Allison raised her hand to get Kingman's attention. "I think I understand what you're saying. According to you, this man, Phillip, had one personality who brought him to your seminar, another who lashed out violently, and another who talked to you after the outburst."

"Close, but not quite. You're right about the personality who came to the seminar and the one who didn't know what was going on. But the violence was caused by demons. Remember, the attack occurred after I identified the demon of Murder. Let's get back to the video, and you'll see the difference between the personalities and the demons."

Kingman hit PLAY again. The screen went to black and the scene shifted. Kingman was having an intense conversation with Phillip. The young man described his upbringing in tearful terms. "My parents were good people, but they never said they loved me." His voice cracked from the strain. "I was an accident, an unplanned child. I guess they never adjusted to my interruption of their lives. They split up when I was about seven. My dad was a heavy drinker who often took me to the bars. For hours on end he sat there, drinking one beer after another, while I was left alone in a corner. He told me to play, but there was nothing but ashtrays, smoke, tables piled with empty whiskey bottles, and wooden chairs. No one wanted anything to do with a kid, least of all my father. At home I developed an imaginary inner world to escape that awful hellhole."

Kingman put a reassuring arm around Phillip's shoulders.

"Finally, I found a neighborhood man who showed me attention. I found out too late that his 'attention' was sick, but I was easy prey. He . . ."

"I know what he did," Kingman said as Phillip burst into tears. Kingman changed the tone of his voice. "That mean man hurt you, didn't he?" Phillip nodded. "He made you feel like a dirty little boy."

"Nasty. He made me feel nasty," Phillip said in a waiflike, quivering voice. "I'm a bad little boy. I deserve to be punished."

"No, you're not," Kingman said firmly. "That man was bad to you. You're a good little boy."

"I'm so bad that even God doesn't love me," Phillip cried.

Kingman knelt in front of him. "That's a lie. And I know who told you that lie. It's the creatures hiding in the darkness around you."

"How did you know about them?"

"Because I know how they operate. Don't be afraid of them. They can't hurt you if Jesus is your friend."

"I want to be a friend of Jesus, but I don't know Him."

"Then we're all going to sing you a little song." Kingman lifted his arms in the air like the director of a mass choir and led the audience in singing "Jesus Loves Me."

Video cameras panned the crowd. There wasn't a dry eye in the entire room. Tears streamed down the faces of everyone from children to grown men.

As the refrain "Little ones to Him belong, they are weak but He is strong" drifted softly through the auditorium, Billy felt a lump in his own throat. He remembered sitting in Sunday school back in Cody, after his dad left, wondering if there was a God who loved him.

Allison sniffled and took a handkerchief from her jeans pocket. Even

Gabriel wiped his eyes. Billy swallowed hard as a camera zoomed in on Phillip's smiling face, which reflected a childlike quality.

Arghhh!!!!

Phillip's soft expression instantly turned into a display of dark rage. Kingman's guards jumped into action and once again grabbed Phillip.

"Jesus doesn't love him. Nobody loves him. He belongs to me. I'm the only one who wanted him, and he wanted me." Phillip looked poised for a fight. His body was tense and agitated. "I gave him the right to be angry," the demon declared, "and I'll give him the reason to . . ."

The hideous voice paused.

"Kill himself," Kingman declared, "after he has killed others. That's what you want him to do, isn't it, Murder?"

"Yes! Yes! Yes! Blood. The smell of it, the sight of it. Blood everywhere. Its crimson flow waters the green, green grass of earth. It feeds the soil. War and destruction come from it. Death to all humanity. Death to every living creature. I hate them all. They must all die. And he must die."

Billy thought he had seen almost everything there was to see in life, but Steinberg was right: this was the most moving video footage he'd ever witnessed. No wonder Steinberg had wanted Gabriel along. If Kingman decided to do an exorcism of Allison, there would be amazing footage to capture.

Kingman paused the video.

"I'm starting to figure this out," said Billy. "Let me guess. That's what you'd call a demon, saying it loves blood and murder. I agree it looks evil, but how do you know it isn't just some kind of madness?"

Kingman let the video resume playing. The demonic voice uttered profane curses and then began speaking in German. Billy was shocked. As a child, his grandmother, who came from the 'old country,' taught him German words and expressions. He didn't understand all that the voice said, but he comprehended enough to know that someone, or something, in Phillip, spoke perfect High German.

Kingman paused the video."Are you ready for the most interesting part?"

Everyone nodded, and Kingman hit PLAY again.

"The curse. That's how you got there, isn't it?"

The voice laughed heartily.

"How many generations? How far back?"

Phillip's face distorted in ways that no actor could mimic. "Ten generations," came the answer in a crisp British accent. "He wanted power, money, and sex. He stopped at nothing. When he killed, that gave the legal right . . ."

The voice hesitated.

"For the curse?"

"Yes, the curse. But you don't know what it is, and you don't know how to break it, do you?" the voice taunted Kingman. "But most importantly, you don't know who created the curse."

"God will show us."

"He'd better show you quickly, because in exactly fifteen minutes, this man will be dead."

Phillip's head suddenly jerked backward. His windpipe thrust outward, and he clawed at his throat as if seeking to remove unseen hands that strangled him. He choked and coughed until he collapsed on the floor. His eyes bulged and his lungs gasped for air. Then his body jerked as if in a seizure, and he went unconscious.

Kingman knelt by Phillip's lifeless body and checked his pulse. He looked directly into the TV camera. "There's no heartbeat," he said. He pushed back an eyelid. Phillip's eyes were rolled back so far in his head that only the whites were visible.

Phillip took one last deep breath, and his face turned blue.

"We'll be at Arapahoe County Airport in ten minutes," said the pilot over the plane's speakers. "Please shut off all electronic devices and fasten your seat belts for landing."

The sound of the landing gear being lowered confirmed the pilot's announcement.

Kingman hit the STOP button and the video screen went blank.

10

Allison rubbed the luxurious gray leather seats inside the stretch limo that transported the four passengers from the Arapahoe County Airport to the downtown Denver Westin Hotel. "You sure know how to travel in style," she said to Billy as she surveyed the elegant surroundings: crystal goblets, champagne on ice, television, plush pillows. Darkened privacy windows hid the occupants from the outside world but offered a clear view of the distant snow-covered peaks. The mountains peeked in and out of the office complexes that lined the freeway.

"Nothing but the best for my guests," Billy responded. "That's Mt. Evans just above the horizon. Look for the tallest peak. The highest paved automobile road in the world goes up there. It's taller than Pike's Peak, but who knows. Pike's gets all the publicity. That Zebulon Pike must have been some promoter. There are more than fifty mountains in the state over fourteen thousand feet, but Pike's is the only one most people hear about. If Pike were around today, I'd hire him as my press agent."

"Didn't the view from Pike's Peak inspire 'America the Beautiful'?" Kingman asked as he bent down to get a better view.

"Maybe. And maybe it was just a publicity stunt. When you're in my business, you have to wonder. You folks in the outside world, apart from promotion and advertising, think you're getting the straight scoop about products, even the news, but you're not. The 'reality' shows, doc-umentaries, the lead stories of 'news at eleven'–it's all managed. Even what you've been told about me is contrived. Why do you think I pay a press agent six figures a year to plant stories and manage the bylines? Don't forget, there's no such thing as bad publicity, just publicity. Say anything you want, but spell my name M-c-B-r-i-d-e."

"What about that home for abandoned children you raised money for last year?" Allison asked. "Was that just for publicity?"

"Partially. I cared about those kids. Who wouldn't? Their plight was pathetic. None of them knew who their real father was. Their single mothers finally gave up and dumped them in homeless shelters or on the doorsteps of hospitals. But the truth is, I never knew that place existed until my P.R. guy came up with the idea of my doing a show on it. At the time, we were taking heat from the network brass about a show I'd done on men marrying transsexuals, and we needed a positive spin in the media."

"I saw that show about transsexuals. Was that for real?"

"Allison, for once I actually did a show on something that wasn't contrived by my producer, Steinberg. We were alerted to the idea by the son of an elderly man who got married just months before he died. After the old guy passed on, the son was upset that his father had left all his money to his spouse. The son did some checking and discovered that his dad actually married a man who had a sex-change operation. The son sued his 'stepmom.' He said the money belonged to him because, by state law, his father, who was a man, couldn't marry another man. No matter what kind of surgery had been performed, he, she, or whatever was still biologically a man."

"Then doing the show on abandoned kids was just a publicity stunt." Allison shook her head in disgust.

"Hey, it's not that bad," Billy responded defensively. "I did raise a ton of money. It was a win/win. The kids won. They were able to remodel their home. I won my battle with the network executives who were about to take me off the air. They backed off when they read the positive publicity my so-called generosity generated."

"I'm grateful those kids were helped, no matter why you did it or what your motive was," Kingman interjected, "but were you troubled by the ethics of your actions?"

"I didn't lose any sleep at night, if that's what you mean. Troubled? Sort of. But I'm not the problem. If you want to get on somebody's case, go after those deadbeat dads. I don't know how you were raised, Reverend, but it's tough without a dad around. Do you have any idea what it's like to grow up without a father, or worse yet, not being sure who your father was?" Billy looked straight at Allison.

"I'll admit I can't personally empathize. I was raised by godly, Christian parents who did their best to affirm me," Kingman said.

"What about you, Gabriel? You're being awfully silent."

"I'm just listening. My answer is like the Reverend's. All I ever knew was encouragement and approval."

"What about you, Allison?" Billy looked her straight in the eye. Gabriel's camera wasn't rolling yet, but Billy wanted to stir the pot a little and get Allison provoked for confrontations that would come later.

Her body grew rigid and her eyes filled with tears. "You know the answer to that!" she said sharply. "Not that it matters. It's what you make of life, not what kind of life someone made for you, or what some P.R. agent is able to fabricate."

Kingman broke the tension. "Abandonment issues are one of the most frequent causes for spiritual problems. When children grow up without one or both parents, a part of them is missing, unless that void is filled with God's love. It's worse yet when the parent deliberately abandons the child. We have an entire generation that is, to a large extent, fatherless."

"What's the difference? You either have a dad or you don't. If you don't, you just get on with life." Billy displayed his usual cavalier attitude toward such topics.

"It makes a huge difference," Kingman replied. "A child can be abandoned because of death or extenuating circumstances, but if a father just walks away and refuses to fulfill his responsibilities, he hands that child over to evil forces."

"Here we go again with the devil stuff, right?" Billy was downright sarcastic.

"Yes, Satan often steps into a child's life when parents abdicate their proper role as protector and spiritual covering."

"Are you actually saying that when children are abandoned, they belong to the devil?" The tone of Allison's voice seemed as much frightened as questioning.

"That's putting it harshly, but the answer is yes. Satan can take control of a child's life in many ways."

"Can a child be possessed by the devil just because of what the parents did?" Allison's face grew more serious.

"That's possible. The child may be ceded to the devil when the parents consider an abortion, or when they say over the womb, 'I don't want this child.' It can also happen when they ignore the emotional needs of the youngster."

"To hear you talk, I'd conclude that half the population has demons. We probably need as many exorcists as we do doctors and nurses."

"That may be exaggerating what I'm saying. The grace of God protects us many times when we would otherwise have been held captive by the devil. I'm not saying that anywhere near 50 percent of the people driving by us on the freeway have demons, but there are a lot more of them than you suspect. Like I said, those who were abandoned by their fathers and mothers are most susceptible."

Allison let out a sigh. "This is heavy. I don't know about the rest of you, but I'd like to see the remainder of that video. We rushed off the airplane so quickly, we still don't know if that guy Phillip lived or died."

"Let me assure you," Kingman responded, "Phillip is very much alive and well. God performed a miracle, almost like raising him from the dead."

Billy rolled his eyes. "Just when I was getting to like you and buy into what you do, you throw that in. First it was demons in abandoned children. Now it's raising people from the dead. Next I suppose you'll walk on water." He turned to Allison. "We can finish the video on the way back to Phoenix tomorrow. Tonight we rodeo!"

The limousine headed up Interstate 25 toward Denver's skyline. Cloudless baby-blue skies enveloped the skyscrapers in a scene worthy of a tourist bureau postcard. The serenity of the scenery contrasted with the bedlam of the traffic. Even at one o'clock in the afternoon, the convoy of cars moved at a crawl. After the intense discussion, the four passengers sat silently for a few minutes, each looking out the window, watching the creeping procession of automobiles. Allison broke the silence.

"I can't wait. I want to know how Phillip survived. I'm too curious to sit in suspense for another twenty-four hours."

Kingman looked at Billy, who shrugged his shoulders.

"All right, Allison, I'll do my best to describe what happened." Kingman turned sideways in his seat and leaned slightly toward her. "Life was being choked out of Phillip. His heartbeat had stilled to nothing. Strangely enough, without any sign of life, a voice spoke from his body. His lips barely moved, just enough to say, 'What will you do now? How are you going to explain a dead body on your hands?' I knew it was the demon daring me, but because it spoke, that meant Phillip's 'death' wasn't real."

"But you said on the video his heartbeat was gone," Billy reminded Kingman.

"Whose heartbeat? That was the question I had to answer."

"What do you mean, 'whose heartbeat?'" Allison asked. "That's an irrelevant question. It was Phillip lying there."

"Yes, but what part of Phillip's body was experiencing 'death'?"

Billy had been lounging back in his seat. Now he leaned forward with renewed interest. "There you go again, heading off into the twilight zone. Phillip's body was Phillip's body."

"Not exactly. A lot of research has been done on what's called the mind-body connection. More and more, medical science is recognizing that there's a strong link between a person's physical health and mental condition. Like the Bible says in Proverbs 17:22, 'A cheerful heart is good medicine, but a crushed spirit dries up the bones.'"

"That still doesn't explain what you mean." There was a tone of frustration in Billy's voice.

The chauffeur slid open the Plexiglass window that separated him from the passengers and glanced over his shoulder quickly. "Is there anything you want before I drop all of you off at the hotel?" he asked.

Billy looked at Allison, Gabriel, and Kingman. They shook their heads. "I think we're all a little tired. We've got a big night ahead of us, so we'll go straight to our rooms. Thanks for checking."

The driver nodded and closed the window.

"Here's my point," said Kingman, resuming the conversation. "Remember, I told you Phillip had multiple personalities. When he appeared to be dying, I had a spiritual hunch that only one of his personalities was experiencing death. So I called out to the other personalities to fight their way back to life."

"Maybe you should tell them just how distinctive each personality can be. That might help to explain the degree of separateness that multiples have," Gabriel suggested.

Billy looked at him curiously. Everyone but Gabriel seemed confused by the talk about multiple personalities. Billy couldn't resist finding out why. "Allison and I are in the dark about all this. How do you know so much?"

Gabriel smiled pleasantly. "I should have mentioned earlier that I've had an interest in the subject of multiple personalities for years. A couple of years ago, I was involved in a videotaping project that explored just how far multiplicity extends into the consciousness. When Dr. Kingman talked about one personality dying while the others were alive, that was a minor example of how incredible this phenomenon is. It's amazing how the mind, especially the wounded soul of a person, can fragment into different identities. When severe abuse or trauma is experienced, forming multiple personalities to repress the memory of the tragedy is the only way the person can survive. The splitting that takes place is a defense mechanism, and the distinction between different personalities in one body is very remarkable."

"He's right," said Kingman. "I've studied cases where one personality is a hemophiliac and someone has nearly bled to death because that particular personality cut the body."

"You mean that a person could bleed uncontrollably if the alter personality that was a hemophiliac was in control at the time of an injury?" Allison asked.

"Exactly. There is some evidence that when going from one alter personality to another, the brain waves differ. Blood types can change, and patterns of addictive behavior can be affected. For example, if one personality in the body is a drug addict, and that alter is conscious, the body will crave the drug that particular alter abuses—but only when that particular personality surfaces."

"Multiples are also gender specific," Gabriel added.

"What he means is that there can be more than one gender in a body." Kingman went on. "A male body can have a female personality inside, and vice versa. Once a group of counselors and I were going to a dinner with a woman who was multiple. She had a male personality inside named George. As the waiter led us to the table, I pulled out the chair, to be a gentleman. At that instant she did a switch."

"What's a switch?" Allison asked.

"That's when one personality switches to another. By the facial expressions and the body language, I recognized the new personality was George. I knew George would be insulted if I treated him like a woman, so I put the chair back under the table and said, 'Sorry, George.' I wish you could have seen the look on that waiter's face.

Everyone, including Allison, chuckled.

"They're also multiracial," Gabriel said. "I've heard that they can have ethnic identities that differ from the body. Is that right, Dr. Kingman?"

"Yes. I once dealt with a woman who had been tortured by a Ku Klux Klan group that was a front for a satanic cult. The torture was so severe, she split off a multiple personality to handle the pain. Her mind needed some explanation as to why she, a white woman, was being abused by a racist group. So she mentally came up with the conclusion that she must be black."

"But that was all in her mind, wasn't it?" asked Billy.

"Yes, but it was real to her. She created an African-American personality, and when it was out, she spoke in an Alabama accent with African-American slang. I asked that particular personality what she saw when she looked in the mirror, and instead of seeing the reflection of a white woman, she actually saw herself with black skin."

Billy shook his head in amazement. "This is really getting complicated. When I did the show on multiple personalities, we never got into any of this. I'm not sure how much of it I believe. How do you know she wasn't crazy?"

"Well, let me give you another example that may answer that question. If what I've told you so far seems amazing, try this on for size. I once worked with a man who attended Yale University. He studied genetics and made a very important scientific discovery regarding genomes. He had multiple personalities, and to get through school, he assigned a different personality to take each course."

"Whoa! This is getting too strange." Billy listened in disbelief.

"I told you it was astonishing. Get this. One personality took languages, another chemistry, another mathematics, and so on. Each personality was responsible for only one subject, so when it came time for tests, the core personality had to make certain the right alter was dominant. One personality was assigned to drive to and from school each day. Once, a child alter came out on the way to school and didn't know how to drive and wrecked the car."

"Are you sure these people aren't mental?"

"Billy, don't forget, these people are extraordinarily bright. They have to remember every trait and idiosyncrasy of every personality, even to the extent of specific wardrobes. Some colleagues and I were once counseling a woman who was a multiple, and we went by her house to pick her up to take her to a meeting. Before we left the house, she made a series of clothing changes. Every time she started to leave, a different personality surfaced and refused to leave wearing whatever particular dress was on at the time. An hour and five different outfits later, we finally left."

"Do you think this is what's wrong with Allison?"

"I don't think. I know! My prayer is that somehow I'll be able to help her so she can realize what a wonderful person she is, and that she doesn't have to hurt herself any more."

For a split second Allison shot a glance Kingman's way, but Billy wasn't sure whether it was a look of anger or curiosity. Then she looked away out the window.

"I'm still not sure what this has to do with Phillip," Billy said.

"If an evil spirit had control over a certain alter, that demon could affect the vital signs of that state of consciousness," Kingman explained. "That could cause the body to die. But if a nondemonic personality surfaced, the state of death could be reversed."

"Let me guess," Billy offered. "You somehow contacted an alter that wasn't dying, and when that mental state came out, life returned."

"You got it. Except, it wasn't that simple. When I tried to get an alter with 'life' to surface, demons interfered. We had to fight off one spiritual attack after another before we could get through to the personality that saved Phillip's life."

"Hold it a minute, Mr. Preacher Man," Allison said. "You keep talking about the demons as if they're real, and that all of us should believe in the supernatural like you. Has it occurred to you that some of us might think your idea of evil spirits is medieval? Maybe you're just dealing with unstable people."

"I can understand why you feel that way, Allison. That's what a lot of people think."

"I agree with Allison. What you call 'demons' and multiple personalities are really figments of your own prejudices," Billy argued.

"Well, Billy, you'll have to explain what you saw on that video."

"I can't explain it. And I don't have to. It's your problem to explain what's going on. You're the one who claims to be an exorcist."

Tension filled the air until Kingman responded. "It's hard to explain a miracle, unless you accept it by faith. Billy, your skepticism won't let you believe what your eyes plainly see."

Kingman directed his attention toward Allison. "You've heard more about multiple personalities in the last few minutes than most people have heard in a lifetime. I'm curious. What do you think about our discussion?"

Allison was put off by the question. She toyed with the collar of her sweater. Her eyes were averted downward. When her gaze did meet Kingman's, a relaxed look filled her face. She tilted her forehead down slightly and looked upward coquettishly. "I'm not sure I really understand what y'all are talking about. It's an awfully serious conversation for a li'l sheltered girl like me."

Billy was caught off guard by the Southern accent. What kind of act was Allison putting on this time?

"Perhaps we can talk about it later when you feel more comfortable," Kingman suggested.

"That would be fine with me." Allison batted her eyes like an antebellum debutante at a plantation ball. "I usually don't discuss such serious subjects, but I'm right pleased to meet you."

Kingman leaned across the aisle and gently took Allison's hands in his. "Thank you, ma'am. Any time you want to talk is fine with me. You just let me know." He spoke with a reassuring pastoral tone and patted Allison's hand as he leaned back in his seat.

Billy was angry. To his way of thinking, Allison was putting on another one of her performances, and Kingman had been suckered right into it.

"So, where's this rodeo, cowboy?" Allison spoke in an assertive and terse manner suddenly different from her Southern belle persona. "I didn't come all this way to spend my time on a freeway. I can do that in Phoenix."

"Be patient. We'll be on our way to the rodeo in a few hours."

"Where is this thing?" Allison asked

"It's held in an arena just north of downtown. Be sure to bring a coat. Even though Colorado is unseasonably warm this time of year, it will cool down at night. The arena is heated, but some of the stock stalls aren't."

"Stock stalls? What are you talking about?"

"I'm going to take you behind the scenes to get up close and personal with some cows and horses."

"Cows I can handle. But I'm not getting near any horses. I hate horses!"

"Why? Did a horse ever frighten you?" Billy asked.

Allison's eyes darted back and forth searching for an answer. "I do remember my mother taking me to a petting zoo when I was a kid and giving me a pony ride. I was terrified. She had to get me off the horse after a few seconds. My dad was furious. He thought I was being a brat. I wasn't. That horse scared me to death."

"I've been with people who were skittish around horses because they were afraid of getting kicked or bucked off, but I've never heard anyone say that horses affected them that badly."

"It's coming back to me now. I was so frightened, I ran away as fast as I could, until . . ." Allison paused. Her mind was lost in deep thought.

"Until what?"

"Until I fell down. No, something knocked me down. I remember it now. Something literally knocked me off my feet."

11

"Ladies and gentlemen, will you please rise for the presentation of the colors."

In unison, thousands of spectators stood as cowboys removed their hats and placed their hands over their hearts. From the far end of the arena, three young women on galloping horses burst into the coliseum. Each held a staff with a flag that unfurled as they raced toward the other end of the arena and back toward the center. One rode a white horse, another a palomino, and the third a gray. The riders crisscrossed at breakneck speed, just missing each other, in a circle-eight pattern. Then they stopped and presented their flags at attention: a Colorado flag, a Canadian maple leaf, and the United States' Stars and Stripes.

The flag presenters rested their reins on the saddle horns as a woman dressed in a flamboyant cowgirl outfit stepped from a box seat near Billy and his entourage. She walked toward the horses, carrying a cordless microphone. The spangles on her brightly decorated vest reflected the glare of a single follow spot that traced her movements. Her flowing western skirt, with embroidered designs of cowboy symbols, moved in waves as she walked.

"Will you please join our rodeo queen, Miss Tiffany Johnson, as she leads us in the singing of our national anthem."

Near the judge's booth, a six-piece band struck up the introduction to "The Star-Spangled Banner." The cavernous coliseum didn't have the best acoustics, and the words to the song echoed off the steel beams and concrete roof, high above the dirt-covered floor.

Billy winced. He never liked hearing an audience of amateurs try to hit those high notes at the end of the song. It grated on him. Worse yet, Miss Johnson was less than talented, and her effort to soar flatted out. The audience happily sang along, creating a tune that barely resembled Francis Scott Key's ode to America. They broke into whoops and cheers as the three women once again galloped around the arena and exited as quickly as they had entered.

Billy, Allison, Gabriel, and Dr. Kingman had the best location in the house, ground-level box seats so close to the action that they heard the wheezing of the horses' breath. The scent of earth, mingled with the smell of horse manure, was overpowering. Small clods of dirt, flung in the air by the horses' hooves, landed in Billy's box. Allison had been told she would be "up close and personal," but this was more than she had imagined.

For Billy, this night was an ambivalent trip back in time. Part of him felt at home with the life that dominated his early adult years. The camaraderie of cowboys, the adrenaline rush seconds before the chute gate opened, the cheer of the crowd at the end of a successful ride— all these rekindled recollections were welcome. Recalling bucking broncos and hard-to-heal bruises didn't bother him. However, he was uncomfortable with revisiting other less pleasant memories. The pain he felt was from the years he wasted trying to find himself in too much booze and too many meaningless relationships. Being so close again to guys who sweated for a living forced Billy to realize how artificial his life had become. In spite of all his efforts to find his true self, he wondered if he had left what mattered most back in the scuffed boots that he once wore to arenas like this.

All around the inside of the arena perimeter, which was slightly smaller than a football field, were hand-painted signs draped over the fence. The advertisements welcomed stock show visitors and promoted beer, real estate companies, agricultural products, soft drinks, and satellite dishes. At the end of the arena, opposite the flag bearers' entry, were the chutes where cowboys would mount their untamed broncs. The public address platform and announcer's booth were directly above. High above the crowd, in the center of the arena, was a large scoreboard to flash the results of each event. Vendors made their way through the crowd, dispensing ice cream, cotton candy, beer, and popcorn.

In preparation for the evening, two gaudily dressed clowns entered the arena and established rapport with the crowd through their comedic antics. One was dressed in a floral Hawaiian shirt with oversized overalls, held up by stars and stripes suspenders. His partner's face was painted white with a large red nose. A dirty, floppy brown hat, a woman's scarf around his neck, and bicycle racing pants completed his wardrobe. They acted silly, slow, and clueless, but Billy knew these men were accomplished athletes. Instead of being the stumblebums they portrayed, they had the daring of a trapeze artist and the cunning of a mongoose.

The lights dimmed, and the spotlight fell on a single rider approaching slowly from the chutes. An unidentified voice signaled the solitary cowboy. "Ladies and gentlemen, please welcome our rodeo announcer, Charley Chestnut, and his horse, Wyoming Wonder."

A cordless lapel microphone was attached to the collar of the cowboy's plaid shirt. A black silk tie hung around his neck, cinched by a shiny silver bolo. His hand-tooled leather chaps were intricately etched with ranch brands, and his polished spurs sparkled in the bright light. His face was etched with deep lines that formed small crevices in his weathered skin. He was lanky, almost skinny, far too thin for a man who appeared to be sixty-plus years of age. He had the look of a man who had lived a hard life: countless Marlboros, too much cheap whiskey, and a slew of lonely nights driving to the next rodeo. His dilapidated white cowboy hat contrasted with the steam-shaped felt and feather varieties worn by the rodeo officials who scurried about making final preparations for the first ride.

"Do you ever watch NFL football?" Billy leaned in front of Kingman, who was seated on his left, to pose the question to Allison. He was surprised at her answer.

"Believe it or not, yes. But with the way the Arizona Cardinals have been playing the last few years, there hasn't been much to cheer about."

"Well, think of that guy on the horse as the color announcer. That nameless voice in the booth will keep things anchored, but the horseman will make it interesting. He'll do more than give the play-by-play. He'll add life and drama to what goes on."

As if responding on cue, the cowboy spoke. His baritone voice boomed over the loudspeakers as his strawberry roan quarter horse ambled about the arena. "The word *rodeo* is Spanish and referred to a gathering place of cattle, like the old roundups. Cowboys gathered in cow towns at the end of a cattle drive and vied to be the best at some skill, like roping a calf. When barbed wire and the railroads curtailed the western way of life, the contests evolved into what we know as rodeos, a regular kind of entertainment in the West.

"Now, there is some dispute about where the first rodeo took place, but you folks right here in Colorado can lay claim to what some say was the first official rodeo, one hundred and fifty years ago, in Deer Creek, Colorado. In those days, you rodeoed to earn five bucks a day and were happy to have it. The purses are a lot bigger now, and the stock is a lot tougher. Some cowboys here tonight are taking a crack at more than $100,000 in total prizes. For one eight-second ride, they'll pocket thousands of dollars. But don't let their superstar status fool you. Many of the riders you'll see have a real western heritage."

Small puffs of dust rose from the arena floor as Wyoming Wonder kicked up piles of deep dirt with each step. Caged rodeo bronc horses snorted, ready for the riders who drew their lot. The faint bawl of calves, combined with the sound of bulls banging against their steel enclosures, created background music more authentic than any Garth Brooks ballad.

"These aren't dime-store cowboys," Charley explained. "Some are direct descendants of the pioneer stock that settled the mountain West. Their forefathers drove herds of longhorns from Amarillo to Kansas City. They ate over campfires every night of their lives, when free range extended from Denver to Salt Lake, from Albuquerque to Casper. Today, the sons and daughters of those brave men and women eat at a chuck wagon with golden arches."

A chuckle rippled through the audience.

"Their bed is a Featherlite combination horse trailer pulled by a Ford F350 pickup, not a moldy sleeping bag stretched out under the stars. But the fire in their bellies hasn't changed in a hundred years. The thrill of spurring fifteen hundred pounds of bucking bronc and the smell of horse flesh and sod are still the same. These aren't urban cowboys. They believe in the West, where men still know the names of their neighbors, even if they live six sections away, and where a man and his gun are constant companions."

A shout erupted in the crowd. The fervor struck city-bred Allison as strange, like the cheering section for a National Rifle Association convention.

"The riders you'll see tonight believe in the real American West. They believe in family values. They believe in each other, and they still believe in God." Charley paused for dramatic effect. "Would you please remove your hats one more time, as we bless this evening and ask God to protect those who compete on this hallowed ground."

The constant chatter of the audience ceased instantly. Even the animals sensed that the order of the evening was different. A sacred silence settled on man and beast as Charley halted his horse and reverently intoned, "Our Heavenly Father, we ask Your blessing on the gathering this evening, as we enjoy America's greatest sport. As cowboys, we don't ask for any special favors. We don't ask to finish our ride or to stop a steer. We don't ask for a bull that is easy to ride or that we never knock over a barrel. We only ask that, when we have finished our duty down here and we make that last ride to the country up yonder, where the grass grows green and stirrup high, that You, as our last Judge, will tell us that our entry fee has been paid."

Polite applause followed, as Charley continued to introduce the evening. "Let me tell you about the people who make this evening happen, the folks you won't think about as you watch the cowboys come flying out of the chute in a few minutes. First of all, give a hand to our stock contractor, Mr. David Lyons. He's the man responsible for seeing that all our animals are healthy and untamed. Don't listen to the propaganda of those animal rights people. Horses and cattle are the love of David's life. In fact, David treats his horses better than his wife." The audience laughed as Charley continued. "Mr. Lyons's horses are renegades. They like to buck. They're fresh off the range and have resisted every effort to break them. No man has ever mastered them, and they'll prove it tonight."

Charley paused for a moment to walk his horse a short distance. Then he halted and resumed. "Next, let me tell you about our pickup men, Kenny Hays and Chuck Kelley. They're responsible for making sure our riders aren't hurt and that they get off their mounts quickly and safely. Finally, our rodeo clowns, Ornery Andy, and Harry Hooligan. They'll make you laugh, but their work is dead serious, especially when it comes to the bulls. They are master 'matadors' who risk their own lives for the safety of our contestants."

Charley nudged his horse away from the center of the arena and a reasonable distance from the chutes. "Now, turn your attention to the bucking chutes for the first bareback bronc ride of the evening. The rider is Chad Reynolds on a horse called Thunder."

Suddenly, the clang of metal, as the gate flew open, hushed the audience. Out of the middle chute flew rider and horse in an explosion of horsepower. Thunder bucked first one way, then the other. When that didn't dislodge his rider, Thunder's back legs flew in the air so high that he almost lost his balance. The dust from Thunder's hooves obliterated the audience's clear view of the spectacle. Before the cloud settled, the horn blew, signaling the eight seconds were over. The pickup men instantly arrived at Reynolds's side, loosening the flank strap that Thunder had been trying to detach.

"Ladies and gentlemen," Charley intoned deliberately, "our first ride was a successful one. Let me tell you, bronc riding is a humbling event. You can ride twenty in a row and never get bucked off, or get thrown every time. If you get too cocky, the Man Upstairs and Mother Nature have a way of putting you face first in foot-deep dirt. But Chad made it look easy."

Chad grabbed the body of a pickup man who pulled him from the back of Thunder and deposited him feet first on the ground. "Chad's safe now and can hear what you think about his ride. Let him know you enjoyed his performance."

The audience applauded enthusiastically.

"And his score is an 84 with no penalties. He did a great job of spurring Thunder, and he's still in the running for all-around cowboy. Let's hear it again for Chad Reynolds."

Allison leaned in front of Kingman and tugged at the sleeve of Billy's shirt. "I can't believe that was only eight seconds," she observed. "It seemed like minutes."

"It feels like a lot more than that when you're on top of a rank bucker like Thunder, determined to send you flying into the next county. I have Gunsmoke to thank for this." Billy held out both his arms, extended full length in front of his body.

"Your left arm is shorter than your right," Allison observed. "You can't put it out completely straight?"

"It got that way when Gunsmoke stepped on this elbow." Billy bent his left arm several times. "It happened at the national finals in Las Vegas, in the last go-round of the competition. Gunsmoke first bucked me off. Then, his front right hoof came down full force on my elbow. Nothing that three operations and six months of physical therapy couldn't cure–almost."

"Is that why you quit competing?"

"No, that decision belonged to Dangerous, two thousand pounds of bull that . . ." Billy caught himself mid-sentence. The memory was so painful that it halted his words.

Chad made his way out of the arena as the pickup men herded Thunder back to the stock pens. Charley resumed his commentary.

"One hand, ladies and gentlemen, that's all the cowboys can use. He holds on to a flat piece of leather called a bareback rigging. It's like hanging onto a suitcase handle, with a stick of dynamite in the luggage. That rigging fits around the horse's midsection, just over the horse's withers. The rider must keep one hand free and never touch the horse with it at any time during the ride. The judges score 1 to 25 for the cowboy, and 1 to 25 for the horse. The cowboy has to spur the horse over the shoulders on every jump. The best you can do is 100, so you can see why Chad's 84 is outstanding. Best score ever in this event was a 95 at the National Finals. Now watch when the next rider mounts in the chute," Charley explained. The sound of a horse hoof striking steel echoed across the arena. "Some horses kick the side of the chute just for fun, to get a little psychological edge on the cowboy."

A second later, the chute gate flew open and another rider tested his mettle. Not for long. One spur and one wave of the arm, and both cowboy and horse went down in a cloud of dirt. Fortunately, rider and horse went in opposite directions.

As Kenny reined his pickup horse close to the fallen cowboy, the horse lost his footing in the loose sod and also went down. Both cowboys lay motionless for a moment, stunned by their misfortune. The rodeo clowns, who had been acting up near the box seats on the other side of the arena, rushed to the side of the fallen cowboys. They obviously feared that the cowboys might be in the way of the bucking horse, who was running wildly about the arena.

As Kenny's partner, Chuck, got things under control, Charley called out to the crowd, "That rider on the pinto mare will have nothing to show for his efforts but your applause and a long ride back to Durango. His name is Luke Greystone, former bareback bronc-riding champion in the state of Colorado. He'll have no score, but you can let him know how you feel right now."

The audience thundered with applause, and a few hundred stood in acclaim. Luke picked up his hat, hit it on his leg a couple of times to beat out the dirt, and waved it at the crowd as he walked, head down, toward the chutes. Luke was the second of eight riders, none of whom topped Chad Reynolds's score.

Between bareback bronc-riding and the saddle bronc-riding competition, the band played while cowboys readied the arena for the third event. Gabriel was quiet, as usual. He focused on what was happening around him. His camera rested in his lap, turned on and ready for action. Kingman watched all the action with avid curiosity, cheering every successful ride and groaning as each failed contestant landed in a cloud of soft, sandy soil.

In his mind, Billy was on top of every horse, right there with the rider feeling every bone-jarring jolt. At times he winced instinctively when a rider's body twisted at unnatural angles to stay atop the exploding buckers. At one point, he was so much into the competition that he leaned sharply right in his seat and flung his arm into the chest of Kingman.

"Hang on, cowboy," the minister responded with a lighthearted laugh. "Just don't take this so seriously that you spur one of my legs in an attempt to win the big buckle."

Billy smiled in response and watched Allison out of the corner of his eye. She appeared to be the most interested of anyone, just as he hoped. She was so enthralled, she hardly seemed to notice the occasional bit of footage that Gabriel shot of her reactions to each horse and cowboy. If she was afraid of horses, it didn't look like it from where she sat. She winced slightly during the calf-roping competition. The sight of a frightened calf, immobilized with three of its feet tied after being flipped into the air by a cowboy, needed some explanation.

"Don't worry," Billy responded to the pained look on Allison's face. "It doesn't hurt the calf. There are strict rules about how stock is handled, and no cowboy would ever mistreat an animal. Remember, he depends on these four-legged critters for a living."

"Which event do the cowboys like best?" Kingman asked, while Gabriel zoomed in for a tight shot of the question.

"The one that's next, team roping," Billy responded. "I suppose that's because it's a team sport. In some ways it has a more complicated skill level. Both cowboys, the roper who heads the steer's horns and the heeler who ropes the hind legs, have to time their break perfectly. See that string tied around the neck of the steer? That's the barrier that can't be broken until the animal bolts first and gets a head start. The chest of the horses should just about touch the barrier, but not break it. If they do, it's a penalty. Watch."

As Billy spoke, two cowboys bolted past the broken barrier toward the speeding steer. One cowboy successfully roped the horns, jerking the animal abruptly sideways. Immediately, his quarter horse dug in all four hooves and turned hard to the left. The heeler did his part by roping the steer's hind legs, while his horse stopped quickly and pulled backward. At the exact point the steer was properly stretched, a judge on the arena floor dropped a flag signaling the time.

"It reminds me of fighting demons," Kingman said to Billy, with a wink. "Taking on Satan works best when it's a team effort. Just like with those steers, if you're not careful, just when you think you've got the devil caught, he slips away if you don't keep a good spiritual hold on him."

"Those demons must be slippery little dogies," Billy said with a touch of humor.

Allison jumped in. "Where did they ever come up with the ideas for all these strange kinds of competitions?"

"Good question." Billy was encouraged by her increasing interest. "Back in the days of the cattle drives, the steers were much bigger than they are now. These steers probably weigh no more than five or six hundred pounds. On the Chisolm Trail, they might have gone as high as thirteen or fourteen hundred pounds. When it came time to brand, one cowboy couldn't do it alone. So they devised a way that two cowboys could bring down an animal, one roping the head and the other the legs."

"What's left?" Allison asked.

"Well, we've seen bareback bronc-riding, saddle bronc-riding, calf roping, and team roping. They'll probably take an intermission soon and finish up with barrel racing, steer wrestling, and bull riding."

Billy noticed some commotion at the far end of the arena. A half-dozen cowboys were trying to haze an escaped steer back toward the catch pens.

"Ladies and gentlemen, while we have a lull in the action, I'd like to make a special announcement." Charley rode slowly in the direction of Billy's box. "I've just been told that we have a national celebrity in our midst."

Allison reached across Kingman and poked Billy in the ribs. "Steinberg," he whispered. "Another one of his ideas to promo the show."

"Now, we have lots of famous people come to our rodeo, and we can't recognize them all. But the man I'm about to introduce is one of us. He's paid his dues in this business and has ridden his share of buckin' horses and bulls." Charley came so close that he and his horse stood no more than twenty feet away from Billy. "Would you please give a warm round of applause to a cowboy who rides the range of talk TV, the former winner of the bull-riding event at the 1990 National Western, Mr. Billy McBride."

Billy stood, took off his hat, and waved to the crowd. Thousands cheered enthusiastically, while several hundred fans seated near the top tier chanted, "Billll-eeee, Billll-eeee!"

As the cheers abated, Charley again addressed the crowd. "We'll be taking a short intermission while our cowboys set up the arena for the ladies' barrel racing event. After that it's steer wrestling and then every-one's favorite–bull riding."

Oohs and aahs swept the crowd in anticipation of the night's upcom-ing encounter with danger. "Go light on the popcorn and beer. We want you folks nice and sober for the grand finale. Thank you for being such a great audience. I'll be right back." Charley reined his horse hard right and headed toward the chutes.

The band struck up "Deep in the Heart of Texas," and half the audi-ence headed swiftly for the exits. Billy turned to his companions, after shaking hands with a few of his fans in the crowd around him. "The restrooms and concessions are right up those stairs," he said, pointing toward a portal that led out of the arena. "Help yourselves. I have some old acquaintances I want to say hello to. I won't be gone long."

Billy opened the box seat door that led to the arena and stepped into the dirt. His boots kicked up small puffs of dust as he slowly walked in the same direction that Charley had ridden just moments before. As he did, dozens of people leaped over the arena fence and ran toward him with pens and paper for autographs. Billy obliged them, while he made his way toward the chutes.

Allison nervously shifted back and forth in her seat. Finally, she spoke. "Don't know about you two, but I could use a hot dog, before the lines get too long."

"I'll get it for you." Kingman stood to his feet. "Mustard? Ketchup? Relish?"

"All of the above. And plenty of it." She shifted her eyes downward. She wasn't used to anyone besides her mother being so considerate. "Would you mind getting me a cola?" She reached into her jeans pocket for money.

"It's on me. Take the opportunity to get to know Gabriel a little better while I'm gone." Kingman headed up the stairs.

In the arena, rodeo hands rolled three large yellow barrels toward the far center, about thirty or forty yards from the chutes. The barrels were arranged in a triangle at precise distances that were paced off by one cowboy. Another cowboy set up two light-beam timers on opposite sides of the floor, not far from the chutes. The sensors were carefully aligned so that the timing of the barrel-racing event could be calculated when horse and rider would break the beam. Allison wasn't sure what to say to Gabriel, so she stared straight ahead as if the lining up of the barrels was of immense interest to her.

"Is it what you expected?" Gabriel asked.

"What?"

"The rodeo."

"Yeah. Sort of. Actually, it's more interesting than I thought it would be. I've seen this kind of thing on TV, but it's a lot different in person. It's . . ." She groped for the right word. "It's . . . smellier."

Gabriel laughed. "Exactly what I was thinking."

"How about you? What do you think?"

"Well, it's a little out of my line of work, but I'm glad I took the job."

"What is your line of work? I'm not sure I know. You shoot video. I know that. But who do you work for?"

"My boss is the best. Not everyone can say they love their job assignments, but I do. There's never a dull moment. I have to admit that with the wide range of projects I've been given, this is one of the most interesting."

"Why is that?"

"You."

Allison wasn't sure how to handle that answer. She said nothing.

Gabriel went on. "You probably don't realize it, but you're a very special young woman. God loves you very much to have seen you through everything you've faced in life."

"Wait a minute. No more of that God stuff. One preacher around me is enough. Anyway, you wouldn't have any idea what I've been through."

"You might be surprised. In my line of work I've learned a lot about human nature and what makes people tick. Like the voices in your head."

Allison looked shocked. "How did you know I hear voices?"

"It comes with the territory. Most people with multiple personalities hear voices, conversations inside their minds."

"Hold it!" Allison was irritated. "Who said I have multiple personalities?"

"It seems likely from what Reverend Kingman said earlier in the limo. I'm not trying to make a psychological diagnosis; I'm just commenting on what I've heard and what I've seen."

Allison folded her arms. "What *have* you seen?"

"You're two different people. Maybe more. On the surface you're tough, cavalier, self-sufficient. But underneath, there's a soft side that has been deeply injured by . . ."

"My dad, whoever he is and wherever he is. I know what you're thinking now. 'Poor little girl. Her daddy didn't love her. Spent her whole life just wanting someone to love her.' Give me a break! I'm glad my old man split. He wasn't worth having around. Ask my mom. As for men, they're all . . ."

"All what?"

"No offense to you. You seem like a nice enough guy. But all, at least most, men are pigs! They take what they want and throw you aside."

"And the little child inside you? What does she think?"

"What child? Do you think you're Freud or something? The only little girl around me is my daughter, Ashley, and she's the reason I survive. And by the way, why should all of this make any difference to you? You're just another media type. Shoot the video. Edit it to your satisfaction. Make it show what you want the people to see, and paint whatever picture you want. Go ahead. Roll that camera now. Let me look into the lens and tell you what I really think. I'm one person. Me. Allison. No more and no less. Next thing I know you'll want to do an exorcism on me like the preach."

"Okay, okay. Didn't mean to make you mad."

"I'm not mad, just spooked. First you show up out of nowhere and act like a know-it-all. Then, you start preaching like a clone of Kingman. I feel a little ganged up on. I don't need another Christian breathing down my neck. One exorcist is enough, thank you. It's like your being here was planned."

"Perhaps it was."

"By whom, Steinberg?"

"No, God."

Allison leaned across the seat and forced herself into Gabriel's face. "Get this straight. I'm not sure I believe there is a God, but if there is, I'm the last piece of trash He'd be interested in." She pulled back the sleeves of her jacket to reveal her wrists. "Perhaps Steinberg should have told you about this."

"God loves you just the way you are."

"Keep your God to yourself." Allison took a deep breath and sat back with a disgusted look. "How *do* you know so much about what goes on inside my mind?"

"I'm not just a cameraman. I've made it a point to learn all I can about human behavior. You might say it's my mission to help the less fortunate. Someday, I'd like to help out at a treatment center for those with emotional disorders. That why I study things like multiple personalities in my spare time."

"Fine. Do what you want on your own time, but leave me alone. That Steinberg slug hired you to take video of me to make a star out of McBride, so get back to your job and quit messing with my mind."

"One mystery-meat frank, loaded with ketchup and mustard, and guaranteed to produce heartburn." Kingman held a tray full of concession stand food. As he dispensed his fare, a booming voice came over

Bob Larson

the public address system. It wasn't Charley. For whatever reason, someone else was temporarily taking over.

"Prepare yourselves to see the finest cowgirls in the mountain West. They'll be exploding into the arena to ride around those barrels in a cloverleaf pattern. If they knock a barrel down, it's a five-second penalty. They've first got to break that light beam and start the timer. The first barrel will be a right turn. The second, a left. The third, a left turn as well. They'll circle all three barrels and ride as fast as they can across the finish line to break that beam again. As these gals hit the stretch, they'll use that little whip or lash the horses' neck with the reins. Our first rider is Natalie Walker from Sante Fe, New Mexico."

Seconds later, Natalie burst on the scene, the whip clenched tightly in her teeth, leaning hard on her horse as the Appaloosa grazed each barrel without upsetting it.

"The trick is not to be too wide off the barrel and lose time, or be too close and knock it over," said the announcer.

Natalie was intense. Her circuitous route was precisely executed. The horse's hip slightly tipped the third barrel. It teetered for a second. Allison nervously put her hands to her mouth, thinking it might tip over. It didn't, and Natalie flew down the home stretch.

As she broke the beam, the crowd cheered. "Seventeen, fifty-nine," the faceless announcer said. "Good enough to be in the running for the championship. Give her a hand."

As the audience clapped, Allison wondered what had happened to Charley, the play-by-play man on the roan. Allison looked around the arena for Charley's horse. Five more barrel racers, and Charley still hadn't returned. Neither had Billy. The rodeo was Billy's idea. Why hadn't he stuck around to see his mission through?

The barrel racers finished and were followed by the steer wrestlers. Still no McBride. Allison wiped the last traces of mustard and ketchup from her hands, took a drink of her Pepsi, and got ready for the bull riding.

"Two thousand pounds of the most dangerous animal in the rodeo,"

144

the announcement rang out of the loudspeakers. "Think about it. The biggest animals and quite often, the smallest cowboys compete. Don't worry about the bulls. If you think that a rodeo abuses animals, think about how these beasts will bruise their riders. Last summer at Frontier Days in Cheyenne, one of our finest cowboys, Jimmy Martindale, was killed when a bull stomped on his back. His wife and kids were in the stands at the time and saw it happen. Moments after he was struck, he went into convulsions. This is serious business."

Where is Charley? Allison couldn't get the thought out of her mind. He seemed a little rough on the edges, a wild West curmudgeon. But she liked him. He seemed honest. The man talking to the audience now couldn't even be seen.

"It's the premier event," the announcer went on. "One ton of animal explosion, with nothing to hang on to but a loose rope wrapped around the bull's middle, with a handhold attached. Before the cowboy leaves the chute, he pulls that rope tightly and runs his glove, which is full of resin, up and down to make it hot. No knots are allowed. Be patient with the riders as they sit in the chute. They're trying to get that rope as tight as they can before giving the okay to open the gate.

Bang! Clang! A bull was snorting and showing off his stuff. One horn after another rattled the steel sides of the chute.

"I'd know that bull anywhere," the announcer said. "It's Trick-or-Treat, and the rider is Scott Linfield. He's leaning forward instead of backward, like with saddle bronc-riding. There goes the gate. Let Scott know you're on his side."

As quickly as the audience let out whoops and hollers, it was over. The bull went one way and Scott went the other. The bull wheeled around and aimed his sharp horns in Scott's direction. The beast pawed the earth in frustration and finally charged, a mass of head and horns. Just in time, a clown in a large rubber-covered barrel rolled in between Trick-or-Treat and the fallen rider. For now, Scott was safe to ride another day.

As Scott stood, the announcer explained, "That's a no-score for our cowboy, but there will be other days and more bulls to ride. In the meantime, let him know you appreciate the risk he took this evening."

As the crowd applauded, Billy appeared from behind. His face was ashen, almost white, as if blood had drained from it. He sat down stiffly and stared blankly into space.

"You look like you've seen a ghost," Allison said.

Billy paused and then spoke, hardly above a whisper. "That's exactly what I saw. A ghost!"

12

"Where in the world are you taking me?"

Allison was irritated. She didn't have a clue where she was going. Worse yet, Billy was acting oddly. For the last five minutes, he had firmly clasped her hand and had briskly led her and Kingman through dense crowds and a series of stairs and corridors at the back of the arena. The video camera rolled the whole time, the lens pointed toward Allison and Billy, as Gabriel walked backward. Allison was amazed at his dexterity. He seemed to have eyes in the back of his head that guided the heel of each shoe as it was planted.

"I promised that you'd be up close and personal with the animals," Billy explained.

"What? The smell of horse manure in the arena was close enough." Allison said.

Billy remained serious. Whatever ghost he saw affected him in a way that neither Allison nor Kingman had seen before.

"Do you want to talk about this poltergeist?" Allison asked.

"No, this isn't the time. We're going to the stock stalls. I'd like to get some shots of you interacting with animals. A little human interest footage. Don't worry, you won't have to milk any cows or brand any calves."

"Just how close are we talking about?"

"As close as you want. You can touch them, even talk to them, if you want to."

"And I suppose they'll talk back."

"As a matter of fact, yes, if you know how to speak their language."

Allison rolled her eyes. "What is the point of all this, anyway? Why am I here? You may love the rodeo, but it's not going to change my life. Do you think I'm going to become a barrel rider? No way! I hate cowboy boots. All I can say is I hope this is good TV for you, because it's a colossal waste of time for me."

Billy was undaunted. "I felt this was the right thing to do. I had no choice in the matter. Let's just keep moving. You never know what we might find."

Billy led his crew down another series of long hallways and winding stairs. The odor of animal flesh grew stronger with each stride. The sounds of cows bellowing and horses whinnying melded with the crowd noise in a cacophony of aural confusion.

Finally they were at the end of the maze. Hundreds of stock stalls were arranged in a checkerboard fashion, with narrow aisles separating them. Nearly every stall quartered an animal with a human attendant. Some of the animals were being fed handfuls of hay while others received buckets full of oats and corn. There were pigs, sheep, ducks, rabbits, chickens, cows, and horses in separate sections. Hoses snaked all over the stalls to spray water on dusty beasts while handlers carefully brushed the coats of prize animals.

Every corner they turned elicited a new reaction from Allison. A turned-up nose at the wallowing of pigs in small pools of straw and water. A bemused fascination with the chewing habits of cattle. A softened expression as she reached out to stroke the luxurious fur of exotic rabbits.

"This isn't your average rodeo," Billy explained. "Like the name implies, this is a 'stock show.' It's the highlight of the year for ranchers in this part of the country. They drive hundreds of miles to have the quality of their livestock judged. If you're a cowboy in the mountain West, this is the Super Bowl and the Final Four wrapped into one. I used to come here every year as a boy. Mom drove all the way from Cody. When I was real little, my dad . . ."

Billy stopped, his face frozen in an expression of pain.

"Over there." Billy pointed toward the horse stalls. "That was always my favorite part of the stock area. Come on, everyone, you are about to get an equestrian education."

Scores of horses of every variety imaginable were in the stalls. The owners busily groomed their horses, checked their shoes, and combed their manes and tails. Some horses were washed down and curried, their sleek hair shining under the harsh overhead fluorescent lights. Cowboys and cowgirls, young and old, scurried about the stalls making sure their horses were well fed and show-ready. The buzz of clippers filled the air as every stray hair was trimmed to exacting lengths. Some cowboys tested the latest halters and saddles that they had just purchased. The scent of freshly soaped leather, from saddles slung over fences, mingled with the pungent odor of manure and hay.

"This looks like a horse spa," Allison said jokingly. "These animals get more attention than I've ever had."

"Most folks don't understand the bond between a man and his horse," Bill responded. "A famous cowboy once said, 'The best thing for the inside of a man is the outside of a horse.' That's the way I used to feel when I would cowboy-up."

"Cowboy-up?"

"It's just an expression. Part of the lingo of the world of horsemanship. There's a lot more to being a cowboy then hopping on a horse. These horses are pampered because they're part of an elite corps. Any one of them is worth thousands of dollars, some tens of thousands of dollars. They're royalty, and get treated like it."

Gabriel and Kingman approached the stalls calmly, occasionally reaching out to stroke one of the horses. Allison was uncomfortable. She kept her distance. She nervously glanced out of the corners of her eyes to be sure she maintained the maximum distance from each steed. "There are so many varieties and colors," she observed.

"Bays, buckskins, palominos, pintos, paints—you name it and there's probably a stall with one somewhere," Billy responded.

"I always thought that a horse was a horse was a horse," Allison commented. "But these come in all different sizes."

"There are three basic sizes," Billy explained. "Ponies, light horses, and draft horses. Ponies are the smallest. Light horses, like Arabians or quarter horses, are what you probably think of when you associate a horse with the rodeo. The big boys are the draft horses. They're not for riding but for hauling heavy loads. They go back to medieval times when heavy draft breeds were used as knights' chargers. They were bred for their large size because they needed the strength to carry the weight of the knight and his armor. If we look around we can probably find some. They're very majestic creatures."

Billy turned and headed down a back lane between stalls of show horses in the process of being fitted with fancy bridles and elaborate harnesses, embedded with sparkling silver.

"Over there." Billy pointed toward a huge sorrel draft horse that towered over its makeshift stall. "That's a Shire. They're somewhat rare in the United States, more common in England. Probably weighs more than a ton. I'll bet his shoulders are at least six feet tall."

Kingman approached the animal's stall. "Look at the size of that chest!"

"He may be the largest horse in this entire area," Billy said, "but his size is deceptive. Most Shires are very gentle. They'd never buck you off. Then again, no one would ever ride one. You're more likely to see one pulling a wagon in a parade than being saddled up. Anyway, how would you put a saddle on an animal that large? It wouldn't fit."

Gabriel shouldered his camera and moved in a slow concentric pattern around the Shire, shooting it from every angle. Kingman leaned down and picked up a handful of hay from a nearby pile of hay bales, and stretched his hand inside the stall. The Shire seemed uninterested at first, but then moved hesitantly toward the preacher. The horse's huge lips reached out for the hay and plucked it from Kingman's hand with amazing gentleness. Billy patted the neck of the horse and turned to speak to Allison. At first he couldn't see her anywhere and wondered if she had somehow wandered off. Then he spotted her. She had glued herself to the vacant stall across from the Shire.

"Don't be afraid, Allison. This is a gentle giant. He's less harmful than the stallions half his size that you saw bucking off cowboys in the arena. C'mon over and get to know him."

Allison didn't budge. She cowered slightly, wrapping her arms tightly around herself in a self-protective gesture. Billy stroked the big Shire's neck and forehead. The horse bobbed its head up and down several times to acknowledge the attention and gently nuzzled Billy's chest.

"Hey, mister. What do you think you're doing? Get your hands off that horse!"

The voice came from down the hallway between the stalls. A burly man with a shaggy gray beard ran toward Billy and the Shire, waving his arms wildly. "Did you hear me? He's not a pet. Leave him alone!"

The man huffed and puffed for air as he pulled his overweight frame faster and faster. His pot belly, covered by an undersized white shirt, hung over his genuine silver, western belt buckle. His girth gave him an uncertain balance as he tottered on the side of his high-heeled, pointed-toed cowboy boots. Billy ignored the man's protestations and kept on stroking the horse.

"For the last time I'm telling you . . ." The red-faced man grabbed Billy's left arm and spun him around.

"Oh, my. I had no idea. It's . . . you, Billy! Billy McBride. Shucks, I'd never yell at you like that. Why, you're my hero. I watched you tame the toughest broncs in seven states. And . . . and . . ." The man was so embarrassed and flustered he couldn't form sentences properly. "I never miss your show."

The man nervously shoved his right hand between his belt and body and tucked in the tails of his shirt, which had jerked out in his haste. He pulled at his beard and took off his cowboy hat to scratch the top of his head. Huge beads of perspiration rolled off the top of his bald pate. He wiped it with the back of his hand and ran his fingers over his head.

"And that little lady over there," he added, pointing to Allison. "Isn't she the one I saw on your show just the other day?"

Allison said nothing.

"Gee, I'm really sorry, Billy, I mean, Mr. McBride. This here's Big Boy. Name's rather obvious. He's the biggest of the Shires. Imported him from the United Kingdom. Tops out over two tons. You should see the frogs on his hooves. Bigger than the entire hooves of most horses. Billy McBride. Can't believe it. My hero. Clyde's the name. Clyde Carsdale."

He took Billy's hand and shook it vigorously.

Gabriel seized the moment and rolled video. The comedic frustration of Big Boy's owner was a photo op he knew would provide great human interest on Billy's show.

"He's gentle, you know. Most docile draft horse I've ever seen. I've raised 'em for years. Have a ranch near Telluride. Big Boy is part of a team that pulls a beer wagon for a local brewery. He's the team lead. Never have to crack the whip on him." He turned again to Allison. "Want to ride him? Not exactly the kind of horse that people think about riding, but it's a kick to sit way up there and look down on the world. Go ahead, little lady."

Billy smiled at Clyde's machine-gun-like, staccato speech patterns.

"It would make a great shot for the show," Billy said to Allison. "Try it. Even I've never been on the back of a horse that size. Imagine, seeing yourself on TV tomorrow, Lady Godiva-like, atop the biggest horse in the mountain West." Carsdale opened the gate to Big Boy's stall.

"Sure, I'll do it!" Allison's demure demeanor suddenly changed. She virtually swaggered toward the horse, "Show me how to get up there. Roll that video, Gabriel."

Billy wasn't sure how to account for her abrupt change of mind, but he cupped the fingers of both his hands together as a hand stirrup and bent over slightly to support Allison's left foot.

"When I count to three, bend your knee and reach up. Grab Big Boy's withers . . . sorry, you wouldn't know what that is . . . just grab a fistful of mane, and yank yourself. I'll pull up with my hands and push you right up on his back."

Allison did what Billy said and, in a split second, was astride Big Boy. The horse acted as if nothing had happened. Billy held the horse's rope halter tightly in his hands. Allison grinned. She shifted from side to side to adjust her position and settle into a comfortable spot on Big Boy's enormous back. The horse swished his three-foot-long tail and tilted his head slightly. Then, he began to stomp his left hoof and rhythmically paw at the straw bed of his stall.

"Whoa, Big Boy," Clyde said reassuringly. "It's okay. She's not going to hurt you."

The horse stomped harder and shifted the weight on his back legs from one side to another, in a slight rocking motion. Then he alternated the stomping with his right foot. First the left, then the right. Faster and faster he pawed at the ground with a pulsating intensity, like the measured beating of a drum. His nostrils flared and his ears pinned back. Billy sensed trouble, but was helpless to do anything. Two thousand pounds of horse can't be reined in like an Arabian. He held the rope halter more tightly. Clyde patted the back flank of the horse and spoke in a calm banter of reassurance.

Suddenly, Big Boy reared in the air. Both front hooves thrust skyward and pawed at the air. Allison flung her body forward and clung to the horse's flowing mane. Her arms were too short to encircle Big Boy's massive neck, but her grip was tight enough to keep her from flying through the air. Big Boy came down on his front hooves simultaneously with a thud that shook the concrete floor. Allison lost her hold and tumbled off the horse's left side and onto the floor of the stall. She lay there motionless, as Billy and Clyde maneuvered their bodies between the horse and Allison's fallen body.

Clyde took the halter rope from Billy and hung on with both hands. Big Boy raised his head and tossed his owner back and forth like a child on a swing. For a moment it looked like Big Boy might break free from his stall and run amok. The commotion drew a crowd that came from every direction to see what was happening. Gradually, Big Boy calmed down, and they led him away from Allison. Billy quickly dropped to one knee next to Allison. "You might be injured. Don't move," he yelled.

Allison grimaced in pain. "That's no problem. I can't," she groaned. She lay on the ground, on her side, and didn't make a move.

Clyde handed the halter rope to another horseman and got down on both knees next to Allison. "He's never done that. I'm sorry, so sorry. Gosh, it was my idea. I should never have said anything. Are you all right? I'll get a doctor. Do you need a doctor?"

Billy put a hand on Clyde's shoulder. "Relax. Don't do anything yet. Let her catch her breath, and we'll see how badly she's hurt."

Kingman knelt by Allison and bowed his head in prayer. His lips moved inaudibly.

"Where does it hurt?"

Allison looked at Billy with pleading eyes. "All over, but especially my lower back. I can't move either of my legs. Oh, God, help me. My little girl needs me. Don't let me die!" Her plea turned to deep sobs.

"Let me help if I can." A lanky man dressed in a tailored western suit approached the stall. "I'm a vet, but I know enough to see how seriously she's injured."

Billy waved him through the crowd. The veterinarian gently touched Allison's back and nudged her.

"Does this hurt?" he said, each time he probed a new spot.

Moments later he stood, motioned for Billy, and whispered into his ear: "It doesn't look good. She appears to have some kind of lower back injury. It could be a fractured vertebra. I'm not sure. Understand, my specialty is horses, not humans. But I know enough anatomy to say that we shouldn't move her just yet."

"Here's something if she's cold," someone in the crowd called out. A brightly patterned horse blanket was passed, hand by hand, over the heads of the crowd. Gabriel laid down his camera, which he had kept rolling to capture the drama. He took the blanket, fluffed it, and lightly laid it over her. Then, he knelt by Kingman and gave Allison's shoulder a reassuring touch and lightly stroked her back.

Billy didn't know what to say, or do, though everyone looked to him for the next move. The crowd recognized him, but no one said anything. All eyes were on Allison.

"Everyone remain calm," Billy said to the murmuring crowd. He turned to the veterinarian. "Have an announcement made over the P.A. system to see if there's a doctor in the house." The veterinarian nodded and pushed his way through the crowd toward the exit.

Billy wasn't sure why he did what he did next. He wanted to believe he was being sincere. After so many years of media manipulation, he wasn't sure. He only knew that the words leapt out of his mouth without thought. "Quiet, everyone, we have a minister here. While we're waiting for medical help, we need him to pray."

Kingman looked up in surprise. He hesitated for a moment, then stood as the men in the crowd removed their hats and bowed their heads. Even Big Boy stood silent, his head stretched to the ground to eat some oats that Clyde had tossed there to quiet him.

"Father in heaven," Kingman intoned in his rich, baritone voice, "one of your children has been hurt, and we need your help. Look down on her with mercy and heal her broken body."

With his eyes closed and his head bowed, Billy felt a firm hand squeeze his shoulder. He opened one eye and turned his head. It was

Charley Chestnut. "I heard what happened and thought you might need some help. I'm sorry it took me so long to be there when you needed me," he whispered in Billy's ear.

Billy raised his forearm to his face and buried his eyes in his shirt sleeve. Tears poured from his eyes.

"Satan meant this for evil, but we believe that right now, dear Lord, You are going to bring good out of this. We ask for a miracle," Kingman concluded.

A chorus of soft amens drifted through the crowd.

Gabriel once again gently touched Allison's back and rose to his feet. "She'll be all right. It's not as serious as it looks."

As he spoke, Allison opened her eyes. She lifted her head and looked straight at Billy, whose entire torso heaved with deep sobs. Charley put his arm around Billy as the two men embraced.

This was no theatrical moment. Even Allison knew it. Until now, she had thought of Billy only as a crass manipulator. In her opinion, she was merely a means to an end, and whatever role she played in his purposes was purely selfish. To see him weep moved something inside her, emotionally and physically. She wiggled her legs and took a couple of deep breaths. Then, she abruptly sat up and stretched out a hand for someone to assist her. The stunned crowd let out a collective sigh of amazement.

Kingman took her hand in his and pulled her up. She stood and brushed the straw off her jeans. With her right hand she reached to rub her back. "It doesn't hurt anymore," she said. "I must have just had the breath knocked out of me. I'm fine now."

Billy wiped the tears from his eyes, as his expression turned from shock to puzzlement. He looked at Gabriel out the corner of his eyes. He shrugged his shoulders and reached down to pick up his camera.

"Well, Preach," Allison said to Kingman. "That was a close call. There must be something to that prayer stuff. Only next time, pray before I get on a horse, not after!" She looked in the direction of Big Boy. "What do you think possessed him to do that?"

Kingman gave Gabriel a knowing glance.

Billy reached out to take Allison's hand. "I can't tell you how glad I am to see you're all right. That Kingman sure must have Someone listening when he prays."

Allison nodded her head in agreement.

Billy turned to Charley. "I want you to meet Allison Owens. She has been on my show the last two days, and I invited her to the rodeo, never knowing I'd also meet you here."

The cowboy touched the brim of his hat with a gentlemanly gesture. "Pleased to meet you, ma'am." He reached to shake Allison's hand. His skin was weathered, but it had a firm, pleasant feel.

Allison smiled. "I've enjoyed your narration of the events. I'm happy to make your acquaintance, Mr. Chestnut."

"Oh, that's just my stage name. You can call me Brogue. Brogue McBride."

13

Allison smiled and shook Brogue's hand. He had such a natural and warm way about him, the kind of person who drew children and animals to him everywhere he went. She wasn't sure she heard correctly. She thought she heard him say he had the same last name as Billy.

Kingman looked equally nonplussed. Gabriel acted as though he hadn't heard a thing. He was busy brushing straw and dirt off the camera he had laid on the floor.

Allison tilted her head to one side. "Did you say McBride?"

"Yes."

Allison stepped back a little and glanced first at Brogue and then at Billy, sizing them both up. "Are you . . . you can't be . . ."

"His brother?" Brogue answered.

"Yeah, I guess so."

"No, I'm not his brother."

"Uncle?"

Brogue and Billy smiled at each other.

Kingman reached to shake Brogue's hand. "You're just what I imagined Billy's dad would look like. Pleased to meet you."

Gabriel had the camera back on his shoulder, and videotape was rolling. No one had to direct him to capture the moment. His expertise was capturing television gold—pure, raw emotion.

Allison still didn't quite know how to respond. Then she nodded her head knowingly. "I get it now. You weren't going to the chutes to talk to old friends. You went to talk to your father."

"Close, but not quite right," Billy interrupted. "When I walked back to the chutes, I really was looking up old friends. I had no idea that this man was my . . ." His voice choked. He bit his lower lip and brought his left fist to his face to hide his eyes. Tears streamed down his cheeks, and his body lurched in deep, silent sobs.

There was silence for a few seconds. "Why didn't you tell us what happened?" Allison asked. "At the very least, you should have rushed back to be with your father after you returned to us, instead of leading us on this wild animal chase."

"I guess I didn't know how to handle it," Billy explained. "I've spent my whole life running away from the pain of missing my father, and when I finally found him, I started running again. Maybe it was one more way of living in denial. When I'm emotionally jolted by some-thing, I resort to a flurry of activity as my way of dealing with it."

"Let me tell you what happened," Brogue said. "I was checking my contestant sheets to see who was up after the break when I saw Billy coming toward the chute where stock is loaded back on the trucks. I knew he was my son, but he had no idea who I was." He put an arm around Billy's shoulders. "All these years I watched him from afar, afraid to ever contact him. I was too ashamed."

Brogue's eyes grew moist. He threw both arms around Billy, and the two men embraced again. Brogue went on. "It was my idea to have him return to you without saying anything. The whole thing was too emo-tionally overwhelming for both of us. We exchanged phone numbers and agreed to talk later. Your accident with that horse over there prompted me to come here."

Kingman took Allison's hand. The crowd, sensing they were intrud-ers on a private moment, gradually drifted away. Carsdale and his part-ner stepped back quietly and nudged Big Boy to the farthest corner of the stall. Gabriel pulled back his camera presence to be less intrusive and let his zoom lens take over the close-ups of the moment.

"God has strange ways of moving our lives in the direction He has planned," Kingman offered. "This is an even greater miracle than your quick recovery," he said to Allison. "Think about it. If it hadn't been for your appearance on Billy's show, there would have been no trip to this rodeo, and no meeting like we're witnessing. Plus, God arranged for Brogue to be at the very rodeo Billy would attend. Allison, whether you realize it or not, you were an instrument of God's grace in Billy's life."

Allison was uncomfortable with the thought. It was enough to experience the intense emotion of the moment, but to put these events into the context of something supernatural was stretching it.

"Coincidence, that's all," she shot back, minimizing her reaction to the moment.

Kingman smiled. "Providence," he responded.

"Let's not argue about this," Billy interjected. "I'm not sure what to think. All I know is that I had no idea where my dad was and what he did. Something, or Someone, brought me here today. This is no accident."

Brogue flashed his easy grin. "Billy, I was afraid to come to you after the mess I made of things. I had no idea what your mother told you. I was fearful you'd reject me, hate me, want nothing to do with me. I felt like I didn't deserve to be your dad, so I just prayed that someday before I died there would be a way to tell you all the things I never had a chance to say."

"So what happened when you saw each other back in the arena?"

"Well, Allison, I just saw Brogue—I mean, Dad—staring at me while I talked to some old buddies. Then he walked over and made some small talk. But from the moment our eyes met, I felt this strange tug toward him. It was like some kind of vortex was pulling me deeper into who he was or what he represented. Finally, I said, 'Do I know you from somewhere? Have we met before?'"

"That broke the ice," said Brogue. "We both knew there was a connection, and it was up to me to spill the beans. I had to take the risk of being rejected one last time, or being reunited with the son I left behind nearly forty years ago."

"So, just like that, you said, 'Hi, I'm your father'?"

"No, ma'am. I hem-hawed around for a while, making small talk. Finally, I worked up the courage. I asked some personal questions, like I was interested in knowing more about Billy's background. I thought that if I came right out and told him who I was, he wouldn't believe me. It was when I asked about his mother, Madalyn, that I broke down. He must have thought I was a blithering idiot to be standing around a bunch of tough cowhands and crying. After that, I had nothing to lose."

Big Boy walked around in his stall with his halter still on. He swished his tail but seemed calm.

Billy patted his dad's shoulder. "I knew that a man like you wouldn't be that emotional unless there was a very good reason for it. At first, I thought I might have reminded you of someone, perhaps a son who died." Billy turned to Allison. "I didn't want to believe it at first, and I'm still in shock. It was when he mentioned my mother that I knew there was something to this. If only you could have seen my father's eyes. There was no question, this man was for real."

"It was as if you had died, and suddenly had been brought back from the dead," Brogue said to Billy. "At that moment there was so much I wanted to tell you, stuff that's been pent up for decades. Things about me and your mother, and you and me, and what I remembered from those few brief moments when your mother and I tried to make it after I returned from the war."

Kingman stepped closer and put his arms around both their shoulders. "I don't think either of you can comprehend what this means spiritually."

Billy realized he hadn't introduced Kingman. "I'm sorry, I was so caught up in my emotions, I forgot to tell you who these other people are. That's Aaron Gabriel over there with the camera. He's along to shoot footage for the show. And this is Joseph Kingman. He's a seminary professor, a minister."

"Pleased to meet you, Reverend," Brogue said. "Glad to hear that Billy is keeping some good company." He shot a half-joking disapproving look in Billy's direction. "From what I read in the newspapers I get at the 7-Eleven, he's sure in need of good advice from a preacher now and then."

Billy's face turned red.

"Just what do you mean about spirituality?" Brogue asked.

"Don't get him started," Allison said, rolling her eyes. "You're hitting a hot button that will put him on fast-forward, and we'll spend the rest of the evening in this smelly place."

"Let him answer," Billy said, with a hint of irritation in his voice.

"Well, I don't want to lay anything too heavy on you now, but the person that Billy became was a direct result of your not being there for him. I don't know the whole story, so I'm not judging what happened, but the bottom line is this: you weren't there to show Billy how to be a man, how to handle life from a father's perspective. So, he was left to find his own way, without your spiritual covering."

"Covering?" Brogue looked puzzled.

"That's a term that speaks of the role a parent plays as the spiritual protector of a child. The Bible tells children to obey their parents for a good reason. God has placed parents in authority over their children, to speak for them until they are of an age of consent when they can speak for themselves. So if a child has no parent to declare what is good and right on his behalf, someone else lays claim for the right to speak for that child."

"Like another relative?" Billy asked.

"No," Kingman answered with a serious look on his face. "The devil."

"Here we go again," Allison said. "Look out, cowboy, or the preach here will wave a crucifix and start an exorcism."

"Not exactly," Kingman corrected. "I'm just saying that Billy never had a male identity to tell him who he was, and he never had the protective hand of a father to spiritually shield him from the enemy."

"Back to the devil stuff."

"Yes, Allison, the enemy is the devil."

"I know I haven't lived the best lifestyle," Billy admitted, "but are you telling my father that because he wasn't around, that Satan took over my life?"

"Not entirely. You made a lot of decisions on your own, good and bad. But, yes, I am saying that a lot of what you did, and who you became, was controlled by Satan."

Allison was getting more irritated by the second. "Hold it. Billy's not some voodoo doll with unseen forces sticking pins in him. I'm not crazy about the guy, no matter how good he was at riding bulls, but even I'm not ready to say he's got a curse of some kind on him."

"Very perceptive," Kingman replied. "Because that's exactly what I'm saying."

"A curse? I was just using that as an expression. I didn't mean it literally."

"But it is literal."

"Wait a minute. You're saying that from the day my dad drove off I was cursed?" Billy demanded. "If I was, it's a strange curse. Have you forgotten you flew here on a private jet, and that I'll make more money in one month than you'll make in a lifetime? No offense intended, but those are the facts."

Kingman was unfazed by Billy's logic. " 'What good will it be for a man if he gains the whole world, yet forfeits his own soul?' " he said, quoting Scripture.

"Did I put a curse on my kid?" Brogue asked, looking at Billy with a touch of anguish in his face.

"You didn't intend to, but, yes, you did. The curse of abandonment and rejection. Abandonment because you weren't there, and rejection because of the way Billy felt about your leaving."

"And because I wasn't his . . . what did you call it?"

"Covering."

"Okay. Because I wasn't his covering, bad things happened to him. Is that what you're saying? So what about his mother? She was a good woman. I'm sure she did her best."

"That was certainly a mitigating factor, but nothing takes the place of a father in a family."

"I suppose I'm cursed too, especially since I don't know who my old man was. Oh, don't forget, I was also illegitimate," Allison said angrily. "Remember, my mom didn't even marry the guy!"

Kingman spoke softly. "As long as we're being blunt about these matters, you're right. In fact, the Bible says that the curse of illegitimacy lasts up to ten generations. Chances are, your mother was born illegitimately."

"She was, and so what?" Allison interjected.

"In all likelihood, her mother was illegitimate, and probably her mother and so on. That's the way these things work."

"As a matter of fact, from what Mom has told me, you're right. But that doesn't mean I'm cursed or that my mother is cursed, for that matter. You're no better than that pathetic psychic. You both get some perverse pleasure from claiming to know what secretly goes on in people's lives and then lording it over them."

"Allison, I'm not out to make your life miserable. I'm just being honest. The good news is, neither of you has to live under any curse. God has the power to instantly break that curse and turn things around in your lives."

"How? With a little love potion number nine? Is this where the Kool-aid comes in?"

Kingman grew serious again. "I'm not talking about some cult thing or any hocus-pocus. You break a curse by declaring it null and void. By refusing to let its effect continue. But you've got to do it through the power of Christ by letting Him take control of your life."

Brogue took off his hat and held it in front of him with both hands. "Preacher, I once turned my life over to God. It was a long time ago, but I've never forgotten. One cold winter's day in December, I was down in

Casper buying cattle and I went to a little country church on Sunday morning. Couldn't have been more than a dozen people there. After the pastor finished, I walked to the front and kneeled. Something came over me that I'll never forget. For a while my whole outlook on life changed, but I'm sorry to say, it didn't last very long." He glanced at Billy. "Rodeo life is rough, and I went back to doing things I knew were wrong. It was hard being without Madalyn and always wondering what I could have done to keep her and Billy. The guilt got the best of me." Brogue looked at his hands. "Most of all, I couldn't forgive myself for what happened during the war." He looked straight at Billy. "Son, I've got to tell you . . ."

Billy smiled warmly. "It's okay, Dad. I know."

"You know? How?"

"Some stuff Mom left behind when she died."

The harsh lines on Brogue's face seemed to grow deeper. "I didn't know your mother was gone." He paused. "I guess no one knew where to find me."

Billy nodded.

"Did she say anything at the end? I mean, were there any last words about me?"

"Nothing. I'm sorry, Dad."

"It's all right. Can't blame her. But you need to know why I did what I did."

"Excuse me, someone asked for a doctor." A middle-aged man in a white shirt, jeans, and sneakers stood a few feet from the entrance to Big Boy's stall. "I'm Dr. Johnson. I'm sorry it took so long for me to get here, but I was all the way out in the parking lot when someone tracked me down. I was told a horse injured someone."

"Everything seems to be all right now," Kingman responded. "A few minutes ago we weren't so sure."

"Where's the injured party?"

"That's me," Allison said calmly. "It was just a bad fall that knocked the wind out of me."

"I think we should at least let him take a look at her, as a precautionary measure," Kingman said.

"Okay, but I'm all right, really," Allison said.

Johnson pointed toward some bales of hay outside the stall. "Please sit down over here. It will only take a few minutes for me to see if anything serious is wrong."

Allison sat down on the hay while the doctor pulled a stethoscope out of a backpack he was carrying. "I'm glad I grabbed this from my car," the doctor said.

Brogue walked over to Carsdale. "Mind if I take a closer look at your horse? He's as fine a specimen of horseflesh as I've ever seen. And he's big, even for a draft horse."

"Yes sir," Carsdale replied. "That's why we call him Big Boy. Be careful. I'm not sure what spooked him when that lady mounted him. Why, I let my grandkids ride him all the time, and we've never had a problem. He's a gentle giant if there ever was one. Must have been something unusual he heard or saw."

Carsdale held the rope halter tightly as Brogue approached the animal with the experience of a lifelong horseman. As he did, Big Boy perked up his huge head and pinned his ears back.

"Whoa, Big Boy. Take it easy. I don't mean you any harm. You're a good horse. I just want to look at you up close for a minute."

Big Boy jerked at the halter. Carsdale vainly tried to keep his animal under control as the horse nervously moved backward, away from Brogue.

"Drop the halter." Brogue instructed.

"But . . ."

"It's okay, trust me. I know what I'm doing."

"You don't understand. I'm responsible for the horse, and I can't have another accident on my hands."

"You won't. Drop it."

Carsdale looked at Billy and then reluctantly let go of the rope.

Big Boy stood still. Then, as Brogue came closer, the horse backed into a corner of the stall and began pawing the ground. Brogue made unusual sounds with his mouth but didn't say a word. Strangely enough, he turned sideways to the horse and moved around it at various angles. Big Boy began circling the stall with a deliberate pace, bobbing his head up and down. Occasionally the horse whinnied as if talking back to his stalker. Then Brogue turned his back and walked away, acting uninterested in the horse. He stopped in the middle of the stall, facing away from the animal.

Billy was stunned. He'd been around horses all his adult life and had never seen anything like this. Big Boy began moving slowly toward Brogue's back, then stopped just inches from his body. Brogue didn't move. The horse snorted a couple of times, as if irritated that he was being ignored, and then forced his nuzzle into the middle of Brogue's back, nearly knocking him over. Brogue turned around and put out the palm of his hand. Big Boy's big tongue licked his palm and nudged his hand as if to say, "Pet me."

Brogue put an arm around the underside of the horse's neck and rubbed his chest. Big Boy gave a soft whinny, like the purr of a cat, shivered for a moment, and then relaxed his whole body. He bent one back leg in a relaxed stance.

"Good boy, good boy. Mind if I look you over?" Brogue slowly encircled the large animal, glancing up and down to survey every inch. His hands moved up and down Big Boy's body as if he were giving a massage. As Brogue approached the horse's hindquarters, he stooped down to stroke the underbelly.

Then Brogue ran his hand over and over the same portion of the horse's belly as if he were feeling for something. He paused, a serious look on his face, and bent down to look.

Carsdale grew tense. This was the same horse that earlier had uncharacteristically gone berserk. What if Big Boy decided to act up now? He'd surely trample his examiner and seriously injure him. To the owner's amazement, Big Boy stayed relaxed.

"Look here, Billy," Brogue said, bending down and looking at the horse's belly. "Ever check under here?" Brogue asked Carsdale.

"Not really. I have a groom, and I suppose he has looked everywhere there is to look on Big Boy. But me, no. Can't recall that the groom has ever said anything unusual about his belly. Why? What's down there?"

Billy bent over near his father to look under the horse. "Dad's right. Looks like some kind of brand," he explained.

"A brand? The breeders I got him from in the U.K. never said anything about a brand. Never heard of such a thing. I've had this horse since he was a colt, and I certainly never branded him, especially in a place like that. Whoever heard of branding a horse on the belly?"

"Well, someone has branded this horse. I agree, it's a strange place." Billy motioned to Kingman. "Do you have a piece of paper? I'd like to jot down what this thing looks like. I'm just curious. I've never seen a brand that looks anything like this."

Kingman reached in his coat pocket and took out a small notebook and a pen. He knelt by Brogue and Billy.

"Thanks," said Billy, taking the pen and paper. Meticulously, he sketched what his father had discovered. "Here, you look at it." He handed the paper to Kingman as he and his father stood up. "What does it look like to you?"

Kingman said nothing. His right index finger traced the lines on the paper. With each stroke of his hand, his expression grew more reflective. There was a long silence.

"She's all right," Dr. Johnson said, getting up from the hay bale and offering Allison his hand to stand. "I am concerned about that lower back, though. Have you ever had a lower back injury?"

"No," Allison responded.

"That's what bothers me. Mind you, I'm talking without the benefit of an X-ray, but I'd swear you had broken some vertebrae, by the way it feels. I had a patient one time who fractured several lower back vertebrae. After surgery, her back felt just like yours does. Are you sure you haven't had any back surgery?"

"No. Why do you keep asking?"

"It's just so unusual for someone's back to feel like yours without there being some very serious injury that was corrected by surgery. Anyway, I'm glad to have been able to look at it for you. Be grateful that you're walking around. You may want to stay away from horses."

Allison nodded.

"Make sure you see your regular doctor for a checkup as soon as possible."

"Thanks," Allison said.

Billy and Brogue also thanked the doctor, who stuffed the stethoscope in his backpack. As the doctor walked away, Billy looked over Kingman's shoulder. Kingman stared intently at the brand Billy had sketched.

"Have you ever seen anything like that?" Billy asked.

Kingman nodded. "Yes, as a matter of fact, I have."

"Well, what is it?"

"Not here, not now," Kingman said with a tone so solemn that Billy knew to drop the subject. "Strange, very strange," Kingman mumbled as he folded the paper and put it in his pocket.

14

"Wow! What a cool place! I've never seen a hotel room like this!"

Allison was the first of Billy's group to step inside his room at the Westin Hotel; Kingman, Brogue, and Gabriel were not far behind her. She walked slowly, reaching out to touch the faux-painted walls that lined both sides of the entry. "You have your own private dining room!" she exclaimed. "This place must be at least twice the size of the apartment I share with Mom and Ashley."

She walked into a large, gracious living room, furnished with a couch and two chairs made from delicately stitched soft leather. Allison patted the fabric on one of the half-dozen exquisitely embroidered silk pillows on the couch. "All this and no TV?" she asked.

Billy pushed a button, and a six-by-eight-foot screen dropped from the ceiling at the far end of the living room. He pointed to the ceiling at the opposite end of the room. "That's a video projector. It's got surround-sound with Dolby."

"It's like your own private screening room," Allison commented, shaking her head in amazement.

"Go ahead, look around the rest of the place if you want to," Billy said. "Just don't go in the bathroom. It's a mess. I left towels all over the floor and dumped some dirty clothes there."

Allison disappeared into the bedroom. "Wow!" She emerged with a handful of chocolates in gold foil. "These were on the bed. Godivas. And there are two TVs in there, one for watching in bed and another just over the sink in the bathroom. Sorry, I couldn't help but peek. "

"Please be seated." Billy motioned Kingman and Brogue toward the couch. "Is your unescorted tour over yet?" he asked Allison.

"I haven't had a chance to see the stable and pool," Allison said.

Billy smiled. "It's not *that* big."

"Does that sign on the door mean what it says? Do presidents really stay here?"

"I don't know. 'The presidential suite' is a designation lots of high-class hotels use for their top-of-the-line rooms."

"Like the honeymoon suite?"

"Yes, Allison, only better. There's no rice on the floor of the presidential suite."

"So who pays for this?"

"The television network. Actually, the advertisers. More specifically, you do. If you buy what's being pitched on my show, your dollars end up providing me with gold-plated faucets and . . ."

"There are gold-plated faucets in the bathrooms?"

"Okay, you can look if you don't believe me."

Allison again went into the bedroom and disappeared for a few seconds. Kingman and Brogue sat down on the couch, while Gabriel positioned himself in an easy chair opposite them. He kept the video camera ready in his lap.

Allison walked back into the living room shaking her head. "It's amazing what sleaze will buy."

"Hey, watch it," Billy said. "Remember, you're the sleaze, if you want to put it that way. People watch me to watch people like you."

Allison shrugged her shoulders.

"Mind if I help myself to a soft drink from the wet bar?" Brogue asked.

"I'll get it." Billy took out five wine glasses from an upside-down wooden rack. "Pepsi and 7-Up are the only drinks they stocked in the fridge. If anyone wants booze, we'll have to call room service," he added.

"Just plain water for me," Kingman responded.

"I'll take a Pepsi," Brogue said.

"What'll you have, Gabriel?"

"Nothing, thanks."

"And you, Allison?"

"7-Up."

Billy bent down to the mini-fridge and took out a half-dozen cans of sodas, popped the tops on three of them, and began pouring.

"Why did you invite us up here?" Allison asked, plopping herself down on one of the living room chairs. She draped one leg over an arm and rested the other leg on an ottoman.

"I thought it might be good to come back to my hotel room and wrap up the evening with a little conversation," Billy said, handing out the drinks. "Especially since the Reverend opened a can of worms with his talk about you and me living under some kind of curse. It didn't seem like the right kind of conversation to have alongside cattle and sheep."

"The real issue isn't whether we talk about it, but whether we do something about it," Kingman said bluntly. His directness caught everyone off guard.

Billy finally reacted. "Just exactly what do you mean by 'doing something' about it?"

"It depends on what the curse is, how long it has been in effect, and whether it has been effective. A curse is removed by renunciation, a verbal declaration that repudiates it. At least that's where we start. Sometimes we have to find out what the curse is, how long ago it was spoken, who declared it, and a lot of other things. But we've got to begin somewhere, so the best place is to have the person who is cursed start renouncing all curses, and then move from the general to the specific."

"But what if you don't know if you've been cursed?"

"Approach the subject as if you have been. There is no harm in having some spiritual insurance. You buy car insurance and health insurance for 'what-if' reasons. That's the way you deal with the possibility of a curse. You pray that if you have one, it will be broken. If you don't have a curse, you've lost nothing by praying that kind of prayer."

"You're not talking about a philosophical discussion of good and evil," Billy said. "You're talking about speaking directly to demons."

Kingman nodded in agreement.

Billy set down his glass and walked around the room, pacing in deep thought. Finally, he leaned over the couch and looked seriously at Kingman. "Let's suppose that I do live under a curse? What next?"

"Tell Satan that his right to curse you is nullified," Kingman explained.

"Wait a minute. First you say that I might be cursed because I was abandoned, and now you want me to talk to the devil and tell him what to do. Allison may have a curse, but not me. She's the one who cuts herself. I haven't done anything really bad. Even the bizarre behavior on my show is calculated to get ratings. It's not real."

"If you have a curse, it wouldn't be obvious. The legal right of the curse may be limited to some part of your mind or emotions."

Billy looked at Kingman skeptically. He moved away from the couch to lean against a stool by the wet bar. "I'm not the one you're supposed to be talking to. I brought you on this trip to help Allison. She's the one you should concentrate on. She's got the body piercings and tattoos. I don't even know if I accept this, but if I do, it's Allison who has problems."

Kingman got up from his seat and went over to Billy. "I'm not telling you that you do have a curse, but it would be clever for Satan to attack you. We expect Allison to have spiritual problems."

Brogue stood and walked toward Billy. "Son, I don't know much about this stuff, but I'd want to know if something evil was attached to me. What's the harm of getting some kind of checkup, like going to a doctor?"

"Hold it! You two are talking to me like I'm some weirdo who's about ready to bounce off walls and scream incoherently. I told you, I don't know if I believe this stuff."

Allison smiled. For the last few days, she was the one everyone wanted to fix. Billy was the famous TV star calling the shots with his expensive airplane and fancy hotel room. Now he was on the hot seat, and she loved it.

"Preacher, you can test me if you'd like," Brogue offered. "See if I've got the devil attached to any part of my life. I'm not afraid. I've always wanted to do the right thing for the Lord, and I'm truly sorry I never followed up on that night in Casper. Maybe it's time now to get real with God. Tell me what to do, and I'll do it. I have something to live for now."

Billy moved between Kingman and Brogue. "Wait a minute, Dad. Don't let Kingman's smooth way with words get you to embarrass yourself. You don't have to protect me. I can handle myself." He looked Kingman straight in the eye. "I'll play your game. You can confront any curse on my life right on the spot. Hey, I've faced down tougher challenges than that in the rodeo arena and in front of a TV camera. I guess after riding bulls and bucking the Hollywood system, I can handle an exorcist."

"That sounds like the Billy McBride I respect," Kingman said.

"Want me to videotape it?" Gabriel asked.

"Sure, why not? My audience would love it. I can see the headlines now: McBride takes a Curse and Survives!"

"Normally, I wouldn't try to administer emotional healing under these circumstances. I don't pray with people in spiritual bondage to prove anything. It has to be in God's timing and His leading. I don't want you to get the idea that my accepting your dare is the result of cockiness on my part. But I'll take you up on it, because I believe God wants me to."

"Shake, Preacher." Billy put out his hand, and Kingman clenched it tightly.

"So, what do I do? Wait for you to bless some holy water and unpack your crucifix?"

"No, none of that. Just sit on the couch. Allison, mind if I borrow that ottoman to sit on?"

"Sure. You can have my chair if you want it. In fact, I'd give you most anything to watch this."

Billy shot her an annoyed glance and made his way to the couch. Gabriel put the video camera on his shoulder and tested the lens for focus. Brogue leaned on the back of Allison's chair, facing Billy. Kingman pulled the ottoman close to the couch and sat down directly in front of Billy.

"Do you remember how you felt as a child when your father left you?"

"That's a strange way to deal with a curse," Billy said. "How should I know? It's been thirty-eight years since I laid eyes on him, and I don't remember what I thought back then."

"Some of your consciousness does."

"Anyway, why are you asking me about my father? I thought you were looking for the devil."

"Are you angry with your father?"

"Angry? I told you, I don't even know him. I suppose a part of me is upset with how he left me. It was difficult growing up with all the other kids having a dad who did things with them. Moms are great, but they don't take you to football games, or play catch with you, or go hunting and fishing. I guess I learned to get by, but that part of my life is missing."

"You were robbed."

"If you want to look at it like that. I didn't think so at the time. That's just the way it was."

"What went through your mind that day at age four as your father drove away?"

Billy squirmed with irritation. "Reverend Kingman, I respect you, or I wouldn't have invited you along on this jaunt. But asking me what I remember from the age of four is ridiculous." He waved his arm toward everyone in the room. "Which one of you can remember much of anything that young?"

There was silence.

"See, what did I tell you?"

Kingman pulled a knee toward his chest and clasped his arms around it. He leaned back slightly. He spoke softly and kindly. "Just tell me what you can remember, and Little Billy will fill in the rest."

Billy looked at Brogue, seeking some kind of assistance, but the elder McBride stared back with equal uncertainty. Billy tilted his head inquisitively. "Little Billy?"

"That hidden part of you that was traumatized when your dad left. Close your eyes, go back the best that you can to what you remember of the last time you saw your father, and we'll go from there."

Billy sighed heavily, relaxed his body, and closed both eyes. For a few moments, Kingman said nothing. With one hand, Gabriel steadied the front of his camera for a tight zoom. His shot was so close that he framed Billy's clenched eyelids in the full frame of his lens. Allison watched carefully, with curiosity and apprehension. What if she were to visit some distant place in her past where buried memories of her own biological father resided? How would she go there, and what hidden hurts might come rushing to the surface? Until now Allison had related to Billy with a mixture of irritation and fascination. Now she felt sorry for him.

"I'm doing the best I can," Billy said softly. "My mother is next to me. She cradles my hand in hers. Her skin is soft. She's wearing a long, brightly colored gingham dress. My other arm is raised, just above my eyebrows, to shield my eyes from the sun. I can't see my father. He's walking away with his back turned, heading toward a car. It's an old Chevy, a late '50s model, the ones with those flared-out fins. An Impala, 1959, that's exactly what it is."

Allison was astonished at the detail in Billy's recollection. She expected some vague, meaningless description. Now she was hooked by the story. She flipped her leg off the arm of the chair and planted both feet on the floor. She leaned forward with elbows on her legs, her chin in the palms of her hands, and watched intently.

"The wind is blowing. It does that a lot in Wyoming. Dust is swirling. It's a warm day, and the heat from the sun is intense."

"Is anyone saying anything?" Kingman asked. He glanced at Brogue, who was motionless, reliving that painful day.

"No. It's quiet, except for the wind, and the barking of some dogs in the distance."

"What are you doing? Are you feeling any emotion?"

"None. I'm just standing there. I keep looking up at my mother to see how she's reacting, but she's expressionless."

A tiny tear formed in the corner of Billy's right eye, and it began to meander down his cheek. "He's just standing there at the door of the car with his back still to us. His hand is on the door handle. He starts to open it. He stops and turns around. I can't see him. I must be crying. My vision is blurred. Maybe it's just the glare of the sun. I can't make out his face, just his lanky form standing there next to the car. Now he squares his shoulders and starts to take a step back toward the porch."

"How does your mother respond?"

"She doesn't do anything at first. She just stands there. Wait a minute. She's raising her arms as if telling him to stop."

Another tear formed from beneath the left eyelid and began its slow journey downward.

Brogue sniffled and cleared his throat. Shakily, he walked to the far side of the room. He stared at the wall with his back to the others.

" 'It's over.'" Billy paused. "That's all she's saying. 'It's over.' Dad shakes his head in agreement and gets in the car. The dust from the dirt road swirls in the wind and blots out my line of sight. I can barely see the car now. It's disappearing on the horizon."

"How do you feel?"

"Empty. Alone. Sad. And . . ."

"And what?"

"Angry."

"Angry at whom?"

"I'm not sure. Both of them, I guess. My mother for not letting my father come back, and my father for leaving me like that."

"How intense is that anger?"

"I'm mad enough I want to kick something, or hit something."

"Do it. Go to that anger. Be the anger. Let it be you."

"No, I don't like what I'm feeling. I don't want to stay there."

Now both of Billy's cheeks were stained with tears, and he choked on his words.

"Trust me, go there. Be that angry Little Billy whose daddy has just walked out of his life, the daddy who will never take him fishing or throw him a ball, or pick him up when he's bruised a shin. Feel what Little Billy feels." Kingman's voice was insistent, even pushy. He was forcing Billy to face the moment in the now, something Billy had spent a lifetime avoiding.

Billy's whole body began to shake. His arms quivered.

Billy's fist came down hard on the arm of the couch. "Why are you leaving me, Daddy? Why? Don't you love me? Am I a bad little boy, is that why you're leaving? What did I do wrong? Tell me!" The words poured out like a torrent from a breached dam. Both of Billy's fists were doubled, and he pounded the couch on either side of him. His voice turned from a whimper to a scream of indignation. "Am I bad, Daddy? Is it my fault?"

"You're doing great. Go on, say what Little Billy wanted to but couldn't." Billy's body was a fury of emotions. Kingman pushed him further. "Go there, be the pain, be the anger. Be Little Billy, right there on that porch with a daddy you'll never know, the one who is driving away, abandoning you."

Billy's body shook in convulsive spasms. "I hate you! I hate you! I hate you!" he screamed in a voice was at least an octave above his normal baritone. Both arms flailed in frenzy. "You don't love me and Mommy. I want to hurt you like you hurt me. You're a mean daddy. I hate you!"

Allison was stunned. Billy spoke with the voice of a child. This wasn't some hazy memory. Billy was that little boy on that Cody, Wyoming, porch.

"Stop it! Stop it! That's enough!"

It was Brogue. He turned around and came toward the couch with an angry look in his eyes. "Do you have to drag up all this stuff from the past? It's over. It's done. Can't we all just move on with life? What's the point in all this?"

Allison curled back in her chair and wrapped both arms tightly around her shoulders.

Gabriel flipped his camera in the direction of the elder McBride to catch the action. Brogue stopped just short of Kingman and hovered over him. "Blame me if you want, but not Billy. I'm the one who messed up his life. I've hurt him enough. Stop this replay of the past. It won't change anything."

"Please don't interfere, I'm talking to Little Billy." Kingman never moved his eyes, which were focused on Billy. "If you want the curse broken, we've got to get to the pain. Billy's life was scarred indelibly the day he stood on that porch, and we've got to go back there so God can meet him at that time in his life!"

Brogue quivered with emotions that he, too, had hidden for years. He was fighting his own inner battle of the soul.

"Little Billy," Kingman said, his voice abruptly changing from demanding to quietly solicitous. "I know you're a very angry little boy, and you have a right to be. But you can't be angry with your daddy forever. He was a bad daddy, and he left you. But someone else will be your daddy and take his place."

"Who?" Billy's voice was gentle and childlike.

"God. The Bible says he's the father of the fatherless."

"I don't like God. He took my daddy away."

"It isn't God's fault that your daddy left."

"Then it's my fault. I'm a bad boy. That's why Daddy left. I deserve to be punished."

"No little boy deserves to be hurt. You don't have to go on the rest of your life believing nobody truly loves you. There is a way to heal that hurt in your heart."

"How?"

"Do you know Jesus?"

"Not really. I learned about him in Sunday school, but I didn't believe like the other kids."

"Jesus is your true friend. He died for you, and He loves you. If you let Him be your friend, all the loneliness you feel inside will go away."

Allison noted how Billy had taken on the mannerisms of a small child. He hunched over and flopped his arms occasionally, just like a four-year-old.

Kingman glanced around the room. "We're going to sing a song for you. Keep your eyes closed. When we sing, someone else is going to come walking toward that porch. You watch for him carefully, okay?"

"Okay, Little Billy will watch."

"Jesus loves me, this I know, for the Bible tells me so." Kingman sang barely above a whisper. At first he was solo. Then Gabriel rested the video camera on his shoulder, took his eye away from the eyepiece, and joined in.

Brogue's deep baritone blended. "Little ones to him belong; they are weak, but He is strong."

Allison nervously added her voice to the choir. "Yes, Jesus loves me. Yes, Jesus loves me."

A smile crossed Billy's lips, and his entire body became less tense. "I see someone. Is that the person you said would come to the porch? He's dressed all in white. I like his smile. He's a nice man."

"Ask him his name."

Little Billy nodded. His smile grew wider.

"He said his name is Yeah . . . Yeah something. It's so hard to say. I never heard the word before."

"Yeshua," Gabriel said quietly to Brogue and Allison.

Billy paused. Then he spoke conversationally. "Oh, I understand. All right, if you say so."

"Are you talking to that nice man?"

Little Billy nodded.

"What did he say?" Kingman asked.

"He said he would be my daddy until my real daddy came back again some day. Then, He would still be my friend forever."

Brogue sat down next to Billy on the couch and put his arm around his son. Billy leaned over and cuddled to his father. Allison's eyes were wide. Even though he was a grown man, Billy responded to his father just as Allison imagined she would if her real father were to show up.

"You can make God your father by saying what Yeshua wants you to say. Just repeat after me."

"Okay."

Kingman spoke slowly, phrase by phrase, sometimes word by word. Little Billy bobbed his head in agreement with each utterance. "I, Little Billy, renounce all the sins of my daddy, and his daddy, especially the sin of abandonment." The last multisyllable word made Little Billy stumble slightly, but after four tries he finally mastered it, syllable by syllable, "a-ban-don-ment."

Kingman led him further. "I want Ye-shu-a, Jesus, to be my friend forever," Little Billy repeated.

"This next part will be a little harder to say, but you can do it. Jesus will help you. Say it slowly."

"I can do it. Jesus picked me up in His arms, and He's holding me." Suddenly Little Billy's expression became sober. "What about Ronald Thomas?"

Brogue's body jolted. He jerked away from Billy and jumped to his feet. Frantically, he paced the room. Kingman got up and walked toward Brogue.

Brogue shook his head in disbelief. "I didn't think he'd remember what happened. He was so young at the time, just a little baby."

Kingman put an arm on Brogue's shoulder. "I can't go any farther until you tell me what you're talking about. Speak softly if you don't want Billy to hear."

Brogue looked at him seriously. "Is this all real? What are you doing? How did he know about Ronald Thomas?"

"I'm doing what's called 'inner healing,' getting in touch with that childlike state of innocence that was emotionally injured. Part of Billy's consciousness is locked up in that child who was traumatized the day you left the family."

"What's all that stuff about renouncing curses? I thought God only judged us for what we did, not what someone else did."

"That's true, unless that someone is in spiritual authority over us. Brogue, when you abandoned Billy, the devil took over part of Billy's life, specifically the part of his life that was locked away as an abandoned child."

"But I didn't abandon him. I didn't even want to leave him. I begged Madalyn to let me stay."

"Satan doesn't play by our rules. He takes advantage of the innocent and unprotected. Whatever you did that made Billy's mother send you away caused Billy to be spiritually vulnerable. Not every abandoned child is cursed, but I suspect you did something with serious moral consequences."

"I admit what I did was very wrong, and I've asked God to forgive me."

"But did you break the curse?"

"What curse? I didn't even know there was one."

"As I said, Satan doesn't play fair. Right now, that's not the issue. Do you know who Ronald Thomas is?"

"Yes. No. Well, I'm not sure. Perhaps it's just a coincidence that . . ."

"Don't hold back. Your son's spiritual freedom depends on it."

Brogue looked at Kingman. "I guess Billy knows. How much, I'm not sure. During the war, the Korean Conflict, I had an affair while I was overseas. I had gotten hitched just before they shipped me out, and I didn't even know that Madalyn was pregnant before I left. Anyway, I was just a green kid from Wyoming half a world away from the sheltered life I'd known. I was lonely, scared, confused. Madalyn seemed like a dream. I was up on the 38th parallel. With the way the fighting was going, I didn't think I'd ever make it back alive. They gave us two weeks off from the front lines for some R and R, and I headed down to Seoul. While I was there, I got involved with a woman, a Korean national. Her parents found out and made me marry her in some kind of ceremony. The sons in the family were involved in an Asian crime clan, and I was afraid that if I didn't go through with the marriage, they'd kill me. I didn't take the 'wedding' seriously. I did it to save my neck.

"I went back to the front lines and resumed my duty. A couple of months later I found out my 'bride' was pregnant. She wanted an American name for the baby, so I told her Ronald Thomas. Ronald was a school friend back in Cody. Thomas was a barracks buddy I went to basic with."

"Something still doesn't make sense," Kingman said to Brogue. "Is that all there is to the story of Ronald Thomas?"

Brogue looked embarrassed. "Not quite. I thought I could just walk away from what happened in Seoul. In some ways I did. I paid off the family with a large sum of cash I had from an inheritance, and the baby was eventually adopted by an American couple. But I was tormented by the thought that my baby, the child that I fathered but never saw, was still alive somewhere. I couldn't escape the guilt."

Brogue wept. Kingman put an arm around him. "It's all right. The Bible says, 'All have sinned and fall short of the glory of God.' You've admitted your error. God has forgiven you."

Brogue wiped his tears. "I know He forgave me. I never doubted that. I just couldn't forgive myself. I guess that's why I kept Ronald Thomas alive. It was my way of having both sons live in one body."

"I don't follow you."

"When I got back from Korea, in those few months before Madalyn opened the mail and read the letter from the Defense Department, explaining what I'd done, I loved Billy with all my heart. But I loved Ronald Thomas too."

Brogue looked in Billy's direction. Little Billy had faded away, and the grown consciousness of Billy McBride had returned. Billy took his feet off the couch and settled back comfortably, not exactly sure what had gone on.

"I think I see where you're heading," Kingman said knowingly.

"When Madalyn wasn't around, sometimes I held Billy in my arms and pretended he was Ronald Thomas. I know it sounds odd, but it made me feel better, less guilty. I suppose that was okay. Perhaps I carried it a little too far when I played a game with him and actually called him Ronald Thomas."

15

This is all too weird." Allison jumped out of her seat. She waved her arms in the air as if she were flagging down a train. "I've had enough. You're all crazy. Billy has an inner child known as Little Billy. His dad called him by another name when he was a baby." She looked at Kingman. "I even wonder if you are mentally stable. I was really into this when you started to do your inner healing of Billy. I was glad to see him on the hot seat. But then you veered too far into the twilight zone. Before this is over, I may be the only one left to call the guys in the white coats to come and take everyone away."

"Calm down," Kingman said. "I agree that this has been a little intense. Let's take a break so that everyone can get some perspective on what's happening." He glanced at Gabriel. "Are you doing okay?"

Gabriel smiled. "It's not the first time I've seen something like this, so I'm not taken aback like Allison. I'm the last person to worry about."

"Good. Everybody relax for a few moments."

Billy had returned to himself and was trying to understand what had happened. He finally collected his senses enough to talk. "I'll refresh everyone's drinks," he said.

Allison headed to the bathroom. Gabriel put his camera down and stretched his arms and legs to loosen the stiffness in his joints from being constantly locked in position to steady his camera. Brogue walked to a window overlooking Denver's skyline and watched the sparkling lights of the downtown office buildings. Billy popped the top on another can of soda and drank it.

After they had all taken their turns in the bathroom, Kingman asked the group to be seated again. Billy returned to his position on the couch, and Allison went back to her easy chair.

"Mr. McBride," Kingman said to Brogue, "would you mind sitting next to Billy again? If I'm going to continue ministering to the child inside Billy, I'd like you next to him as a source of comfort."

Brogue consented. He gave Billy a pleasant smile and squeezed his son's arm as he sat down.

"This is all a mystery to me," Billy observed, "but for some reason, I feel better, all the way down to my core. I feel lighter and more peaceful."

King made his way to the ottoman. "Perhaps I should recap things so we're all on the same page."

"Please do!" Allison demanded. "Earth would like to know what's going on with all you extraterrestrials on Planet Strange."

Kingman smiled. "Before I give a synopsis, Mr. McBride needs to share something with his son." He motioned to Brogue. "Tell Billy what you revealed a few minutes ago."

Brogue took a couple of deep breaths to steady himself and told about the incident in Korea and about his other son. Billy listened expressionlessly, digesting it all in a logical, detached manner. When Brogue was finished, Kingman spoke. "Billy, do you have any questions for your father?"

Billy looked aside to gather his thoughts. "Do you have any idea what happened to my half brother?"

Brogue shook his head. "I only know that his adoptive parents were Americans. They flew over to take him back." He dropped his head. "I only saw him once. It was a small black-and-white photograph." Tears filled his eyes. "He was a cute little guy. Not bragging, but he looked a lot like me. I guess he's living somewhere in this country, but it would be next to impossible to trace him. I'd have to go to Seoul to do that, and wartime records aren't that easy to come by. Plus, it's a chapter of my life I want sealed for good. Until tonight, I've pretty much pushed it to the back of my mind. He's probably better off without me anyway."

"Here's what we do know," Kingman said. "Billy, you've got an emotionally injured inner child. It's a separate part of your soul. You're not crazy. Many people have an undeveloped part of their emotions that was frozen in time from some trauma, especially if the unfortunate situation occurred at a developmentally sensitive time in life. In addition, both of you are living under a curse that is rooted in abandonment. We need to break that curse."

"I'm not going to argue with you, Preacher," Billy said. "If you had told this to me an hour ago, I'd probably have asked you to leave. Strangely enough, I know a little of what went on a while ago. It was like a movie in my mind. I saw this little kid on a porch, and I'm aware of what happened after that." He looked intently at Kingman. "Do you understand what I'm trying to explain?"

"Yes, I've had many people I've taken through inner healing tell me the same thing. The human mind is incredible, and it holds many corridors of consciousness that God has created to shield us from those memories that would destroy our ability to function successfully."

"Okay, Preacher," Allison interrupted. "For the sake of argument, let's suppose that this isn't a page torn from a Clive Barker script. Now that you've got Mr. Trash TV babbling like a baby, what are you going to do next?"

"Allison, if it depended on me to work this thing out, I'd fail. This is one of those times when I'm totally dependent on the Lord."

"Well, if He's watching, He'd better send an angel quickly to help out."

"He already has, Allison, he already has."

Allison glanced around the room as if she expected to see wings fluttering in the air. "What's that supposed to mean?"

"You'll see," Kingman replied.

The minister turned to face Billy and Brogue. He reached into his pocket and took out the sketch Billy had made of the underbelly of Big Boy. Then he unfolded the paper and held it in front of the two men. "I believe this is related to the curse. Think hard. Has either of you ever seen this symbol before?"

Billy shook his head. Brogue contemplated the drawing for a moment. "Maybe, I'm not sure. Something clicks, but I'm not certain what."

Kingman put the paper back in his pocket. "No problem, we'll deal with that later. Now, are you both ready?"

"I could answer that better if I knew what I'm supposed to be ready for," Billy said.

"Ready to be set free from Satan. Ready to experience life as you've never known it."

"I'm ready," Brogue responded. "I've been ready since that night in Casper."

"Billy, you need what your father found in that little church. Jesus is holding Little Billy in his arms. He wants to hold you too."

"Is this where they start singing 'Just As I Am?' Even a reprobate like me has seen Billy Graham on TV." He gestured around the room. "There's no sawdust trail for me to walk down, Preacher."

Kingman smiled. "I appreciate your humor, but I'm serious about this. I can't break the curse on your life unless you first ask Jesus to take control. It's Jesus who makes the devil go, not me. It's time to quit acting like Billy McBride, the shock-talk host, and be the real Billy that God always meant you to be."

Billy's eyes softened. He looked at his father and then at Kingman. "I'm sorry. I'll cut the sarcasm. Even I have to admit I'm sitting next to a miracle." He looked first at his father and then at Allison. "You too, sweetheart. You're a miracle."

Allison rolled her eyes.

"No, I mean it. Somebody up there sent you across my path to get me to a rodeo in Denver so I could find my father. There's no way all this could be a coincidence."

Gabriel put his camera down. "Mr. McBride, God arranged for all of us to be in this hotel room for this very moment."

"You too? You're in league with Kingman?" Billy said in surprise. "Wait until Steinberg hears about this. He'll be floored to know that he, as an agnostic Jew, sent you to help save the soul of America's trash TV king."

"Steinberg didn't put me on this job—God did," Gabriel replied.

"Don't get him started," Allison interjected. "While you were heading toward the chutes back at the rodeo, Kingman left me alone with this religious zealot, and he started preaching to me."

"Billy, the choice is yours," Kingman said. "Will you or won't you join Little Billy in the arms of Jesus?"

Billy swallowed hard. "Yes," he answered softly. "I will."

"Do me a favor. Close your eyes, and let's go back to that porch."

Billy bowed his head.

Several minutes of silence passed before Kingman spoke. "Are you there?"

After a brief pause Billy replied. "Yes. In the far corner of the porch, there's a man dressed in white. I guess that's Jesus. He's holding a child in His arms."

"That's Little Billy," Kingman explained.

"Wait, there's more." Billy's eyes were closed tightly and his brow furrowed intently. "I can see my mother from the corner of my eye. She's sitting on a swing at the other end of the porch, swinging back and forth, back and forth." Sobs stopped his words as he struggled to speak. "That Chevy Impala is coming back down the road. It's getting closer and closer. It stops. It's Dad. He's getting out of the car and walking toward the porch."

Billy's body heaved uncontrollably. "Mother is walking toward him with outstretched arms. They're hugging. Kissing. Oh, God, this is the way You wanted it to be. I don't want to make the mistake my father and mother made. Take me in your arms like you did Little Billy."

Billy hunched over and wept. Brogue put his arms around Billy's shoulders and hugged him. Gabriel wiped tears from his eyes. Even Allison was quiet.

"Both of you, repeat after me," Kingman said softly to Brogue and Billy.

The two men responded in unison as Kingman led them in prayer. "We submit ourselves to God and His will. We renounce the devil and his kingdom of darkness. We break every curse of our ancestors and renounce each of their sins that led us into spiritual bondage. The curse of abandonment is lifted. We declare this for ourselves and all future generations. In the name of Jesus, every legal right of Satan is removed."

When the prayer was finished, Brogue and Billy looked up. For the first time, Allison saw Billy as someone she didn't resent.

"I've got it!" Kingman exclaimed.

"Got what?" Billy asked.

"This is incredible. Now it all makes sense. I knew I'd seen that symbol on Big Boy's belly before. Everything is falling into place."

"Well, let the rest of us in on what's so dramatic about a brand on a horse's belly," Allison insisted.

"It was approximately twenty years ago," Kingman answered. "I was on sabbatical doing extension studies in the British Isles. The rector of a small Anglican country church invited me to investigate a haunting that had been reported in a remote section of the British countryside, an area settled by Irish immigrants who had worked the fields for centuries. A spiritualist and a parapsychologist had been called in by a family that reported seeing and hearing strange things on their farm. When the two psychics got nowhere, the owners of the farm, an elderly man and his wife, turned to the church for help.

"In those days, I was young and just out of seminary. I had no experience with the supernatural. None of my professors ever talked about demons. Fortunately, the rector had some experience in that sort of thing, and I followed his lead."

The room was completely silent as Kingman continued.

"When we got to the farm, the couple who lived there was frantic. They lived in constant terror of nightfall because that's when the ghost was most active."

"What did the ghost do to the farmers?" Allison inquired.

"It appeared in the form of a horse that galloped at night through the woods. They said you could hear its hoofbeats far in the distance before it ever came on the scene."

"How do they know it wasn't a real horse?" Billy asked.

"First, it never had a rider. It came from somewhere in the trees and disappeared again into the forest. Second, it only appeared when there was a full moon—every full moon. Besides, Shires aren't common anymore in the English countryside."

"A Shire? Are you suggesting that this ghost horse is somehow connected with Big Boy?" Billy asked.

"I'll explain that," Kingman answered.

"How long had this haunting gone on?" Brogue asked.

"No one knows. Scores, perhaps hundreds of years."

"And no one ever did anything about it?" Billy wanted to know.

"Apparently not. It was part of local lore, the Legend of the Shire."

Allison jumped in. "So why did this couple suddenly think they needed help?"

"They retired with a large sum of money and decided to breed horses. Everything was fine, except on the nights when the Shire romped through the countryside. All the horses in the stable would spook, some violently. This went on until one of their prize studs tried to bolt his stall and broke a leg. The couple decided that was enough and started looking for help."

"So that's how you got your start as an exorcist, with horses?" Allison asked.

"Sort of. The rector suggested we look around the farm for clues to the legal rights of the ghostly Shire. Since the reactions happened in the stable, we started there."

"Legal rights?" Billy said with a puzzled look.

"Just like demons need legal rights to enter a body, they also need legal rights to control certain territory, such as a building or a geographical area like a city, a state, or a country. The rector suspected the legal right might be located in the stable, so we searched it top to bottom."

"Did you find anything?"

"Not at first, Allison. But we prayed, and God led us to the tack room in the back of the stable. Keep in mind, this building was hundreds of years old. England isn't like America. We rip things down when they go out of style, but over there they place a premium on quality of construction that has stood the test of time. Many of the buildings on English farms have been there for centuries. Well, we looked everywhere. We were about to give up when we heard a strange sound. It was faint, and at first we thought one of the horses was acting up in a stall, but we checked and they were all out to pasture."

"What did it sound like?" Allison asked earnestly.

"Tapping, pounding, very rhythmic. It actually sounded like the beat of a horse's hooves. What puzzled us was that it seemed to come from down in the ground, somewhere under the tack room. So we grabbed some shovels and started digging. Most older stables in England have dirt floors. But our shovels couldn't budge the dirt. That's when we realized that the floor of the tack room was actually wooden. It had just been covered over with an accumulation of dirt that had hardened through the years. When we scraped off the dirt, and got down to the floor, we saw a sign carved into it."

"What was it?"

Kingman reached in his pocket and once again took out the piece of paper he had sketched earlier that evening, the brand on Big Boy's belly.

"You mean that what you saw in that English stable was the same upside-down cross with a spike through the crossbars?" Billy asked in shock.

"Yes, exactly the same. But there's more. We got permission from the owners to tear up the floorboards and see what was underneath. After an hour of ripping up half-rotted old planks, we found a cavity a foot or more deep. Once we found the cavity, the sound stopped."

Kingman paused.

"Well, don't leave us in suspense," Allison said, thoroughly intrigued by the tale. "C'mon. What did you see?"

Kingman responded soberly. "Bones and ashes. The large bones obviously belonged to an adult. The smaller bones, and there were lots of them, belonged to children, young babies."

"Was this some kind of old burial ground?" Allison asked.

"Not exactly. According to the Legend of the Shire, it was more of a sacrificial chamber."

Allison shivered. "Are you saying sacrificial as in 'killing'? These babies were human sacrifices?"

"Yes. The legend says that more than four hundred years ago a certain man, an Irishman by ancestry, owed a gambling debt to a powerful English landlord. When he couldn't pay, a curse was put on his family line. The firstborn child of each successive generation had to be sacrificed, literally or symbolically, by possession of the Shire spirit. The Irishman was killed by a horse to ratify the curse, and his firstborn male son was slaughtered to pay the debt. The curse was so powerful that even the witch who invoked the oath was himself murdered, the very night he called upon the powers of the Shire."

"And the Shire was . . .?" Billy wanted to know.

"A demon, an ancient spirit that inhabited animals, especially horses." Kingman paused. "The rector had performed exorcisms on buildings before, so he knew how to drive out the evil spirits from that place. We had a special prayer over the stable, especially the area beneath the floorboards. I checked back with the rector several years later, and the couple never had any more problems. The Shire never returned."

"There are still some missing pieces," Billy said. "What about her?" he asked, pointing to Allison. "The horse threw her off, not me."

"I can't answer that question, but your connection seems very clear. Look no further than your name, McBride. I assume you have Scottish or Irish ancestry."

"Actually, both," Brogue responded. "Scottish on my father's side, and my mother was Irish. They settled first in Nebraska, then moved on to Wyoming."

"Chances are," Kingman explained, "that an ancestor, way back, was in the bloodline of the Shire curse."

"Is that why Dad and I were attracted to the rodeo and horses?"

"Perhaps."

"And what about Gunsmoke?" Billy stretched out his short left arm. "When that horse did this, was he possessed by some kind of demon, or was it just chance that he stomped on my elbow?"

"There are lots of things that happen in the spiritual realm we have no way of knowing about, but when you belong to a bloodline that's cursed, everything is suspect. The man, the father who brought on the curse of the Shire, abandoned his child by the gambling debt he incurred. When a parent does something that inherently shows disregard for the safety or care of a child, it's the same as abandoning the spiritual welfare of that child. My guess is the father was so obsessed with gambling that his family suffered deprivation and hardship. So, the spirit of the Shire manifested itself in future generations as a demon of abandonment, which is what you did, Brogue."

"So what's next? Let's get on with this," Billy said impatiently.

"Now that we know the curse has been broken, we need to find out why that horse bucked Allison off," Kingman declared.

Suddenly, Allison's body jolted as if an electric shock had struck her. Both arms shot out stiffly and her entire torso contorted violently. She flew out of the chair and staggered across the room. Then she fell to the floor so hard that everyone was afraid she might be seriously injured. She lay there for a moment without moving.

Then her eyes opened, and a grotesque sneer crossed her face. "You'll never figure out how I got here, or how to break the curse over this body. The Legend of the Shire lives on!"

16

The return flight to Phoenix was completely different from the departure twenty-four hours earlier. Emotionally and spiritually, this was a very different group. For each of them, life had taken a major turn. The discovery of Billy's father, the uncovering of the curse, the knowledge that Allison had demons—once the plane landed, all these things would thrust each of them into a new relationship with reality. Billy's face had even changed. The hard edges seemed to have softened.

There was little conversation on the plane. Gabriel used his camera viewfinder to preview the footage he had shot and logged it with detailed notes indicating which videotapes contained which scenes. Kingman slept, exhausted from the stress of the previous night's spiritual encounters. Allison stared out the window. Brogue joined the entourage for the flight back to Phoenix.

Billy was the only one who was alert and animated. He constantly shuffled in his seat and made several trips to the snack tray. He had a lot to think about. Finding his father forced new considerations. Would Brogue go on with his life in the rodeo or relocate closer to Billy, perhaps move in with him? Billy also wondered what to do with his new commitment to God. Would he keep silent about his faith or jeopardize his career by drastic changes in behavior that would be professionally threatening? What kind of ongoing counseling or therapeutic intervention would he seek to resolve the raw issues that he confronted while undergoing Kingman's episode of inner healing?

The most imminent uncertainty centered on Allison. Nothing had been done to resolve her demonic outburst the night before. When the evil within her spoke, revealing that she was cursed by the Legend of the Shire, Kingman simply prayed that the power of Satan would be held in check until a plan of action regarding her spiritual dilemma could be implemented. Allison herself had been so confused by the strange turn of events, she had been unable to express any feelings about what she wanted to do.

Billy faced an urgent decision. Steinberg would meet him when the plane landed wanting to know immediately what would happen on the show today. The day before, a show had been pulled from the archives for airing. Billy knew that the network, and the advertisers, wouldn't stand for that happening two days in a row. Too many millions of dollars were at stake. Love him or hate him, Billy was the center of the universe for multinational corporations whose product sales, and stock value, depended on who watched *McBride* and how they responded at the marketplace.

"We'll be landing in about thirty minutes," the copilot informed everyone. "Last call for drinks and snacks."

Gabriel continued logging, while Kingman shifted in his seat, awakening from a refreshing nap.

"Think I'll have one last cookie and Coke," Brogue said, getting out of his seat. "Anything I can get for you, ma'am?" he asked Allison.

Allison shook her head. She didn't take her eyes off the window as the view of the landscape below grew closer.

With the landing minutes away, Billy no longer had the luxury of mentally rambling. He had to have a plan of action ready. Billy began to pray silently. It seemed such a natural thing to do. As he centered his thoughts on God, he realized how remarkable the exercise was. He couldn't remember that he had ever earnestly asked God for direction for any decisions in life. Sure, he had prayed in times of trouble, fox-hole prayers to get him out of a bad situation. But this prayer was different. He really wanted to know God's will for his life today, and the future. He didn't know exactly what to say, but the inner language of his thoughts flowed smoothly.

Lord, I don't know where You are taking my life from here, but I do know I'm not proud of where I have been. Help me make the right decisions. You sent Allison into my life for a purpose, and now I see that part of that purpose was for me to find You. Whatever else You have planned, let me be willing to accept Your will. Show me what You want me to do with the rest of my life, and help Allison to receive healing like I did. God, now I know how good it feels to be free, and I want that for her too. The darkness, the heaviness, and the anger is gone. Thank you. Amen.

Billy felt peaceful. The burden of being "McBride" had been lifted. His reunion with his father had begun the healing of his soul. Until today, he had been unconnected to the past. A part of him had never known where he came from and couldn't find the way to where he was going.

He remembered the last thing that had happened the night before, and the stillness of his soul, when he looked directly at his father and said, "I forgive you."

Billy couldn't claim that all the feelings of bitterness and betrayal were settled, but he did forgive Brogue for abandoning him. That declaration by itself was liberating. When he heard his father say, "I'm sorry," as they said good night, his emotional healing came full circle.

Billy was surprised that he could so easily offer clemency for a scar that his wounded spirit had carried for so long. But how could he hold forever the anger that festered inside his soul when God had forgiven him for all the wrongs he had done?

As the jet descended for its approach to the airport, Billy brushed aside any doubts about what went on when he met Jesus on that porch. If the whole world said he was crazy and imagined it all, Billy knew inside his soul that it was real. Being held in the arms of Jesus wasn't an induced fantasy. It wasn't the power of suggestion that pried open the prison of his emotions. It was a miracle. Billy knew he had to keep that miracle in motion.

"Listen up," he said to get the attention of the other travelers. "I need your cooperation. The vacation is over, and I've got to head straight to the set of my television show when we land. I'm counting on all of you to come with me. The audience is waiting to hear our story of the trip to Denver, and we owe it to them to report on what happened."

Everyone, except Allison, looked in his direction. She continued staring out the window, absorbed in her inner world. Billy went on. "I assume you can come with me to the television studio," he said to Gabriel.

"No problem. Do you need any of the video footage I've logged? I've got everything coded and ready to roll, except for a few minutes that you probably wouldn't use anyway."

"I definitely want certain segments." Billy handed Gabriel a sheet of paper on which he had scribbled some notes. "This will tell you what I'd like to put on the show, where each video goes, and the approximate length of what I need."

Gabriel glanced at the paper and nodded his head as he read through Billy's scribbles. "I don't see any problem here. I'll just need fifteen or twenty minutes at the studio to tell your production people where each section is cued. We won't be able to run with edited footage, so there will be a few camera glitches, but it's reality TV and showing raw footage will give it a gritty feel."

"That's exactly what I want," Billy said. "Action as it happened, including some camera shakes, out-of-focus zooms, and quick pans. You know, *Blair Witch* stuff, the avant-garde camera style."

Gabriel grinned. "It definitely has that feel. It's not the best video I've done, but considering the circumstances, I think the audience will understand. It's the kind of thing they're used to seeing on the news

when footage from some late-breaking story is rushed on the air without the luxury of sophisticated editing."

"I've arranged for two limos to meet us. Dad, you'll come with us to
the studio, all right?"

Brogue agreed. "And where else would I be going?"

Billy looked at Kingman. "I have no doubts you're ready for anything. I'm hoping your schedule is clear for the rest of the day."

"I called my wife before we took off and told her that I'd see her later
today."

"Allison?"

There was no response at first. Then she turned and smiled sweetly.
"I've never been on television before, so this will be a new experience.
I've been mostly sheltered my whole life." She batted her eyes with
innocent charm.

This was the same Southern belle personality Billy had seen in the
limo the day before. Only this time, Billy knew it wasn't an act.

Then, Allison blinked and abruptly changed expressions. Her face
was sober. A different part of her was back in control. She had switched
to being the Allison everyone had known since she first stepped on the
McBride set.

"Until today I haven't taken any of this stuff seriously," she said. "I'm
not ready to say I buy into this whole business of God and demons and
multiple personalities, but I've been doing a lot of thinking on the
flight back. You all know what a mess my life is, and something has definitely happened to my thinking since yesterday. Even I know that the
way I recovered so quickly from that fall off Big Boy was strange." She
shifted back to a defensive tone of voice. "Now, I'm not saying that for
sure it was God or anything like that, but . . ."

"I hear what you're saying," Kingman interjected. "You're not sure
you believe, but you're not so sure of your doubts anymore."

"Yeah, something like that."

"That's good enough. God takes us one step at a time, Allison. You're starting the journey at point zero. After what you've been through in life, no one expects an overnight change in your outlook. I'm just happy to see that you're moving in God's direction."

Allison looked apprehensive. "I don't know about God, but let's say I'm moving in Ashley's direction. I'm still not certain I care that much about myself, but I do care about Ashley, no matter what my mother thinks. If my life never gets fixed, I don't want my little girl to go through what I've had to deal with."

"Does that mean you'll do the show?" Billy asked.

"Look, Mr. McBride. I've been your foil twice this week, and I'm not looking to make a career out of this. One more time, that's it. And I don't want Mom onstage this time. She can watch from your Green Room with Ashley. I've got to have my little girl with me today after being away from her. I can't just say 'hello' and run off to do your TV thing. Got it?"

"Got it. I assume your mother and your daughter will be at the airport?"

"I'm sure they will be."

The jet jolted slightly as the landing gear greeted touchdown. Billy was back in the world he left behind one day ago, but in ways it seemed like a lifetime ago. In moments he would know if God heard and answered his prayer.

Allison was the first off the plane.

"Mommy, Mommy!" Ashley ran toward the plane as fast as her tiny legs would allow. Allison ran toward Ashley and swept her in the air. In that moment, Allison Owens wasn't a troubled woman with drug dependency problems or a victim of an ancient curse. She was a mother, warm and loving, who responded to one of the most primal instincts of humanity—parenting.

"Mommy missed you so much," Allison said.

"Ashley miss you," the child repeated over and over.

Jenny smiled. Certainly her daughter was a source of distress, but she was glad to see her return from this enigmatic journey.

"What was the rodeo like?" Jenny had an anxious look on her face.

Allison shrugged her shoulders at Jenny's question. Ashley clung tightly to her mother's neck. "It was all right. Just about what I expected. But it wasn't the rodeo that turned out to be the interesting part of the trip."

"We've all been on an emotional roller-coaster ride," Kingman said to Jenny. "Please give us a few minutes to sort it all out. The main thing you need to know is that everyone is safe and sound, and in a lot better spiritual condition than before they left. Soon, we'll be recounting the whole story of what happened in Denver, and we want you to be involved. "

"Hey, Billy Boy," Steinberg called out as the entourage crossed the tarmac and neared the Executive Travel International lounge. "Your limo is waiting. If we push it a little, we'll have just enough time to debrief before the start of the show. Anything I need to know?"

Billy pointed to Gabriel, who had just disembarked and was checking his duffel bag to be certain all the video he had taped was readily accessible. "Yeah, the cameraman shot some great video that I want to open the show with."

"But there won't be time to do much editing."

"It's all ready to go. The B-roll I want to use is self-explanatory. Trust me."

"No problem, boss. What are your thoughts about the show today? I thought you'd be doing some kind of report on what happened in Denver."

"I want to pick up the pieces from two days ago. I assume you got my voice mail last night and have a second limo ready."

"It's parked right behind yours," Steinberg answered.

As the group settled in the lounge to await their luggage, Billy and Steinberg moved off to one side to talk. Jenny, Allison, and Ashley carried on their own animated conversation about what had transpired with Ashley while Allison was gone. Kingman and Gabriel exchanged thoughts about the spiritual significance of what had happened the night before.

Soon luggage handlers set the passenger bags, one by one, on the curb where the long, white stretch limos were parked. As the group made their way toward the cars, Billy spoke. "If you don't mind, I'd like to ride alone with Mr. Steinberg. We've got a short amount of time to talk about the show, and we'll be discussing nothing but business the whole way. There's plenty of room for the rest of you in that second limo. All right?"

Everyone nodded their head except Jenny. "Just exactly where are we headed?" She looked directly at Allison. "Aren't you coming with me in our car?"

"Sorry, Mom," Allison said. "I didn't have a chance to tell you. Mr. McBride wants to do one more show about the trip to Denver, and we're all on our way to the television studio."

Jenny frowned and put her hands on her hips.

Billy broke the tension of the awkward moment. "Let me make a suggestion. You come with us, Ms. Owens. Give me the keys to your car, and I'll send a couple of assistants back to the airport to pick up your vehicle and bring it to the studio. That way, when the show is finished, you'll have your car. In the meantime, you can ride in the limo and be with your daughter."

"I guess that will work, but . . ." Jenny had a fearful look on her face. She had been burned by what had happened, and she was resentful toward Billy. She had come to him for help. In the aftermath, she felt that Allison's dangerous and life-threatening actions were at least partially the result of Billy's provocative behavior on-camera. She didn't want a repeat, or worse yet, something even more alarming. But before she could object, something inside held her back. Perhaps it was the tone in Billy's voice. He seemed to be much different from the brash, cocky talk show host who had taken her daughter on a jaunt to Denver the day before. Maybe he was just exhausted from the trip and more laid-back. Or maybe it was a clever trick to lure her into yet another exploitive encounter to wring one more ratings point out of the personal tragedy of her daughter.

Billy sensed Jenny's apprehension. "I know you're probably worried about a repeat of what happened earlier this week, but I assure you, this show today is going to be much different. Please trust me," he said.

"I don't know . . ."

Dr. Kingman put a hand on her shoulder. "It will be all right. Billy is telling the truth. I don't know exactly what Mr. McBride has in mind, but I'm confident you'll be happy with what takes place on today's show. Your daughter is in no further danger."

"There you go, Mom, a clean bill of health. Your sweet, adorable daughter is all fixed," Allison said sarcastically. "That should make you happy."

Kingman looked at her seriously. "Not fixed *yet*, but on her way."

"Want to tell me what's going on?"

Billy and Steinberg were finally ensconced in the back of the limo away from the others, and Steinberg was more than a little irritated.

"Hold it, Jeff. Have you forgotten what you did to me earlier this week? Remember, it was your idea to get Allison and her mother back on the show. After that suicide attempt, I thought we'd move on. You were the one who went behind my back to book them again the next day. Well, this is a little taste of your own medicine."

Steinberg was angry. "Listen, you may be the hot-shot, high-paid talent, and I know there's no show without you, but the network execs hold me accountable for what airs. We've been a great team, until now. And teamwork means communication. I can't turn on those cameras until I know at least something of what you have in mind. A follow-up report would be expected, but where's the hook? You haven't told me a thing about what went on. You can keep some surprises to yourself if you want, but we've got to build the graphic bylines before you start."

Billy nodded in agreement. "I understand. And I'm not trying to sneak anything past you. It's just that things have changed."

Steinberg had been leaning forward assertively. Now, he settled back in his seat to make himself more comfortable for what was coming. "Changed? So what's different about Allison that's going to affect today's show?"

"It's not Allison, Jeff. It's me."

"You? Oh, don't tell me you're going to do something crazy like return to the rodeo? Wait, I know. Some Texas cowgirl in tight blue jeans got your attention, and you're going to get back on a bucking bronc to prove you're still a macho man."

Billy laughed. "No, you're way off base."

"You got drunk and did something stupid? What was it?"

Billy smiled. "It wasn't women or booze. It was God."

Steinberg jerked forward in shock. "God? Oh, no. That's over the top. It was Kingman, wasn't it? I knew I never should have left you alone with a preacher. What did he do, throw some holy water on you and drive out the devil? Hey, you need some devilishness in you. It's that satanic spunk that makes you so irascible and unpredictable."

Billy shot Steinberg a stern look. "Knock off the attempt at humor, please. This isn't a laughing matter, Jeff. You're so focused on the show, you're clueless as to what else is going on around you. Get a life!"

"Billy, you are my life. I eat, sleep, breathe *McBride*. That's why you're so rich. Don't knock my obsession with you and what you do. Remember, you're a star because of me." He motioned to the inside of the limo. "Perks like this, to say nothing of your private jet and presidential suites, are because I have given my whole life to making you an American hero. So what did I miss?"

"You never said a word about the man in the cowboy hat who got off the plane with me."

"I just figured it was some friend you met at the rodeo and let tag along to see your show. I'm sorry, but all I could think about was getting you in this car and whisking you off to prep for the show. I'll apologize to the guy, whoever he is, when we get to the studio. Right now we're going to talk about the show today."

"Jeff, that man is my father."

Steinberg's eyes widened. "I thought he was dead. I mean, I just took for granted that it was an off-limits subject. You never talked about him, except one time, when you had one too many bloody Marys and started yelling about how he left you high and dry. How in the world did you know he was going to be in Denver? Is that why you wanted to go there?"

"Not at all. I thought he was dead. I had no idea where he was or what happened to him. The last time I saw him, I was four years old."

"So that's the surprise for today's show. You're going to introduce your dad to the audience. That's a great idea. Why didn't you tell me in the first place?"

Billy sighed in frustration. "Jeff, if you'd stop talking and start listening, I'll be happy to tell you part of the reason today's show will be unique. Yes, I do plan to introduce my father to the audience, but not because I have some cheap, melodramatic motive in mind. I want people to hear the miracle behind finding my father, and the miracle God did in my own life."

Steinberg was silent. He wasn't sure what to say.

"Jeff, I've turned my life over to God."

By now, Steinberg was too numb to respond. His mind raced with thoughts of all the possibilities that *this* turn of events might mean. Finally, he could no longer hold back.

"Okay, people find religion all the time. So, you're going to clean up your act a little. I've got no problem with that. Frankly, I have been worried that your life has started to imitate 'art.' I wondered myself if you had lost the distinction between the wild and crazy man on-camera and the real you off-camera. No one is going to be upset that you've gotten a dose of sensibility in your private life. Then, you'll probably get over this, just like you did the rodeo." Steinberg forced a smile. "I'm happy for you. Hey, even I go to the synagogue on Yom Kippur and during Hanukkah."

"I appreciate what you're saying, but I'm not sure you understand how profoundly this has affected my life already. Let's talk about it later. We need to deal with the technical aspects of the show right now. I've got a lot of B-roll lined up." Billy took a piece of paper from his pocket, unfolded it, and handed it to Steinberg. "I've already covered the bases on graphics. I scribbled down a few ideas of what we might say while footage from Denver is rolling."

"So, how many chairs do we want on stage?"

"Just three. We'll let Jenny stay in the Green Room with Allison's little girl, Ashley."

"Okay, and how does the show start?"

"I'll do my usual monologue, though I've revised it a little. I won't need a teleprompter. I'm going to wing it. Then, when I give the cue, we'll go to that first B-roll segment I picked."

Steinberg looked carefully at the paper. "All I see here is the byline, 'National Western Stock Show & Rodeo.' It really doesn't tell me anything about what the audience will be seeing."

"Don't worry about that. I didn't have time to write out everything. Besides, like I said, it's going to be a surprise. I can tell you one thing, that guy you hired to accompany me and shoot video was a great help. He really knows his business."

"Pardon? What are you talking about?"

"You know, Aaron Gabriel, the video cameraman you hired at the last minute, just before we left Denver."

"I have no idea what you're talking about. When I saw that guy with the video camera get off the plane, I thought it was someone you arranged to shoot footage. I've never even heard of an Aaron Gabriel."

17

And now, the host of America's most unscripted hour on television. The man whose boots are made for walking into your living room with the unusual, the outlandish, and the outright insane. Take a wild ride with the host who hog-ties topics others won't touch. Welcome him back from the National Western Stock Show and Rodeo, Billlleeee McBride!"

"Billll-eeee, Billll-eeee!"

The chant from the audience raised the roof. After a rerun the day before, Billy's crowd was primed for his real, live presence. Their exuberance was electrifying. Billy bounded onstage looking like the same old McBride.

But something was different. Billy didn't milk the crowd as he usually did, and he calmed them down more quickly. "My fellow Americans," he began.

The opening line was the same, and upon hearing it, the audience was on their feet again, chanting, "Billll-eeee, Billll-eeee!"

"As you may know, I've been away from the cameras for a day going to a rodeo. I wasn't alone." He looked soberly into camera one. "Allison Owens, the young woman who attempted suicide three days ago, right on this stage, was with me. I also took along the minister who tried to help her, Reverend Joseph Kingman, a seminary professor and . . . an exorcist."

The audience grunted and punched their fists into the air in mock acclamation.

"Before we welcome Allison and Reverend Kingman back onstage, I want you to see what it was like to attend one of America's premier rodeos . . . Roll the videotape."

In the control booth things were more frantic than usual. Steinberg normally went through precise rehearsals of everything that would take place during *McBride* and scripted it to the second. Today, he was unable to do that. Gabriel stood by his side to indicate which tape had the footage Billy would call for. The three of them had agreed that Billy would cushion their cues with adequate talk-up time that hinted at which video clip would be next, so they could load it into the Beta SP video machines.

The studio audience tilted their heads back to look up at the monitors. On the screens above them were rodeo scenes. Bucking broncos and wailing steers. Roaring bulls and nimble barrel riders. Spurs flew and cowboys tumbled in the dirt. All this was interspersed with human-interest shots of the McBride bunch.

In the control booth Steinberg leaned close to whisper in Gabriel's ear. "Good job. Some of the best on-location shoulder cam stuff I've seen, especially without a lot of cutting. It looks like this footage spent a day in the editing bay instead of a couple of hours in a viewfinder on an airplane."

Gabriel smiled.

"Say, I was wondering," Steinberg said, "Billy and I were talking on the way from the airport, and both of us were curious who hired you. Billy thought it was me, and I thought it was him. Finally we both figured out it must have been Kingman, since according to Billy, you both are strong religious types. So why didn't Kingman say anything about getting you for the job? I didn't realize he knew anything about the media."

As the rodeo scenes continued, Gabriel responded. "There's a lot you don't know about Dr. Kingman and me."

"So, he was the one who got you the job."

"Yes, in a roundabout way, I did get the job because of him. He's the one who told my boss that you'd need someone to capture what happened on video, and I was the one who knew the most about the subject of exorcism."

"Well, like I said, great stuff."

The floor director counted Billy down to the end of the video clip and cued him back to camera one. Andy Mallory, Billy's sidekick, exhorted the audience to applaud as the video ended.

"That's what we went to Denver to see," Billy said, "but our trip turned out to be a lot more interesting than we expected, especially after the rodeo was over and we went to see the animals in the stock stalls. Roll that clip, please."

Once again Steinberg and Gabriel sprang into action. They already had the video cued on the second Sony deck and hit PLAY.

Gabriel's deft, backward footwork was apparent from the creative shots of Billy leading Allison and Kingman down the corridors to the stock area. Then the scene cut to Big Boy and that scary moment when the huge Shire reared and tossed off Allison. The footage ended with Allison cringing in pain on the floor.

"Ladies and gentlemen, I am happy to report that our own queen of the rodeo, Allison Owens, is alive and well. Would you give her a warm welcome back to another ride with *McBride*."

As Mallory again exhorted the audience, Kim Usher gave Allison, who was standing offstage, a gentle push toward Billy. "You know the drill, sister," Kim said to Allison. "Get out there and do your thing."

Allison stumbled slightly and smiled weakly as she made her way to center stage. Billy shook her hand and motioned toward a seat.

"And I also want you to welcome back a man you've already met. Right here on this show he's taken on a psychiatrist and a psychic and sent them both hightailing it outta here. He's a seminary professor and exorcist, and the man whose prayers made it possible for Allison to be back on her feet and with us here today. Welcome back a man of God, and my friend, Dr. Joseph Kingman."

That comment made Steinberg nervous. It was okay to get religion behind the scenes, but Billy had a "reputation" to maintain. Saying he was friends with a preacher would not endear him to his core audience—males of ages 18–34 who bought the beer and blue jeans advertised on his show.

As the applause, and a few boos, for Kingman faded, Billy directed him to his chair.

"The last time these two were on our stage, just two days ago, there was a violent outburst from Allison, and she threatened Dr. Kingman's life. Some of you saw how I had to tackle her and knock the knife out of her hands. Well, today Allison has no knives; we've made sure of that before she came onstage. Many of you have been wondering why this lovely young woman and mother have been on such a self-destructive course. Why did she cut herself? Where did her bizarre behavior come from? Yesterday we learned a lot about her that explains her conduct. More importantly, and unexpectedly, we learned a lot about yours truly that no one knew, including me. Let's begin that part of the story by introducing a man I haven't seen in nearly forty years, a man who is responsible for my being here today, my father, Brogue McBride."

At first the audience was stunned. Then, they jumped to their feet without any prompting from Mallory and erupted with enthusiasm. Brogue stepped slowly in front of the cameras, and took off his cowboy hat to wave it at the audience. He grinned broadly and moved toward Billy with the gait of a man who had spent a lifetime on the back of broncs and bulls. As he neared Billy, both men stretched out their arms and fell into a firm shoulder-to-shoulder embrace. When they pulled back from each other, Billy directed Brogue to the remaining chair.

As Billy turned to the lead camera and looked directly into the lens, he wiped a tear from his eye. "Since the age of four, I've been looking for me, the real me. Not the man you've watched every day on TV.

That's not who I am. That's who I became to hide the hurt inside from feeling abandoned by a father I never knew. Now, thanks to Dr. Kingman, and the Lord, I have found my father, and I've found myself."

Steinberg cringed. *He's doing a great job of wringing emotions out of people to set up this show, but if he doesn't lay off that religion stuff, he's going to blow it.*

"I want to apologize."

Those words ripped through Steinberg. He wanted to stop Billy in his tracks but had no way to do it, at least not until there was a commercial break.

Billy waved in the direction of his studio audience. "To all of you, I want to say, I'm sorry." Billy pointed directly at the camera. "And to all of you, America, I want to say I'm sorry. I took advantage of you. I manipulated and exploited you for my own gain. I wasn't evil or corrupt. I was just part of the system, the same system I bragged about leaving behind in L.A. A system that appeals to what's worst about our society and sensationalizes the most eccentric and aberrant kinds of behavior to get your attention. I could have showcased the lives of those around us who are courageous and good. Instead, I paraded before you the worst examples of indecency and immorality, all for the ratings."

The studio audience was totally silent. Billy was their man, the embodiment of their anger and rebellion. He said what they wanted to say to those in politics and the pulpit. That's what they liked most about him. This kinder, gentler Billy was someone they didn't know and weren't sure they wanted to.

Billy looked at his father. "This man made some mistakes when he was young, and it cost him his family. It cost him the love of a woman and the companionship of a son." Billy turned and stepped toward the studio audience as the television camera followed his methodical movements. "Don't you make the mistake he made. It took a miracle for me to see him again, and there may not be enough miracles to go around for every one of you if you choose to mess up the life God's given you."

Billy paused and walked back toward center stage. "I finally know who I am." He pointed at Brogue. "I'm that man's son, and the rejection I felt from his abandonment made me bitter against the world. I sucked you into my own inner world of moral confusion. I'm saying this because you thought I was your friend when, in truth, I was your enemy. Like I said, I'm sorry. I want to be real with you, and that's why I'm talking to you the way I am now. We're going to a commercial break, and after that I'm going to show you, what may well be the most amazing video footage you've ever seen in your life."

Billy dropped his head in silence.

For a moment no one made a sound. Then a single person clapped. Then two. Three. Five. Ten. Suddenly the whole studio audience exploded into cheers and the loudest applause anyone on the production staff had ever heard.

Steinberg shook his head. *I can't believe it. He spilled his guts like a repentant convert at a revival meeting, and they're going nuts.*

Everyone in the control booth scrambled. They had been so captivated by what Billy said, they forgot about the clock. When he gave the commercial cue, everything on screen went black for a moment before the commercials could be punched up.

Billy knew that Steinberg would be at point D, damage control central. As he walked across the stage to the back of the set, Brogue stood and patted Billy on the shoulder. "I'm proud of you, son," he said softly.

Allison nervously shifted her weight back and forth in her chair. She was as uncomfortable as Billy had ever seen her, but she managed a faint smile as he glanced her way.

Billy approached Steinberg, who wasn't sure what to do. His first reaction had been irritation at what Billy had said, but the response of the audience softened his stance. As he gathered his thoughts, he decided this wasn't the time to scold Billy. More than half the time was left, and there was still an opportunity to salvage the show.

"You're doing all right," Steinberg mustered.

Billy looked at him skeptically. "You don't really mean that. But thanks anyway. Hang tight. The show isn't over yet, and there are more surprises, so save some shock for the last segment."

"I suppose Billy Graham is going to show up and give an altar call," Steinberg said.

Billy grinned. "You just can't cut the sarcasm, can you? No, I'm not turning *McBride* into a tent meeting, at least not yet." Billy jabbed Steinberg. "Just stay on the job and keep the video clips tight. Do what Gabriel tells you to do with the footage he shot."

"Hey, it's your show today. I take no responsibility for this one. Oh, by the way, I found out who hired him. Kingman."

"That's what he said?"

"Not in those exact words, but yes, he admitted Kingman was responsible for his being called in to shoot the video. Hey, I don't care if God himself gave him the assignment, it's some of the best footage I've seen, and that's good enough for me. What's next?"

"Me."

"You, and who else?"

"Just footage of me."

"Doing what?"

"You'll see."

The sound of *McBride* theme music called Billy back to the set. As he jumped in front of the cameras the cheers of the audience, unassisted by Mallory, were as ardent as before.

"Thank you. Now I want you to prepare yourselves for some footage of me. This wasn't shot at the rodeo. It was taken that same night, after we returned to my hotel suite. You're going to see Dr. Kingman take me back to the time my father left when I was four years old. Roll the tape."

Gabriel tapped the technical director on the shoulder to cue him for the next clip. Gabriel's videography captured, with stunning close-ups, the intense emotions Billy experienced as his mind traveled back in time. Some in the studio audience sniffled and wiped tears from their eyes as Billy's voice raised a register and he spoke as Little Billy. Then, when Little Billy was embraced in the arms of Jesus, audible weeping could be heard.

As Little Billy asked, "What about Ronald Thomas?" the video clip stopped and the live camera returned to Billy on the set.

"Dr. Kingman," Billy said, "from the sounds of what's taking place in the studio audience, I'm not the only one who has stuffed away hidden hurts. For those here, and those out there, please tell all of us what we can do about past emotional injuries."

Camera two did a slow zoom toward Kingman as he spoke with compassion and the wellspring of years of ministry. "The truth makes us free, John 8:32 declares. When we live a lie, we're not free," he explained. "Many of you are in bondage to a pain in your past. Someone, or some circumstance, deeply wounded your heart. You tried to put it behind you, but you couldn't. You said you forgave them, but you didn't. You moved on with your life, but you never escaped the memory. When you think of it now, it's still happening in your mind. That abuse, that injustice, that rejection still stirs up frightening emotions and feelings of resentment and bitterness. Sometimes the thought of what happened makes you so angry that you go into deep depression. At other times, you explode in a violent rage."

Kingman pointed at Allison. "Some of you cut yourself like this young woman. You abuse alcohol and drugs. You experiment with promiscuous sex. You are anorexic or bulimic. Something down inside wants to get even with those who hurt you. If you want to get free, you've got to get to that pain. Stop the secrets. Admit what happened and face your fears. Only then can God turn your life around. The Bible says, 'Confess your faults to one another and you will be healed.' Find a friend, a pastor or priest, a counselor of some kind, and talk about what's eating you from the inside out. Get free, and live free! That's what God wants for your life, and that's why He sent His Son to die for you."

The audience was on its feet again. Cheers mingled with tears as everyone, including the production staff, stood to applaud. Some hugged a weeping friend near them. Others embraced a spouse or significant other. Tissues and handkerchiefs were passed around freely as one person after another broke down sobbing.

Steinberg couldn't believe it. Even the seasoned taping crew who had seen it all was caught up in the fervor. This *was* a revival meeting on national TV, and everyone loved it.

Except Allison.

She was frozen in her chair, immobilized by some fearsome force that had overtaken her. Suddenly she stood, doubled her fists, and flailed the air, her long black hair flying in every direction as her head shook violently.

"No! No! No!" a voice that was not Allison's own screamed. "Stop it, you fools. Don't believe what he says. You have a right to hate. A right to get even. He's trying to deceive you. It's all lies, lies, lies!" Her eyes bulged out, and the color drained from her face.

The shriek of her voice startled everyone to silence. Kingman got out of his chair and locked his eyes on hers. Without speaking, he moved slowly in her direction like a cat stalking its prey. When he was no more than a foot from her face, his countenance took on a seething expression of holy indignation. Allison and Kingman were like two enraged animals preparing to lunge at each other.

"I know you," Kingman said firmly. "Now, everyone will see you for what you really are. You've invaded this creature of God to destroy her, but the hour of your judgment has arrived, and you will receive the wrath of God!"

With that, Kingman took the leather-bound Bible he was holding and thrust it in the air like a sword. Swiftly it came down in the direction of Allison's head. In the split second before it reached her, the voice inside her cried out with the most bloodcurdling scream Billy had ever heard. He couldn't believe his eyes. Kingman never touched

Allison's body, but the blow was like a falling sledgehammer. Allison hit the floor with a thud so loud that Billy wondered if she was injured.

The studio went abruptly silent.

Kingman stood over Allison, his whole body shaking as if he had taken on Tyson in a fifteen-rounder and floored him.

Then Allison started to move. She tucked her knees to her chest and cried with a tiny, thin voice. "Daddy, Daddy. Why don't you want me? Why don't you love me?"

Steinberg had left the control room and was standing just out of camera range looking perplexed. Billy motioned for him to go to a spot break. The bumper music came over the house speakers announcing four minutes of commercials. Billy knelt with Kingman by Allison's side.

"I think I can help."

The voice came from behind Billy. He looked upward, over his shoulder, into the face of a handsome man who appeared to be not much younger than himself. He was stockily built with curly dark hair that accented his swarthy skin. He knelt down on the other side of Kingman, who was positioned between the two men, and took Allison's hand in his.

"I'm sorry," he said as his eyes misted with tears. "Please, forgive me."

Billy looked the stranger directly in the eye and spoke quietly, but firmly. "Who are you?" he demanded.

The man smiled warmly and reached out to shake Billy's hand. "I'm Allison's real father, Bud Coleman."

18

Bud Coleman had arrived just moments after the network switched to commercials. Billy knew that the unannounced appearance of Allison's biological father wouldn't make sense to the viewers. He tried to figure out a way to explain who Coleman was and how he appeared, though Billy really didn't understand it either.

So much had happened on the show already. The strange appearance of Coleman, Allison's demonic episode, and the new Billy persona. Billy knew his audience was confused, but for the first time the viewers weren't foremost in his mind. He was having a life transition, internally and in front of the cameras. It took everything within him just to hold it together and stay focused. When the show was over, the audience would either love or hate him. The network execs would cheer him or give him his walking papers. There was so much at stake, and yet he felt fully energized. Years had melted off him, and the cobwebs that had clouded his thoughts were being pulled away. The weight that always pressed on him had been lifted.

Billy looked over and saw Allison still lying on the floor curled up in her frightened childlike state. Coleman knelt next to her, uncertain as to what he should do. Kingman stood beside them, with a Bible in hand, poised at the ready if the evil surfaced again. His eyes were cast upward in prayer. Brogue sat in his chair and watched but said nothing.

When Kingman had swung the Bible toward Allison, many in the audience had jumped to their feet for a better look. Now, after the break, most of them were settled in their seats, whispering about what had happened. They seemed to love this show because it was unlike any *McBride* they'd seen before. This was the first time they had seen real emotions and genuine miracles from God.

Camera operators jockeyed for different angles, trying to capture the best shot of Allison's facial expressions. One man with a shoulder-cam crawled on his stomach toward Allison, with the lens at ground level, pointed toward her face. Her eyes were closed, but her countenance had a softness to it. Her hair tumbled to one side on the floor, and her hands were curled near her chest. Though her body lay in a difficult position with her head bent forward, she appeared peaceful.

Coleman gently stroked Allison's hand. "It's okay. I'm here for you," he said over and over. "You'll be all right. Please try to forgive me."

Billy knew he had to cover Coleman's appearance right after the commercial break. Hoping that Steinberg had an answer, he walked over to his producer before the last commercial.

"This is great!" Steinberg exclaimed. "An attempted suicide, a threat on a preacher's life, and now this–all in one week! If we can pull it all together today, this show will go down as the most dramatic week in the history of daytime TV. If that doesn't double your ad rates, I don't know what will." He ran his hands over his head.

Billy shot Steinberg a disgusted look. "Are ratings all you think about?"

"Hey, great share points and more money never hurt your feelings before. Did you get kicked in the head by one of those broncos when you were at the rodeo?"

"Nothing Kingman couldn't fix, I assure you," Billy said. "We're in to countdown now. I've got to explain Coleman off the top."

"Yeah, what's that all about? You know I don't let just anyone . . ."

"I know," Billy said. "That's why I'm going to find out how he got in here."

Billy bounded back to the stage just as the break ended. "We've had a strange turn of events," Billy told his television audience. He pointed toward Coleman. "That man kneeling by Allison says he's her biological father. We didn't even know who he was when he walked onstage. He's our miracle guest, if someone can prove he's really her father."

"I can prove it."

"What?" Billy looked around. Jenny stood just offstage, holding Ashley in her arms. Kim Usher quickly stepped to her side and reached out for Ashley, handing her off to an assistant. Then Jenny walked slowly into the show lights, her face flushed. She headed toward the man who had deserted her little girl so many years ago.

Sheepishly Coleman stood to face her. He muttered an apology and said softly, "I was wrong to abandon you and Allison. It ruined my life, and I'm nothing because of what I did. I have asked God to forgive me, and now I need you to do so."

Jenny shook as she bit her lip and wiped the tears that flowed from her eyes. "How dare you show up here! When the TV cameras are on, you swoop in like a knight in shining armor and save the day. Please, just walk away, because that's what you're good at." Her whole body quivered with anger. "You never called. Not even a letter or card on Allison's birthdays. There's no way I can forgive you now."

Coleman dropped his head. "I wouldn't blame you if you never wanted to see me again, but Jen, I've changed. I'm not the man who walked away from you and Allie."

"First of all, don't call me Jen." She gestured toward her daughter's fallen body. "You made her like that. She hates herself because you, her father, never cared enough to take one moment to be concerned about the people you left behind. You never wanted her, and now she doesn't want herself. Please, leave now!"

Kingman moved behind Jenny, talking in a slow and comforting tone. "Jenny, I know your pain. You have borne the burden of Allison's anguish and torment all these years. But the only way to get truly free from what this man did to you, and to free Allison, is to forgive him. You're behind the bars of your own bitterness, and mercy is the key that will free you."

"I can't forgive him," Jenny said.

"Maybe *you* can't, but with God you can. No matter how you feel, say the words. By faith declare what you know is right. The resentment in your heart won't hurt him, but it's a toxin in your soul that will eventually destroy you and the daughter you love so much."

Jenny looked squarely at Kingman. Her voice softened. "You're right." She turned to face Coleman. With trembling lips she said, "I forgive you." Then she paused. "I can't say that I mean it with all my heart. Maybe if I say it, because I know it's the right thing to do, my feelings will catch up with my words."

Coleman approached Jenny and spread his arms wide. At first Jenny hesitated, then she gave in as he pulled her tightly to him. Gradually, she dissolved into Coleman's embrace and drenched his shirt with her tears.

Billy motioned for the cameras to move away from the distraught couple, to allow them some privacy. He focused everyone's attention back on Allison, who still lay unconscious. The audience was quiet. They weren't sure where to watch next.

"Please explain what happened when you waved your Bible at her and she fell down," Billy said to Kingman.

The minister walked over to Billy and spoke with carefully measured words. "The voice that accused me of lying wasn't Allison's. That was an inner evil. When I thrust my Bible, as the sword of the spirit, the demon was supernaturally smitten by the power of God's Word. I did that to torment the demon and weaken it."

"So what do you do next?"

Kingman gestured toward Coleman. "He's part of the answer. As her father, he has the right to break the curse. When he abandoned her, he ratified it. As her spiritual covering, he must nullify it."

Billy turned to the cameras. "Let me show you a short clip of what we're talking about. Come with me to the hotel room last night when Dr. Kingman explained the curse that's affecting Allison. It's called the Curse of the Shire. Roll the video."

In the control room, Steinberg scrambled. Gabriel wasn't there to tell him which tape was next, so he frantically grabbed one video after another. After a harrowing few moments, he found the correct one, labeled THE CURSE OF THE SHIRE.

As footage from Kingman's tale of the trip to England played over the air, Billy took advantage of the lull to approach Coleman, who still held Jenny in his arms.

Away from the glare of the cameras, Billy asked, "How did you get in here?"

"A guy named Gabriel called me out of the blue. He talked like he knew me, and told me it was a matter of life and death. He said I should come down to your show today. Then he told me about Allison and Jen and what had happened earlier in the week. When I heard about Allison trying to kill herself, that was it. I had to get here. Can you blame me?

"Anyway, Gabriel met me out front and escorted me to the studio. That guy sure is something special. From the moment I saw him, I felt like I had known him from somewhere. I'm so grateful that he made it possible for me to be here today."

"Didn't you think that was a little strange, maybe a trick of some kind?"

"Well, I figured that someone on your staff had tracked me down as part of research for the show. I had watched your show at other times when you reunited people with old lovers or lost family members, so I assumed that's what this was about."

Jenny stopped crying and moved back a couple of steps. She had forgiven Coleman, but her emotions were still raw. She continued to wipe her tears with tissues that several staff members handed her.

"Why didn't you do something to patch things up before now?" Billy asked Coleman. "It seems odd that you'd be so interested in your daughter all of a sudden."

"I'm not sure that I have an answer. I suppose it was fear, plus guilt and shame. I knew how Jen felt about my leaving her, and I thought it was better for me to stay out of her life."

"Ten seconds, Billy." The words of the floor director interrupted Billy's conversation.

As the countdown back to "live" began, Allison stirred. She came to, and her body stiffened. Her face contorted and a deep voice growled as her eyes flashed with bulging pupils.

"Are you going to obey now?" Kingman asked sternly.

Allison's lips snarled. "You may know about the Shire, and *he* may be here," the voice said, pointing to Coleman, "but you're still missing a piece of the puzzle." The demon arrogantly taunted Kingman. "You don't know who holds the key to breaking the curse."

People in the audience shifted in their seats and began murmuring to one another, but Kingman remained firm. "I've had enough of your mockery. Hold your tongue and go down. I want to talk to Allison."

The demon contorted Allison's body in a vain attempt to resist, then submerged into her subconscious, and Allison's awareness returned. Kingman knelt beside her and spoke gently. "I want to talk to the child inside you who was so hurt by not having a father."

Allison immediately reacted. She went from snarling to being submissive and tucked her knees to her chest. With one hand she tugged at her hair and twisted it nervously.

"I know you're in there," Kingman said with a soothing tone.

"What do you want? Go away." The voice was thin and childlike. Her eyes squinted, and she curled up, as if she were trying to make herself disappear.

"You're sad because your daddy left, aren't you?"

"It doesn't matter. I have a new daddy. He's much nicer," she said as she jutted out her chin.

"Oh, and who is that daddy?"

"I can't see him very well, but I hear his voice in my head. He promised me that if I'd let him be my daddy, I'd never hurt again."

"That voice is evil, and it's from the devil!"

"No, it isn't. It's God who is evil. He took my daddy away."

"And how do you know that?"

"The voice told me."

"I'll prove to you that voice is evil and is lying to you. Where is it?" Kingman asked as he put his arm around her to give her support.

"Behind me. It's always behind me."

"Turn around and look at it."

"No. The voice said I must never do that, or it will have to go away."

"It lied. It said that because it doesn't want you to see what it really looks like. It isn't a nice daddy. Please, go ahead and turn—now!"

Allison's eyes were shut, but she slowly turned her head, as if literally looking behind her. Then she emitted a terrifying scream. "No! Get away from me!" she cried out. Her body jerked, and she jumped to her feet in terror as if to escape the horror she'd seen. Kingman put both his hands on her shoulders to reassure her.

"You saw the voice, and he was ugly, wasn't he?"

Allison's head nodded.

"Your daddy did a very bad thing when he left you, but he's sorry, and you need to forgive him. The man beside you now is your real daddy."

A shocked look shot across Allison's face. With her eyes still closed, the child in Allison hesitantly reached out to Coleman. She softly touched his arms, then reached toward his face. Like a blind person feeling her surroundings, she gradually moved her hands over Coleman's head and upper body, seeking comfort in his presence. Satisfied that she was safe, she relaxed.

"I forgive my daddy," the child said. "It's not very easy, but his arms feel so nice." She leaned her head on Coleman's chest as tears came down his face.

"What's going on here?" Jenny looked at Kingman and asked. "What is happening to my daughter?"

"This is what we call an alter, or multiple, personality," Kingman explained. "When your daughter was abandoned at a young age, the child within her was so traumatized that a portion of her mind split off to handle the hurt of the rejection. She couldn't bear to keep that memory as a constant reminder, so her inner child held those feelings of abandonment."

Suddenly everyone heard the sound of the *McBride* theme music. Steinberg had only preempted Billy's lead-in to the commercials twice before, but a quick glance at the studio clock, which hung under the lens of camera two, told Billy why his producer had acted so precipitously. The airing schedule was already five minutes past the appointed break, and the amount of show time was slipping away. Billy had been so engrossed in what was going on, he'd lost his sense of pacing.

Steinberg rushed to grab Billy. "Sorry to break in, but I had no choice but to punch in a spot break without your usual segue," he said. "Look. We've milked this subject enough for one go-round. I don't think we can keep the interest over the weekend, so you've got to find a way to give closure before the closing credits. What's your plan?"

Billy hesitated. He didn't have a plan. He knew he wasn't in control. Only divine intervention would resolve this.

"Billy," Brogue spoke up, "there's something I've got to tell you. I think I'm the one the demon was talking about. I'm the missing piece of the puzzle to Allison's freedom."

Brogue had been silent until now, so his voice commanded attention, and each person onstage, and in the audience, turned toward him.

"The demon was right," he said as he stood up. With both hands he tugged at the front of his western vest. The heels of his cowboy boots clomped on the floor as he walked toward Billy. "Someone holds the key to breaking the curse, and I'm that person."

Billy frowned. He had no idea how his dad could possibly have anything to do with this, but stranger things had already happened. "Dad, do you know what you're saying?"

Brogue lifted his bushy eyebrows. "Yeah, I'm fine. Now I realize all too well what is going on."

"Ten seconds," the floor director called out.

Billy welcomed the television audience back to the show and tried to let them know what was happening. "During the break my father made a strange comment. Even I'm not sure what he meant. All he said was, 'I'm the one the demon was talking about.' Then he said he was the one who held the key to breaking the curse." Billy turned to his father. "Please explain what you're talking about."

"I had my suspicions," Brogue replied, "but I wasn't certain enough to say anything. I had to wait and watch. What if I was wrong?" He hung his head.

"What do you mean about being wrong? Wrong about what?"

"Him." Brogue pointed toward Coleman. "I sensed it the moment he walked onstage, but it was just so impossible to believe that I ignored it. But I've been watching him carefully, and I can't deny it any longer."

A look of bewilderment flashed across the audience. No one had a clue what Brogue was talking about. Deliberately the cowboy walked toward Coleman, who was standing to one side of the stage with Jenny and Allison. "Give me your hands," he said softly.

Slowly Brogue examined Coleman's hands, turning them first one way, then the other, nodding his head as if in some inner agreement with his own soul. He stared straight into Coleman's eyes and firmly grasped his shoulders and upper arms as if testing the strength of muscle and sinew. Then he studied the outline of Coleman's features like a doctor carefully examining a patient. Finally he pointed to Jenny. "She knows too."

Jenny reacted with shock. She gave Billy a baffled look. "I have no idea what he's talking about."

"His name," Brogue said. "You know his name."

"Of course I know his name. We lived together for two years."

Brogue smiled and patted Coleman on the shoulder.

"Billy," Brogue said, "they both know his name, but neither of them knows what it means. You do, but you won't believe it unless you see it in black and white. Have him show you his driver's license."

Billy looked around for a clue from anyone as to what was going on. "Okay," he said to Coleman, "can I see your license?"

Coleman fished for his wallet, pulled out his license, and handed it over. As Billy scanned it, he knew what his father had been talking about. He stared at Coleman and Jenny for a moment before he said, "There aren't many times I don't know what to say, but I'm speechless."

He extended his hand to the man he had met only minutes before and shook Coleman's hand firmly. Then he turned around to look at Brogue. The three of them stared first at one and then the other in disbelief. No one said a word, but the audience sensed that an unspoken bond was being forged that only the three men fully understood.

Gabriel walked out of the shadows from a corner of the studio to whisper in Kingman's ear. When he did, a broad smile filled the minister's face. He walked over to Allison, who had returned to her adult consciousness.

Kingman took Allison's hands and held them reassuringly. "Your father's nickname is Bud, but his full legal name is Ronald Thomas Coleman."

19

I wish I had never come on this show!" Allison blurted out as she stared at the man who claimed to be her father.

She shut her eyes to blot out the confusion. Then Ashley's face shot through her mind. "The only reason I've hung in there is because of my little girl. Whatever I have to go through is worth it for her. Whatever this Shire curse thing is, I want it over!"

The audience applauded her decision, and then Kingman signaled for quiet. "Now we know how Allison got the curse," Kingman said. "Brogue, you abandoned Ronald and Billy, and Ronald abandoned Allison. She became the symbolic sacrifice for the Curse of the Shire."

"If all of us were affected by the curse, why didn't all of us get demons?" Billy asked.

"Not everyone who is vulnerable to a demon gets one," Kingman replied. "The common grace of God protects us, even though we're all fallen creatures. Satan could snatch any one of us if it were not for God's love." He paused. "There's another reason. Because of your sin, Brogue, the curse of your ancestors fell upon Ronald. For some reason we don't understand, Ronald, you were affected but not totally dominated by the curse. Allison, as your firstborn, was. Ashley is also at risk, and we're going to take care of that right now.

"We must move quickly," he said to everyone. "Satan knows we've uncovered the key to removing the Curse of the Shire, so he'll begin a counterattack." He looked at Allison. "I need your full cooperation to confront the demons inside you. This battle for your soul is almost over. Now we must remove the legal rights of Satan and completely break the curse."

"I don't understand everything that's going on," Allison responded. "But I'll do whatever you ask—for Ashley's sake."

Kingman looked at Brogue, Billy, Bud, and Jenny. "I want all of you to hold hands and surround Allison and me in a circle of prayer. We're going to free Allison. Each of you search your hearts for any uncon-fessed sins and make a full surrender of your life to God."

The studio audience broke into spontaneous applause as the four positioned themselves just as Kingman had requested. They watched with rapt attention.

"Look me in the eye, Allison. I want to see straight to your soul as I confront the evil inside you."

Allison did her best to relax her body and stare at Kingman without blinking. At first Kingman said nothing. He simply fixed his unmoving gaze on Allison, who nervously shifted her weight, back and forth, from one leg to the other. Her right eyelid twitched, and her right eyebrow lifted ever so slightly. Then it happened. Her eyes totally changed, as if a switch had been thrown, and another state of consciousness appeared. Her eyes distended again and her pupils dilated. Billy felt like he was looking directly into the pit of hell.

"Come to attention and face the judgment of God!" Kingman declared.

Allison's neck stiffened and her jaw jutted out. Her arms tensed and the veins stood out on her neck.

"Who are you?" Kingman demanded.

"The Shire."

"What are your legal rights to this woman?"

"The curse."

"What else?"

"Drugs. Rejection."

"What's your stronghold?"

"Her hatred for herself."

"Spirit, go down. I call back Allison."

Allison's eyes closely briefly, then opened again. Her eyes were back to normal, and she didn't seem agitated.

Kingman spoke tenderly to Allison. "Before we can break the curse, you have to assert your will against the evil that's in you. Will you do that?"

Allison looked at her mother, then at Bud. Thoughts of who she really was and where her life was going reeled through her mind. Drugs. Despair. Suicide. Momentarily she wavered in her resolve. Then she realized what was at stake. "I'll cooperate fully. Just tell me what to do."

Kingman smiled, and Billy uttered an audible "Amen."

"In your own words, tell God how you feel about your life and what you need to do," Kingman directed.

Allison bowed her head. "God, You and I haven't talked much, but here I am. You know what a mess I've made of my life. I've got a drug problem. I really don't want to cut myself, but I don't know how to stop. Until the past couple of days, I wasn't sure I wanted to go on living. But that's changed, thanks to the people You sent into my life. Take this evil out of me. I don't know much about this curse, but break it for me and my little girl."

Sniffling and sobbing could be heard all over the studio. Steinberg paced, watching the crowd's reaction. Gabriel lifted his arms up in the air.

Kingman hugged Allison and spoke to the others. "Brogue, Bud, Jenny, each of you must renounce the Curse of the Shire to free Allison. Will you?"

Everyone nodded. "Just tell us what to say, and we'll say it," Bud responded.

"Repeat these words after me as an affirmation. 'Dear God' . . ."

"Dear God," the trio began, "we all renounce the Curse of the Shire. We renounce the sins of our ancestors, which brought this oath upon all of us. We break off the influence of witchcraft, abandonment, and rejection on us and on all future generations. We nullify the effect of this curse upon ourselves, Allison, and Ashley. In the name of the Father, the Son, and the Holy Spirit."

When the prayer was over, Kingman paused. A holy Presence filled the entire studio, so compelling that everyone was afraid to move or speak. Even Steinberg calmed down. Cameramen momentarily locked down their lenses. Not a single person in the studio audience moved.

Finally Kingman spoke. "Because he has no further right to this child of God, I command the spirit of the Shire to come forth."

Allison's body shook as if a jolt of electricity had hit her.

"Stand back, everyone," Kingman said. He gestured for those who encircled Allison to step away. Then, he fastened his eyes on the evil spirit that once again manifested itself. "Do you have any further right to this woman, yes or no?"

"No!" the demon screamed.

"In the name of Jesus, I bind all of you together as one, under the authority of the Shire who speaks for you. I command that you leave all the parts of Allison's consciousness, her soul, and her body. Declare your doom."

Allison's body staggered back like a boxer headed to the ropes. Kingman strode toward her, waving his Bible like a threatening weapon.

"See this demon for what it is, Allison," Kingman said. "Even though it's in control right now, you can hear me. Fight. In your mind, tell it to go."

"I can see it!" Allison's voice took over. "It's hideous. It has claws and huge fangs. It's covered with filthy, long hair. I can see its eyes. They're bloodred. It's as black as night with the hooves of a horse and a huge bump on its back. It stinks. Oh, dear God, I can't stand the smell." She reached for her nose. "Get it out of me—now!"

"I'm not leaving," the demon cackled.

"You have no choice," Kingman answered. "I command you. Say after me, 'I, the spirit of the Shire!'"

"I, the spirit of the Shire."

"Release this woman from the ancient curse!"

The demon backpedaled in fear. "No, I won't say it."

Kingman stalked the demon. "Say it!"

"Release this woman from the ancient curse."

"And go now!"

The demon cringed. Allison's hands formed like claws. "And go now," it repeated.

"To!"

"To."

"The!" Kingman said.

"No, I won't go there."

"The!" Kingman repeated.

"The."

"Pit!"

"No, any place but there. I'll remove the curse. I'll loose her child. I'll do anything you want," the demon pleaded, "but not the Abyss."

"Say it now, THE PIT!"

"The pit."

"When you go, take with you every desire for drugs, death, and suicide. Loose her from all the feelings of self-hatred, abandonment, and rejection. Leave now, in the name of Jesus!"

Billy had never heard a more menacing growl or hair-raising shriek. Allison's eyes nearly bulged from their sockets. Her hands clawed the air in torment, and her body contorted at unimaginable angles. Her facial features twisted in a grotesque grimace, and her skin became flushed. Then, just as suddenly as the fury within her erupted, it left. She collapsed lifelessly on the floor.

Jenny and Bud ran to her side. Jenny cradled Allison's face in her hands. Bud knelt on both knees, his arms around the women.

Kingman got down near Allison's face and dipped his finger in a vial of anointing oil he had taken from his pocket. He made the sign of the cross on her forehead. "In the name of the Father, the Son, and the Holy Spirit I ask that you be filled with the presence of God. Where the evil of the Shire and all his kind dwelt, let there be peace."

The entire studio audience was on its feet, cheering. Some shot their fists in the air as a sign of victory. Others, who spiritually understood what was happening, raised both arms, their palms heavenward in praise. Even Steinberg gave a thumbs-up sign to the entire crew as the *McBride* theme music started and credits began to roll.

Allison gradually came to, a smile on her face so beautiful that Billy couldn't believe this was the same young woman. She struggled to her hands and knees, and then slowly stood with the aid of Bud and Billy. Once she was on her feet, she blinked and broke forth in exuberant laughter, a joy that was undeniably supernatural.

"I'm free! I'm free!" she shouted over and over. "I feel lighter. It's like a ton has been lifted from my shoulders!"

"Mommy! Mommy!" Ashley cried out. Usher's assistant had brought Ashley to the stage as the show ended. Now she put her down, and Ashley ran to her mother's arms. Allison picked her up and swung her around and around in a circle of joy.

Gabriel. Where is he? Billy had almost forgotten about the man who had made this miracle possible. He was the one who somehow knew about Bud and arranged for him to be here today. *He's got to be somewhere around here. He was just here.*

Billy knew how tight security was since that day a year ago when a stalker had crashed the set and charged him with a loaded gun. The network brass had given strict orders regarding the safety of Billy, his crew, and the audience. Metal detectors had been installed, and entry to the *McBride* portion of the production facility was limited to one door where two armed guards stood. No one could get in or out without passing by them.

Billy ran toward the only way out of the building. He turned two corners of the corridor and came face-to-face with two guards who stood by the sole exit. One was spindly and clumsy, a Don Knotts stereotype. The other guard was a huge man with muscled shoulders and pectorals so oversized he could barely move his arms. His head was completely bald. Billy wasn't sure he'd trust either of these guards in a genuine life-threatening situation, but at least they weren't blind. If Gabriel had exited, they would know.

"Mr. McBride," the larger of the two said nervously as Billy approached, "aren't you supposed to be doing your show?"

"It just finished," Billy responded. "Has anyone gone out of the building since the show started?"

The men looked at each other and shook their heads.

"No one, you're sure?" Billy pressed them further.

"No, sir. You can trust us. No one gets in or out without us knowing," the small man answered. "Once the studio audience is inside, the doors to the building are locked, and this is the only way in or out. We're here to keep you safe, Mr. McBride. I'd stake my life on it. Not a single person has even approached us."

Billy turned and walked back to the studio. On the way, he passed by the entrance to the control room. *That's where he is!*

Above the door there was a bright red light, and below the light a sign that said AUTHORIZED PERSONNEL ONLY. Billy grabbed a plastic security card from his pocket and slid it through the reader. The door clicked open, and he looked inside. No one was in there. Then he heard a familiar sound. The rhythmic pounding of hoofbeats.

The room was dark. The only light came from the glare of a dozen video monitors, all glowing with the same image: a beautiful white horse galloping across a lush meadow. Billy noticed a caption moving across the bottom of the screen. He couldn't read the words from the doorway, so he walked over to the monitors. Over and over the words were repeated:

I saw heaven opened, and behold, a white horse. And He who sat on him was called Faithful and True.

Revelation 19:11

Billy stood unmoving for a moment. He took a few deep breaths and bowed his head.

"All I can say is thank You, God, for the miracles we witnessed today. Kingman said You are a God of miracles, and now I believe." Billy grinned. "I'm glad You didn't give up on a stubborn cowboy like me. Gabriel, I must have been quite a challenge, but God sure knew what He was doing when He picked you for this job."

Billy opened his eyes again to watch the magnificent white stallion run across the screens. Billy never imagined that a setting like this could be so sacred. This control room was holy ground.

Reluctantly, Billy returned to the studio just as the crew was breaking down the set and the studio audience was being escorted out. Bud, Allison, and Jenny were seated on the edge of the stage with their arms around each other, smiling and laughing. Ashley sat in Bud's lap dangling her feet. She looked happy to meet Grandpa. Kingman and Brogue had been talking, but as Billy entered the studio, they walked toward Allison.

"You still need some serious counseling for issues we didn't have time to deal with today," Kingman said to Allison. "There are several multiple personalities inside you who need to be part of the healing process you've started. I suspect that sweet Southern belle we met is a state of innocence in you that was created to ward off the hardness you developed to escape the hurts you've had. The other personality that did the cutting now has to understand there's no longer a need to release emotional pain in a self-destructive way. You'll also require some addiction counseling to deal with your drug problems. I know an excellent church with a pastoral staff of licensed professionals who will be able to help you. You're not at the end of the road yet, but you've started the journey to healing and wholeness."

"Come here," Brogue said to Ashley. "Your great-granddad would like a hug too."

At first Ashley wasn't sure who this guy was.

"It's all right. He's a good man," Allison said. She turned to Brogue. "I want you to meet my little cowgirl."

Brogue gave his best great-grandpa grin and tilted his head to one side. "Come to Paw Paw."

Ashley ran to Brogue, who threw her in the air and grabbed her again to shouts of glee. "Yee-haw," he whooped, to Ashley's delight.

For the first time Jenny looked peaceful. The guilt and fear she had carried for so many years had faded. She reveled in the moment. Ashley had needed a male influence so desperately. Now there were Billy, Brogue, and Bud, even if they were an interesting bunch of characters at that.

Jenny looked at Billy. "Has it dawned on you yet that you're a great-uncle?"

Billy laughed. "I've been called a lot of things in my time, but never that."

Away from all the others, a lonely figure sat in the shadows at the back of the studio. His head was bowed in his hands. It was Steinberg.

Kingman noticed him and approached the producer. "Why don't you join us?"

Steinberg looked up. "Thanks for the invitation, but I think I'll stay here. This looks like a family affair."

"You're welcome to join the 'family.'"

Steinberg dropped his TV tough-guy front for a moment. "I understand what you mean. Maybe someday. Right now, I don't think you all could stand one more miracle."

Kingman reached in his pocket and handed Steinberg a card. "Here's my number if I can ever be of help."

Steinberg nodded and took the card without saying a word.

Then Kingman walked back to the stage and headed toward Billy to shake his hand. "Allison isn't the only one who has begun a journey. How about you, cowboy? Any idea where the new trail is taking you?"

"No, but I sure do know what horse I'll be riding."

Kingman looked inquisitively at Billy.

"It's a white one."

Author's Note

This book is a work of fiction and should not be considered a complete guide to spiritual ministry or therapeutic counseling. If you or someone you know suffers from demonization or dissociation (MPD—Multiple Personality Disorder or DID—Dissociative Identity Disorder), please seek appropriate professional help. Our ministry provides assistance for these issues through our Do What Jesus Did (DWJD) Teams. Please contact our ministry offices at (303) 980-1511 for further details.

The accounts of this book are fiction based on fact, and the instances of demonic and dissociative behavior included are representative of real-life situations I have encountered. Names and particular circumstances have been changed from the original. Because this work is fictional, it should not be considered theologically definitive. I believe that we have often "unwittingly entertained angels" (Hebrews 13:2), but I do not intend to convey the idea that the Gabriel of this book is *the* Gabriel spoken of in Scripture. My experience in spiritual warfare indicates that demons have rankings with names that indicate their standing, such as Satan or Lucifer. This is similar to the military in that there may be more than one general, colonel, sergeant, and so forth. Angels may also have names indicating a position of rank in the celestial hierarchy (for example, Gabriel and Michael).

It is my hope, and the hope of the people who minister with me, that this book will spur a further interest in the subjects of exorcism, deliverance, and inner emotional healing. If you need further help, consult the Bob Larson Ministries Web site at www.boblarson.org for a complete listing of ministry resources, as well as the updated schedule of Spiritual Freedom Conferences.

About the Author

Bob Larson, a popular author, lecturer, and commentator, is an expert on cults, the occult, and supernatural phenomena. He has lectured in more than eighty countries and has appeared on such nationally aired TV shows as *Oprah*, *Sally*, *Larry King Live*, and *Politically Incorrect*.

Bob hosts a daily one-hour radio show, *TALKBACK with Bob Larson*, that is heard in approximately one hundred cities in the United States and Canada. His incisive commentaries on current events are enhanced by a format of live callers and interesting guests. He also hosts a weekly television show, *Bob Larson in Action*, that is broadcast by more than five hundred stations.

Larson is the author of twenty-nine books, including three best-selling novels—*Dead Air*, *Abaddon*, and *The Senator's Agenda*—as well as several nonfiction titles, among them *Extreme Evil: Kids Killing Kids*, *Larson's Book of Spiritual Warfare*, *In the Name of Satan*, and *Satanism: The Seduction of America's Youth*.

*For more information about spiritual warfare,
don't miss this title!*

"The spiritual battle line of our age is not between believers of different persuasions," Bob Larson says. "Christians are combatants in a conflict between good and evil, light and darkness, and God and the devil."

Larson's Book of Spiritual Warfare is an encyclopedic handbook that contains all you need to know about demons, the devil, deliverance, angels, exorcism, satanism, witchcraft, the occult, and psychic phenomena. After you read this book, you will be equipped with scriptural artillery to effectively combat Satan's influence in today's culture.

ISBN 0-7852-6985-1 * Trade Paperback * 504 pages